Michael Carson was born in Merseyside just after the Second World War. Educated at Catholic schools, he then became a novice in a religious order. After leaving university, he took up a career as a teacher of English as a foreign language and has worked in various countries including Saudi Arabia, Brunei and Iran. He has written two previous novels, *Sucking Sherbet Lemons* and *Friends and Infidels* (both available in Black Swan).

Author photograph by Pinsharp.

Also by Michael Carson

SUCKING SHERBET LEMONS
FRIENDS AND INFIDELS

and published by Black Swan

Coming up Roses

Michael Carson

BLACK SWAN

COMING UP ROSES
A BLACK SWAN BOOK 0 552 99421 9

Originally published in Great Britain
by Victor Gollancz Ltd.

PRINTING HISTORY
Gollancz edition published 1990
Corgi edition published 1991

This book is set in 11/12 pt Mallard by Colset Private Limited, Singapore.

Black Swan Books are published by Transworld Publishers Ltd., 61–63 Uxbridge Road, Ealing, London W5 5SA, in Australia by Transworld Publishers (Australia) Pty. Ltd., 15–23 Helles Avenue, Moorebank, NSW 2170, and in New Zealand by Transworld Publishers (N.Z.) Ltd., Cnr. Moselle and Waipareira Avenues, Henderson, Auckland.

Printed and bound in Great Britain by Cox & Wyman Ltd., Reading, Berks.

For Richard Brown

Part One

Convertibles

1

His Majesty King Fadl, ruler of Ras Al Surra and Keeper of the shrine of the Footprints of Aisha, lay on the day-bed of his rumpus room in the early afternoon of a day in late Muharram 1411, stroking the locks of the Philippino cleaning lady to whom he had taken a shine earlier in the day. While thus engaged, his heavy-lidded eyes, located below a forehead kept always corrugated, betokening ennui – or a legion of other feelings of dissatisfaction to which he was prone – scanned the room, finally coming to rest on the gold, silver, and jewel-encrusted map of Ras Al Surra that hung on the grey suede-covered wall opposite.

The map had originally been presented to King Fadl on a visit to a local primary school. It had not then been encrusted with gold, silver and precious jewels. The children had thought that King Fadl would be pleased to have his kingdom displayed in seashells.

King Fadl had been pleased enough. Handing the gift to an attendant with a smile, he said to the nervous little girl who had presented it to him that it would be given pride of place in his office.

But the map had only survived two days on the wall of his office. For then his chief queen, Noof, had arrived back from a shopping trip to Tokyo and pronounced herself 'appalled' by the crude object hanging on the wall. What would people think were the television cameras to pick it out during one of King Fadl's press conferences? What if a visiting Head of State should spot it? It would not do. It just would not do. She had been deaf to King

Fadl's protestations and had had 'the thing' removed. This had irked the King and he kept reminding Queen Noof about it whenever they met. Any little thing that niggled King Fadl about Queen Noof – and there were many little things daily that so niggled – would immediately set off thoughts of the children's gift.

'Oh, very well,' Queen Noof had exclaimed at last, tired of her husband's importuning, 'you can have it, but first I must make it presentable.'

Off she flew to London, where she had the shell map overlaid with gold on the area of Ras Al Surra and silver over alien territory. The ocean was lapis lazuli. Borders were picked out in tiny rubies and pearls. The site of the shrine of the Footprints of Aisha was marked by an exquisite diamond, which, though Queen Noof did not know it, had been smuggled out of Sierra Leone some months before, secreted in one of the darker orifices of a visiting Swiss powdered-milk salesman.

'Aspreys always make a good job of such things!' Noof exclaimed upon her return.

King Fadl had gazed at the once simple object. 'But it's so . . . *rich* now,' he whimpered. 'What will the children say when they see it in the office? I preferred it before.'

Queen Noof mopped her brow with a Liberty linen handkerchief in white on to which NOOF had been hand-embroidered by peasant women in Northern Italy. Having completed this operation, she discarded the handkerchief in a red, velvet-lined rubbish bin with tassels on it and opened her mink coat. 'Have you been turning down the air-conditioning again?' she asked King Fadl accusingly.

'A shade, yes. It has been so cold in here recently.'

Queen Noof clapped her hands and a uniformed English butler appeared after the fourth imperious clap.

'Turn up the air-conditioning immediately! I am stifling, Jeeves.'

Jeeves nodded resignedly, turned on his heel and, muttering beneath his breath, 'Up and down . . . down and bleeding up,' sauntered out of the office.

'It's too rich for the office, dear,' moaned the King, frowning at the retreating Jeeves.

'One can never be too rich or too thin!' barked back Queen Noof.

'But don't you think it's just a mite overdone, a little too flashy?'

'Better nouveau riche than no riche at all,' replied Queen Noof, wondering on whose royal scatter cushions she had recently read the tag.

'Yes, but I don't think it belongs in the office, dear.'

However, Queen Noof had lost interest, 'Well, do what you want,' she snapped. 'You're the King after all. Put it in your disgusting rumpus room for all I care.'

And that was where the gift of the children had ended up.

King Fadl glanced at his temporary wife – now doing her best to bring the monarch to a royal climax – and then concentrated his gaze on the map once more. Something about it irked him, but he was not for a moment quite sure what was wrong. He gazed at it. No, nothing was wrong. Aspreys never got anything wrong. But there was definitely something not quite right. What was it?

Just then the Philippino temporary wife scratched the King with one of her powerful canines and he felt his lust, fragile at best these days, leaving him.

'Return to your duties!' he told the woman. She adjusted her dress. The King reached into the drawer next to the compact disc player and found a gold Dunhill lighter which he could never make work. This he presented to the Philippino lady with a gesture that turned from giving to dismissal in an instant. She made for the door muttering her thanks. King Fadl divorced her retreating back, reciting the prescribed formula. Then he returned his attention to the map.

There was Ras Al Surra, all in gold, a narrow – though rather bent – rectangle of oil-rich land bounded to the east by a lapis lazuli sea. The trouble was that the neighbouring Sultanate of Zibda insinuated itself across his territory, making one huge bulb-shaped silver incursion that completely spoilt the look of Ras Al Surra.

How had this been allowed to happen, he wondered? He wondered, too, why he had not noticed it before.

He turned over and tried to sleep, but the memory of the map stayed with him. Suddenly, not remembering how, he was sitting bolt upright. Yes! Perhaps the work of the schoolchildren was a message. Perhaps at last it was doing its work!

The King of Ras Al Surra picked up the telephone. 'Get me the Sultan of Zibda immediately!' he called out, inspired.

The telephone rang in the half-ruined fort by the sea which the Sultan of Zibda called home.

Before the Sultan could disengage himself from a tussle he was having with three of his eleven children on the floor of his office, his youngest son, Daud, had picked up the receiver.

'Daud's Hardware,' Daud squeaked.

The words left Daud's mouth, darted down the telephone wire, along some ragged line outside the fort – some of which was decorated with the washing of the Sultan and his family – to a recently built installation just across the border in Ras Al Surra which launched his words into the stratosphere, where they bounced off the Ibn Batuta communication satellite and were deflected back to earth and straight into the dish atop the King of Ras Al Surra's gold-leafed roof.

'Daud's Hardware!'

The King of Ras Al Surra held the headset of his reproduction art deco telephone away from his ear, gazing at it with distaste. He should have known that the Sultan of Zibda's phone would be answered by one of the children. There were children all over the palace of the Sultan. They ran wild. The last time he had rung a girl had answered and wouldn't believe that he was the King of Ras Al Surra.

This time the King decided to be brisk. 'Is Daddy there?' he asked.

'Who wants to know?'

'A friend.'

The receiver was dropped with a clatter that offended the King's ears.

At last the Sultan of Zibda came to the phone. 'Hello?' he said.

'It's King Fadl.'

'How are you, Fadl?' asked Nabil, Sultan of Zibda, in a voice that left his larynx sounding irritated, but whose inflection was neutralized by the bounce off the Ibn Batuta satellite dish.

'Fine, thanks,' replied King Fadl.

'How can I help you?'

'My brother! You are so brisk,' observed the King.

'Well, you know how I hate the telephone.'

'Bought yourself a car yet?' the King of Ras Al Surra, who had forty-eight cars – each with its own mechanic – asked.

'No, not yet. We're still managing with bicycles.'

'Really, Nabil! Your lack of conspicuous consumption is bringing shame on the whole Arab Nation.'

'Look,' replied the Sultan, 'I've got better things to do than go through that again. If I've told you once, I've told you a hundred times that it is my belief that a ruler must be the last of all the people to attain wealth. When every last citizen of Zibda has a car then I shall have a car. And not until. We still have some considerable way to go. Now let me hear no more about it. What did you really want to talk to me about?'

'Sorry, Nabil! I always seem to step on your testicles. Well, truth to tell, I do have a serious purpose in calling. How would you like to sell me your Eastern Region?'

'Al Bustan? What *do* you mean?'

'Well, I was thinking that Ras Al Surra would be greatly improved in every way if you would sell me that bulbous bit of wasteland that cuts my kingdom almost in half. I'd pay you well for it and you know it is a useless piece of real estate.'

'Are you quite sane, Fadl? Sell Al Bustan? What can

you be thinking about? Are you making some kind of joke?'

'I'm perfectly serious, Nabil! I'd pay you well. Nobody lives there.'

'My land is not for sale!'

'Not for two billion jumpas?'

The phone went silent. Nabil suddenly had a vision of what two billion jumpas would achieve for Zibda. He would be able to complete the Barefoot Doctors scheme, get all the schoolchildren out of tents and into proper classrooms, build a library and, of course, there was also the impossible dream . . . the radio station. . .

'Are you there, Nabil?' asked King Fadl.

'I am here.'

'So what do you say?'

'Er . . . no.'

'You don't sound too sure.'

'Look, Fadl, I've got to go now. I have some visits to make later on and my bike's got a puncture.'

'You could buy lots of bikes with two billion jumpas.'

'It's . . . out of the question!' exclaimed Nabil. 'Anyway,' he added with a note of uncertainty, 'my people would never agree.'

'Three billion!'

'No, really—'

'Four billion! And that is as high as I am willing to go.'

The Sultan of Zibda was sweating. 'I really must go.'

'Nabil, I want—'

'I'll call you back!'

Sultan Nabil put down the phone. His children stood quietly around him. They seemed to sense that something momentous was happening and did not at once set about their father as they usually did to get him to rejoin the game.

'Who were you talking to, father?' asked Latifa, the Sultan's eldest daughter.

'A servant of the devil,' replied Nabil. 'Now, who's going to help me mend that puncture?'

The servant of the devil smiled as he put down the

phone. He would let the implications of four billion jumpas work their magic on Sultan Nabil of Zibda. The King felt that even at this distance he could hear the not inconsiderable amount of grey matter inside the Sultan's head churning away at spending the vast temptation he had just placed in front of him.

Zibda, unlike Ras Al Surra, had not been blessed with great quantities of oil. In fact, it had not been blessed with great quantities of anything marketable. There had been miles of unspoilt beaches and, at some seasons, a sea solid with fish. But that was before the oil carriers from neighbouring countries had taken to cleaning their tanks off the coast of Zibda. The sandy wastes of Zibda concealed only more sand and then sandstone rock. The people eked out a living as they had always done, by breeding camels and falcons – and by smuggling. This latter pursuit, while not providing Zibda with anything like the amount of revenue it required to build itself into a country able to emulate its oil-rich neighbours, did serve to prevent Zibda's rice bowls from turning into begging bowls.

As neighbours on all sides grew fat from oil, Zibda had been able to take advantage of different prices for gold and luxury goods, plying them across desert and ocean to neighbouring countries; to India and Pakistan, selling them at unmanned border crossings; making rendezvous at sea and exchanging cheap gold and goods for hard currencies. Zibda lived on the proceeds of this rolling, open-air, duty free shop and Ras Al Surra was pivotal to the trade. Its prices were the lowest in the area and, from time immemorial, the people of Zibda had been granted free access to the shrine of the Footprints of Aisha. Thus, Zibdan pilgrimages to the shrine refreshed both soul and pocket and helped keep the country afloat.

Though devoid of natural resources, Zibda had been blessed in one respect: it was ruled by a most unusual monarch. Sultan Nabil, after a carefree childhood at Summerhill and an involved early manhood at Oxford, had returned to Zibda in the seventies determined to put himself last. Upon assuming the throne he vowed that his income and outgoings would be available for all to see and would serve as an example of frugality for all his people. He used the pitiful trickle of money that came into Zibda's coffers totally for the benefit of his people. He refused hand-outs, but encouraged teachers and medical volunteers from both east and west to come to Zibda to help in its development.

Now, Sultan Nabil lived what he had learnt in the heady atmosphere of the sixties. All around him he saw a world in which rulers – despite all the object lessons available from history – continued to please themselves, to be spectacularly corrupt and indifferent to their people's good. He held on to his beliefs, unable to accept that those called upon to serve the needs of their people – able to do what most of mankind can merely talk about – should not see this as the very pinnacle of privilege. He spent much of his spare time writing letters to leaders whom he believed to be in error. He chided kings, presidents and heads of juntas. And kings, presidents and heads of juntas had learnt to take not the least notice of him. And that was why Sultan Nabil wanted a radio station. With a radio station he could broadcast his complaints and his dreams. With a radio station he could take on the world.

But Zibda could not afford a radio station. So Nabil ruled his little kingdom as best he could and sent his children to live for periods of time with the poorest people in the country so that they would know and never forget how it felt.

The Sultan Of Zibda scandalized his prosperous neighbours. The King of Ras Al Surra, the proud owner of eight palaces in Ras Al Surra, eighteen residences overseas, four private jets – one of which was a Boeing 747 with rooms that aped his favourite suite at the Ritz – three wives, five Swedish nannies, one English butler, three French chefs and several wardrobes packed full of classy clothes, presided over his once-hard, now swiftly-softening half a million subjects. His people did little except oversee the operation of over-stuffed shops and rent out spectacular villas surplus to requirements to the thousands of expatriates from all over the world who did the real work.

Sultan Nabil's rich neighbours, like owners of a smart block of flats let down by one stubborn sitting tenant who insists on his Che Guevara posters and sixties-print wallpaper, offered to give Zibda a lift into the affluent nineties. King Fadl had on more than one occasion offered to build Nabil a housing estate for resettling the bedouin, who had once wandered freely over the land of Ras Al Surra and Zibda. Nabil had politely declined. In Ras Al Surra the bedouin had ceased to wander and had been settled into a spectacular group of high-rise apartments on the coast. Those who had not felt able to accept this kind of life had fled to Zibda, where Nabil let them wander the length and breadth of his country. He was the last remaining ruler in the area to give such untidiness its head. All around him the affluent shook their heads towards Zibda and fretted about how to bring him into line.

The evening call to prayer sounded from all the minarets of the capital of Ras Al Surra. Thirty muezzins choired like a car repair shop, a sound sufficiently astringent to penetrate the sound-proofing in King Fadl's rumpus room. With a sigh, the King turned off the compact disc of Whitney Houston and the Italian pornographic video he had been watching with the mildest of mild interest, closed the current copy of *Fortune* and shuffled into his (unbeknown to him) pigskin slippers to walk to the robing room.

He had to meet the Council of Religious Advisers after prayers were finished. A spectre of the pious, bearded men bubbled up in his brain for a moment and he wrinkled his fleshy features with distaste.

Being King was far from the beanfeast everyone thought it was. King Fadl wondered if any of his gardeners, nannies or mechanics had to compromise as much as he did. He thought of his house on the clifftops just outside Monte Carlo. How wonderful it would be to be lounging on the tiled veranda now instead of having to face all those pious faces. Then he could not remember whether the tiled veranda was in the house in the South of France or the one on the Pacific Palisades. King Fadl shrugged. Either would suffice, he thought to himself.

'Find me something sober!' he commanded Jeeves who had been sitting in a corner of the robing room reading an old copy of the *Sun* with a pink Balkan Sobranie cigarette between his lips. Jeeves nodded, and muttering to himself, made off along the street of wardrobes, cupboards and drawers in search of something sober.

'This do yer?' he announced on his return, holding up a grey worsted robe.

'Thank you, that'll do nicely,' replied the King.

Jeeves resumed his seat in the corner and took up the wrinkled *Sun*.

As the King changed he wondered why he kept Jeeves. The man was insolent and slovenly and smelt bad. But it did not take him long to recall. One night while very drunk he had been photographed by Jeeves's brother, Stan, in a very compromising position indeed in a dive somewhere off the Shaftesbury Avenue. Stan, when pressed with much gold in return for the negatives, had refused all blandishments, saying that he would only consent not to send the pictures to the newspapers if the King removed his brother from his hair.

Ever since then Jeeves had been his personal butler. He was always rude, sometimes disgusting. However, apart from the original reason for keeping him, King Fadl did feel some perverse affection for the man. There was something piquant, refreshing, about being a king and yet being so abused.

The British Ambassador during a visit had once remarked to the King on how rude Jeeves was and the King had replied that Jeeves made him laugh. The Ambassador had gone on to talk about an English king called Lear who had had a Jeeves character in his life too. That was heartening.

Looking serious, King Fadl entered the Council Chamber and faced his religious advisers. The King was surprised to see that instead of the hawkish features of Sheikh Ghani Al Gaz, the head of the Ministry for the Suppression of Vice and the Encouragement of Virtue, he found himself standing opposite a face that was new to him: a tall man with dark glasses, whose pale, almost grey, face was further masked by a white head-dress and thick, ginger beard. This, thought King Fadl, could not possibly be Sheikh Al Gaz. For a second, the King found himself hoping that Sheikh Al Gaz had proceeded to the Garden of Allah, had shuffled off dourly to eternity. Could it be? he mused. If only it could!

However, the King did not let his feelings show. He greeted the stranger opposite. Pious ejaculations were exchanged; Surrahs were quoted from, Hadditbs were repeated, more pious ejaculations were exchanged – and everyone sat down on tubular steel chairs with transparent plastic seats.

'Is all well in the Holy Land?' asked King Fadl as was the custom.

There was a momentary silence, then the strange new presence stood up.

'All is not well, O Guardian of the Footprints of Aisha.'

The man's Arabic was flawless, but still the King had the impression that here was no Arab.

'Explain the ill-doing so that I may chastise it with the scimitar of my wrath!' commanded the King. Then he added, 'And who are you?'

'My name is Abdul Wahhab Higgins, your Majesty,' replied the stranger, 'and I have been requested to attend in place of Sheikh Al Gaz.'

'I see,' said the King. 'And where, pray, is Sheikh Al Gaz?'

'He is in Thailand, your Majesty.'

The King raised one eyebrow. 'In Thailand, eh? And why is he in Thailand?'

'Sheikh Al Gaz is on a fact-finding mission, your Majesty. He heard that the pure Ras Al Surran youth was being seduced into acts of darkness with the infidel females of Thailand. He has proceeded thence in order to ascertain whether or not this is the case and to take the appropriate righteous action.'

'You don't say!' said King Fadl.

Abdul Wahhab Higgins nodded. 'I have been requested by Sheikh Al Gaz to take his place at your Majesty's weekly audience with his loyal religious policemen. I am normally employed as religious policeman for the Ministry for the Suppression of Vice and the Encouragement of Virtue at the Naffa industrial port.'

'I see,' replied the King. 'A fine port, is it not? It is the jewel in the crown of the thrusting expansion of the Ras Al Surran renaissance.'

The King was intrigued by this foreigner. He wanted to ask him many questions, but instead went on to repeat the prescribed formula.

'Is all well in the Holy Land of Ras Al Surra?'

Abdul Wahhab Higgins consulted his papers. 'All is not altogether well. First,' he began, 'it has come to our attention that the pure Ras Al Surran youth spends much time in the evening shopping at Safeway.'

'Yes?' asked the King, perplexed

'Many of the infidel wives also shop at Safeway, O King. Our religious police report that the pure Ras Al Surran youth is being tempted and seduced into flirtatious exchanges with the infidel wives.'

'Is this so?' asked the King, momentarily wishing that he were an anonymous youth with time to lust away in Safeway. 'What do you recommend to stamp out this wickedness?'

'We have drawn up some prophylactic measures, your Majesty. Item the first: all Ras Al Surran youth must be accompanied by their guardians in order to shop in Safeway. Item the second: wives of infidels must be accompanied by spouse and be suitably veiled.'

'But the wives already wear headscarves.'

'We recommend that full covering be applied.'

The King sighed inwardly. Though Sheikh Al Gaz was far away, his influence clearly lived on in this Abdul Wahhab Higgins.

'Is all else well in the Holy Land?'

Once more Abdul Wahhab Higgins spoke.

When Abdul Wahhab Higgins had finished speaking, King Fadl blinked at him with his mouth open.

'You can't be serious, surely!' he said. And, as he spoke, the King realized that his mouth had been open throughout much of Abdul Wahhab Higgins's speech. He controlled his errant lips with a tight pout.

'Completely serious, your Majesty.'

'Well . . . I think you and I . . . Mr Higgins, had better adjourn to my apartments. Some further discussion is required.'

Later, after a strange hour with Abdul Wahhab Higgins in his study, King Fadl fled back with relief to his rumpus room.

Clearly, King Fadl reflected, this Abdul Wahhab Higgins had been poured into the same miserable mould that had fashioned Sheikh Al Gaz. The King thought how he would like to fling Sheikh Al Gaz from the battlements of his fairy castle on the Norwegian fjord. In a sack. With snakes. And a pig. It just was not fair that he, the King, should have to bow to the whims of the religious maniacs of the Ministry for the Suppression of Vice and the Encouragement of Virtue. Not fair at all. 'I should be able to say what goes and what doesn't!' King Fadl told a vase of fibre-optic stalks, cunningly illuminated in Ras Al Surra's national colours, which stood atop a bubbling fountain at the door of the royal rumpus room.

The King threw himself down on to an indeterminate space of soft cushions and beat a cushion covered in peacock feathers with his fist. Then he bit another cushion whose corner had had the temerity to poke him in the eye. 'How dare you!' he told it. 'I am the King after all.' He lay still, fuming for a few moments, then recalled that the Great King, his father, had told him many times why the religious policemen were not to be crossed. He calmed down then and his stomach relaxed. Yes, that was how it was. He survived because of the pact with religion. If he were once to cross Sheikh Al Gaz and his sanctimonious side-kicks, there was no telling what would happen. King Fadl looked around him. His anger had become a dull ache. 'Well, they can't do anything about what I do in my own rumpus room.' His eyes wandered round the room again, seeking something to distract him from his heavy thoughts. He surveyed a pile of new videos and compact discs, but did not fancy them somehow. Then he wondered if fiddling with his television satellite dish would bring him satisfaction, but decided against that too. He closed his eyes and thought of his island off Thailand. Then he opened his eyes and looked bejewelled daggers at the map of Ras Al Surra on the wall. But then he recalled the blank, bearded face of the zealot foreigner.

Circumcision! The very idea! Still, it would be interesting to see the reaction. King Fadl loved a little mayhem. Throwing thousand-jumpa gold coins into a crowd was wonderful. He recalled that he had not done that for some time. The expenditure gave him an immediate return. It was hugely gratifying to see the populace battling for his bounty like the pigeons he and Queen Noof bombarded with bits of croissant and caviare-spread toast in their roof-garden on Park Lane. Moments of mayhem made him feel really regal. His forehead cleared of frustration, the corners of his mouth lifted of their own accord to smile. Circumcision would certainly provide a modicum of mayhem. It would be interesting to see whether those money-drunk expatriates would put up with it. Would they actually submit to the knife to stay in Ras Al Surra?

Lying back and gazing at shards of his reflection in the mirror-mosaic ceiling of the room, King Fadl mused, smiling to himself. Images of the red faces of military types who had helped him win his war against insurgency in the south, and who, all the time, had scarcely veiled their contempt for him and Ras Al Surra, came to his mind. He had not thought that they would have tolerated the limitations placed on them by the increasingly draconian edicts of the Ministry for the Suppression of Vice and the Encouragement of Virtue – but most had. There seemed to be nothing that Ras Al Surra could do to make itself less attractive to the money-grabbing hoards. Freedom – paid for with the price of a lowered income at home – did not seem to stand a chance. Truly, it was delightful to hold the purse strings. With one's hands wrapped around them true insights into human nature were vouchsafed. Nabil could stand on his head and chant Indian mantras his whole life long. He would never attain the enlightenment that he, King Fadl, obtained from a week holding the purse strings.

King Fadl of Ras Al Surra, wondering if he should go along with the wishes of Abdul Wahhab Higgins, and feeling rather inclined to, shivered suddenly. He called Jeeves to adjust the air-conditioning, hoping that his butler would not be too abusive.

Some miles away in Al Rahman, the capital city of Zibda, Sultan Nabil, having lit all the kerosene lamps in his suite of rooms on the top floor of the Portuguese fort by the sea, settled down to another evening of writing and meditation.

Sitting down at his desk, directly in front of an unglazed window which gave on to the sea, he unscrewed his old Osmiroid pen and cleared away a pile of books and papers. Reverently he opened a school exercise book, scanned through the pages of writing until he came to an empty page. He sucked the end of his pen and looked out at the navy-blue ocean.

He remained for five minutes thus. Then he heard the muezzin call the last prayer of the day from atop the old minaret. The sound moved him. It was unassisted by gadgetry, and the man's clear voice soared. The sea seemed to go silent. The Sultan recalled that the muezzins of Zibda must sound the same as that first muezzin, Bilal, had sounded when the Prophet had walked on the earth.

But, though moved by the call to prayer, Sultan Nabil did not get up to pray. He sought a God whom all on earth could accept. Iran lay across the silenced ocean. Once, as a student, he had wept on hearing the call to prayer in the Isfahan Shah Square. Then he had loved Iran. Now he saw it as a stage full of light, colour and wonders across which black curtains of dogmatism had fallen.

And Sultan Nabil prayed.

'He determines the perfect whole; his is the cause yesterday of your composition, today of your dissolution; you are the cause of neither. Leave the stage therefore and be content, for he who releases you is content also.'

These last sentences from *The Meditations of Marcus Aurelius* had long been the Sultan's only prayer.

Now, in the evening quiet, he repeated it again and again as he faced the ocean and the clear white sheet of his exercise book.

At last he wrote:

> 'To be incorruptible while in possession of power is difficult enough but is not enough. We in Zibda remain poor while all around us the countries grow fat. Many people increasingly seek out the wealth across our borders and are not satisfied with the simple life I have laid before them as an ideal. It would be so easy to open the floodgates and let change sweep down on us like a tidal wave.
>
> 'But I believe that "Progress" is often a myth. Man can ascend but he can also descend and there is no limit to the descent. It can continue down past the animals, the worms and the fossils into the realms of hell. Often what is seen by the world as the most "progressive", is in fact the inner circle of hell.'

Nabil paused, gazing out to the now-invisible sea. The sky had become alive with stars as the sea faded into blackness. He looked up at the stars and then down at the blackness below him. And he saw King Fadl projected into the blackness and the King's mouth formed the words, 'Four billion jumpas,' again and again and again.

He tried to blink away his vision but it would not go and soon he gave up the attempt and let himself entertain the thought of what the money could do for his country and for his ambitions. He could build a radio station with the money, perhaps the biggest radio station in the world, and with the radio station in place he could set about broadcasting to the world. He could tell the world all the news they did not hear on other radio stations. He could broadcast the pamphlets that Amnesty International sent him and which made him howl with the torture of frustration and impotent empathy. He could broadcast the books that pointed possible ways forward to a better world. But would another radio station change anything? Did knowing about things ever change the way people behaved?

Nabil thought his thoughts through, hoping that when he had thought them through they would leave him and leave him convinced that King Fadl's offer should be rejected out of hand. Was the offer not, after all, just the temptation to corruption wrapped in virtuous packaging?

An hour later the thoughts were still buzzing through his brain. His hands itched to pick up the phone and call King Fadl. He resisted the temptation, however, and left the palace – his head a hive – to wander the streets of Al Rahman, in order to make sure that his people had managed to get through, without mishap, the day that had just died.

2

The following morning, about twenty miles down the coast from Ras Al Surra's capital city of Fadlabad, two British expatriates were driving unhappily to their work on the Naffa industrial port in a white Toyota.

Neither relished the prospect of the day ahead, which, if days already religiously crossed off calendars were anything to go by, would bring neither a slither of satisfaction nor a whit of whoopee.

Captain Pooley, Merchant Marine retired, and now an expert in port infrastructure, sat hunched forward in his driving seat, nervously scanning the black road in front for evidence of any approaching four-wheel Exocet which might need to be avoided. His companion, Armitage, a man in his early forties given to plumpness, stared at the scenery they were passing with mixed emotions – as a tourist who has been promised a wonderful view if he takes a certain road, but finds that the road has not fulfilled its promise – while pushing what held the promise of becoming a fine second chin back under the tight collar of his shirt.

On several occasions Armitage had opened his mouth to speak but each time thought better of it. However, the opening of Armitage's mouth had somehow communicated itself each time to Captain Pooley, who cocked a ear, while not for one instant relaxing his vigilant watch on the road in front.

When Armitage opened his mouth again, Captain Pooley cocked his ear but Armitage merely licked his lips and closed his mouth again.

'Out with it, Armitage,' barked Captain Pooley. 'Can't stand a chap who doesn't speak his mind.'

'It's nothing, Captain Pooley,' replied Armitage in his tentative tenor voice.

Captain Pooley humphed.

'I mean, I was just thinking.'

'Thinking what?'

'Well, perhaps "thinking" isn't the right word, I was just "wondering" really.'

'What were you "wondering"?' asked Captain Pooley with not a hint of wonder in his voice.

'I was just kind of wondering why the Ras Al Surrans are building all these vast factories and things while we knock all ours down.'

'I see. And have you reached any conclusions?'

'I think it is because they find the vertical perspective exciting. That's what I think.'

'Don't get your drift, Armitage. Sorry,' replied Captain Pooley, wishing he had not encouraged his companion to speak in the first place.

He shifted from fourth to second gear and overtook a truck sporting MECCA OR NOWHERE on its back in bold, luminous yellow letters. As he did so he gave the driver a withering look for hogging the crown of the road. The driver, however, refused to wilt before Captain Pooley's frown and honked on his horn happily.

'Typical,' remarked Captain Pooley.

'What I mean is,' continued Armitage who, now that the manoeuvre was over, felt free to remove his right foot from the imaginary brake he had been pushing into the floor, 'they've been starved of the vertical perspective and now they're making up for it.'

Captain Pooley adjusted his blue plastic engineers' hard-hat and looked over at Armitage for a split second before returning redoubled attention to the road ahead. 'It just won't wash,' he said.

'How do you mean?' asked Armitage.

'Quite simple, Armitage. I, out of the goodness of my heart, give you a lift to work every day. You, for some reason beyond the ken of this humble personage, are the English teacher at this blooming industrial port, yet I never understand a single thing you say. I don't know how your students manage, I really don't.'

'They don't manage too well to tell you the truth,' Armitage sighed. 'But it's quite simple really. Look how flat this country is. I'd say the highest point that I've ever seen is about fifty feet above sea-level. The ground is so salty that it won't support even the weediest palm tree. Take away the industries, the desalination plant, the Bedouin Dawn Towers and the Queen Noof Shopping Precinct and you have two perfectly flat planes of desert and sky – and horizontal planes at that.'

'Like Norfolk.'

'No, not like Norfolk!' Armitage rapped back impatiently, petulantly, like the frustrated teacher he was. Then he added with pedagogic urgency, 'Did you know that there are tribes in Africa who have never seen stairs and when they do can't climb them?'

'Sorry?' asked Captain Pooley, not liking Armitage's tone at all and determining to act obtuse.

Armitage repeated his question.

Captain Pooley delayed answering in order to let his displeasure sink in. He was helped in his delaying tactic by the sudden heading up of two pedestrians walking too far out in the road for Captain Pooley's liking. He gave them the finger as he passed them, then saw too late that they were giving him the thumb – seeking a lift – a lift they had no chance of obtaining from Captain Pooley.

'No, I didn't know that, Armitage. That is a new one on me,' he replied in his own time, watching the shapes of the lonely pedestrians retreating in the driving mirror, 'but it doesn't surprise me. Nothing about foreigners surprises me anymore. I was in Africa myself, Armitage, while you were beavering away at your Eleven Plus or your CSEs – or whatever else it was that gave you your fancy ideas and between you and me and a five-legged frog I wouldn't . . . did you see that?'

A Mercedes Benz had performed a sudden U-turn in

front of them, narrowly missing a pick-up going in the opposite direction. Captain Pooley turned momentarily and muttered at the distinguished rear of the Mercedes. 'No, nothing surprises me,' he continued between clenched teeth. 'You know, we used to have a houseboy in Mombasa who prayed to the fridge. He thought it was such a bloody miracle turning out ice like the clappers that he deified it straight away. He used to put garlands of flowers round it and votive candles on the top.'

'Was he the one who sent half his wage to the Donkey Sanctuary?' asked Armitage, who had heard similar tales of singular servants before.

'No. His brother.'

'It's a funny world.'

'Not when you're stuck in the middle of it, it's not,' replied Captain Pooley.

They had reached the gate of the port. A uniformed guard who looked about fifteen years old was sitting in a sentry box contentedly scratching his crotch through his khaki trousers. He waved the car on with a desultory gesture of his spare hand.

'If he was on my ship I'd soon cure him of that little vice,' said Captain Pooley.

'They do it because they shave the pubic region,' said Armitage, who was always ready to attempt cross-cultural clarification.

'How the hell do you know that, professor?'

Armitage was stuck for words for a moment. He set about stuffing his neck down his collar again before replying. 'A friend told me.'

'Funny friends you have, Armitage. How does he know?'

'*She* actually,' lied Armitage.

'Curiouser and curiouser. How does *she* know?'

'Well – actually – she's a nurse in the RASONGRO hospital.'

RASONGRO was the Ras Al Surra Oil and Natural Gas Retrieval Organization whose expatriate employees lived in some splendour behind forbidding barbed wire where they were free to enjoy forbidden ham, forbidden alcohol and forbidden dubious video-cassettes.

Captain Pooley nodded and smirked. 'A nurse, eh? Well she would know, wouldn't she, being a nurse and everything? I mean, it's their business to know everything about that sort of thing. That's what they're paid for. Fine women, nurses! Nothing they won't do for a chap – if you get my drift.'

He winked at Armitage.

Heartened, Armitage said, 'Well, actually, they use depilatory cream. They don't shave. She says.'

'Still, it comes to the same thing, doesn't it? Had an African first mate once. Fine figure of a man and damned good at his job for a foreigner. Run rings round this lot. He used debilitating cream on his face. If he shaved he came up in the most dreadful bumps and blotches. Not that it showed on black skin. Like wrinkles, you know. They can have them but it doesn't show.'

'Yes, they're lucky that way,' said Armitage, switching his nervous fingers from his neck to his forehead and wondering if he should feel happy or sad about still being a martyr to mild acne in his early forties.

'And not only in that way. The consul's servant in Mombasa had a ding-dong you could tie a knot in. I jest not. Saw it with my own eyes. He did his party piece for us at a consular dinner – after the ladies had withdrawn of course – tied it in a knot no trouble. One time I heard they got him to do it and then showed him a girly magazine. Well, you can imagine. Laugh! Still, you've got to hand it to the African: fine specimens physically. It's just that they really haven't got it together up top. Bit like this lot really. Never be great – not at the rate they're going.'

But Armitage had missed the conclusion of Captain Pooley's remarks. His brain was full of the image of a naked black servant struggling with a writhing snake – while all around him port swilling, red-faced, British colonial types guffawed – their eyes full of derision and envy. It was a potent image for colonialism, he thought, feeling suddenly quite hot in spite of the efficient air-conditioning.

Captain Pooley and Armitage were now driving along a causeway that a Korean company had just completed for the Ras al Surran government. It was seven miles long, three hundred yards wide and tired Armitage merely to think about the labour which had gone into its construction.

Along the centre of the dual-carriageway, blue-uniformed Thais and Philippinos were hanging flags from the lamp-standards. Bothered by the hot wind which blew across the ocean from Iran, the flags fluttered and wrapped themselves around the standards, becoming further entangled the more they struggled to be free. The flags were, or so it seemed to Armitage, forever being raised or lowered. It boded no good, signifying the visits of VIPs – events which invariably heightened the mood of paranoia around the port to near-unbearable proportions. Inspections would be made. Heads would roll. English classes would be visited. Armitage's tongue would cleave to the roof of his mouth. Now, for him and for most of the other expatriates who worked on the industrial port, the flag of Ras Al Surra had become a symbol of anxiety and perturbation.

'Wonder who designed the flag?' Armitage wondered out loud.

'Nestlés, I shouldn't wonder. You know, Armitage, it really amazes me that a country should choose a yellow coffee-pot against a green field to show itself to the world. I wonder if we should replace the Union Jack with a red teapot motif on grey?'

'It might change our image for the better,' observed Armitage.

Captain Pooley reacted angrily. He took his right foot off the accelerator and pumped the brake in time to his reply. 'WHAT in THUNder do you MEAN by THAT?' he exploded, rocking Armitage violently backwards and forwards as he spoke.

Armitage was quite irked to be so rolled and jolted

and saw fit not to reply. Captain Pooley, restoring the car to its normal cruising speed, said under his breath, 'Sometimes I find myself sorely tried by you, Armitage, indeed I do!'

Armitage continued to stare from the window. He wore a gentle, Buddha-like smile on his round face – a Buddha-like smile his self-help book, *Winning Through Sweetness*, had told him would come to mirror the peaceful state within if he wore it long enough and often enough. The smile directed itself to the sulphur prilling tower, the roll on-roll off jetty, the urea plant and the tank farms. The sulphur prilling tower, the roll on-roll off jetty, the urea plant and the tank farms stared back, unmoved. Armitage felt his smile pulling downwards and his chin begin to wobble. How could he, he thought, become sweet and enlightened with all this horror around him? His eyes took in the Manhattan-in-miniature skyline of Naffa, across the bay. Until five years ago Naffa had been a tiny fishing village. Now it was known throughout the world – the centre of King Fadl's race to make Ras Al Surra the Japan of the Middle East in a decade.

Finding no consolation in that direction, Armitage directed his gaze out to sea. Through the narrow channel he could make out the shape of *Big Mother*, the ship that brought the vast constructions of pipes, cylinders, condensers and heat-exchangers to go to the methanol plant that was being erected in the middle of the desert behind Naffa. Another piece of Lego to delight the newly-awakened lust for vertical perspectives. No, there was no place here for smiles. He gave up the attempt as he recalled that by the time they had started on their journey home in the evening, all that equipment would have been trundled along the road on its huge, computerized vehicle and would be standing tall in the desert waiting to be bolted together to form the twenty-first century.

'You've got to hand it to the Nips,' remarked Captain Pooley, who had also seen the ship, 'they keep turning out those great modules like Babycham at a Jewish wedding. Now the Nips have got it up top. No time for them as a race of course. I remember Burma. Doris and I won't have a Nip gadget in the house. But they've certainly got it up top.'

Armitage disapproved somewhat of Captain Pooley's disparaging remarks about the different races on earth. He knew that until the whole world learnt to smile Buddha-like at one another there would be neither peace nor meaningful development. But he had enough common sense to know that the voicing of such sentiments would not cut any ice with Captain Pooley at this particular juncture. So, instead of gently remonstrating, Armitage went along with the mood, and, slotting into a role he had had decades to perfect, decided once again to be one of the gang. 'They may have it up top, Captain Pooley, but not down below, I'm told.'

'My, that nurse of yours really gets around,' replied Captain Pooley with a leer.

Abdul Wahhab Higgins arrived in the parking bay of the port's administration building at the same time as Captain Pooley and Armitage. He adjusted his white Arab head-dress in the driving mirror, making sure that the centre fold of the cloth was exactly two fingers' breadth above the place where his eyebrows met.

It was Abdul Wahhab Higgins's habit to wear the head-dress low, with the sides swept forward, so that little of his face could be seen. A full ginger beard, carved in the shape of a garden spade, obscured his features still further, as did the opaque sunglasses he was never seen without. Only a few square inches of white skin dotted with freckles showed through all this and suggested that he was, perhaps, not the Arab that his clothing and demeanour set him out to be.

He watched as Armitage and Captain Pooley disappeared into the administration building, then he turned off the engine of his car and, making a pious ejaculation for a journey safely completed, got out and walked to his office.

En route the Thai cleaners deferred to Abdul Wahhab Higgins as he made his way along the aerosol-scented corridors of the administration building. One of the more timid Thais pressed himself against the wall as the Great Man passed, hoping thereby to blend in with the beige distemper. But it was a vain hope. Abdul Wahhab Higgins noticed from behind his dark glasses and told the lad in Arabic that (by God) he would harm the wall and that the devil is ever on the prowl seeking those whom he may devour and that why else had they (accursed infidels) been hired from afar and given the chance to labour for much gold if not to devote their labour and their every waking hour to the renaissance of the Holy Land of Ras Al Surra (on whom may God bestow His blessings)?

Of course, the Thai cleaners did not understand a word of what Abdul Wahhab Higgins was saying, but they knew exactly what he meant and at once set about polishing the marble floor with a silent American polisher of advanced design.

Abdul Wahhab Higgins entered his office through a door marked in English and Arabic:

MINISTRY FOR THE SUPPRESSION OF VICE
AND
THE ENCOURAGEMENT OF VIRTUE
(NAFFA INDUSTRIAL PORT)

ABDUL WAHHAB HIGGINS

He sat down at his large desk. The morning's mail was spread out in front of him. A paper-knife, bearing the coffee-pot emblem of Ras Al Surra, gleamed within easy reach.

There were two letters: one from the Ministry for the Suppression of Vice and the Encouragement of Virtue in Fadlabad and one, with an Irish stamp bearing a Castlebar postmark, addressed to REV. FR. PATRICK HIGGINS SJ (Society of Jesus) from a Mrs Norah Higgins.

Abdul Wahhab Higgins scowled, reached for the paper-knife and sliced through the jugular vein of his mother's letter. He lifted out the three pieces of blue Basildon Bond it contained and read:

15 August (The Assumption!)

Dear Patrick

I know you don't like me calling you that, son, but sure it was the name I gave you and I'll never be able to get me tongue round Abdul Wahhab – and wouldn't if I could.

You know I pray daily that you'll finally be able to conquer the devil that got into you all those years ago and give up the wicked heresy that the evil one had put in your way to make you lose your vocation and your soul.

All the parishioners at Our Lady of Perpetual Succour remember you in their prayers. You are now mentioned at the end of every mass along with the lost souls in Russia. I've come to dread the end of Sunday mass, son. I'm sure you can imagine the shame of a poor Catholic mother hearing her son mentioned like that. Still, Father McNally did ask me beforehand and I gave me consent. I just grip the rosary tight and offer it up.

I came back from Knock just the other day. Did you get me card? I know you always had a great devotion to the Sacred Heart, and the picture was so tastefully done that I knew you'd be thrilled to receive it. While at Knock I actually put my hand on to the footprint of the Holy Father. It's awful big feet he has! To do it I had to pay 50 pence to a Sister for the African missions, but, you know, Patrick, ever since I touched the footprint the arthritis in my right hand has improved no end! Oh, I can see you scoffing, don't you think I can't! Anyway, it's true. I hope to go back shortly to touch the footprint with my other hand.

Mrs McNabb returned from a trip to Rome, Lourdes and Fatima last week. Between you and me, I don't know where she gets the money. Her house is really threadbare these days, though I must be fair and say that she does keep it spotless. Anyway, she said that she prayed for you in all the Holy Places. During her audience with the Holy Father she shouted out: Pray for Father Patrick Higgins! She told me that at that instant the Holy Father turned and caught her in that gaze of his. She says she is sure he understood. Isn't it a wonderful Pope we've got now? I always thought that the last one was a bit stuck up but this one is lovely. He really has got the common touch and that's rare in this world. He's so different from all those proud Arabs you see on the vision. They don't look as if they've done a good day's work in their lives. And who irons their linen? Anyway, I would have thought it was worth coming back to the fold just for him. But then I'm just an ignorant old lady.

While in Rome, Mrs McNabb met her cousin, the priest, at the Irish college. I'm sure you remember him. Well, he told Mary that he was sure the Jesuits would have you back if only you saw the error of your ways. She says he says they're so short of new people just now. Of course you'd have to eat a bit of humble pie but isn't that a small price to pay to be back on the side of the angels?

Do you remember Kevin O'Leary? You went to school with him. Well, I'm sorry to say that he's been taken from us. And he only thirty-eight and with seven children! He's the same age you are, Patrick. Sure, it's true. We never know the time. All flesh is glass – as the Good Book says, and you know how easily it breaks, don't you, Patrick? I wish I had a shilling for every glass of mine you broke as you were growing up.

I'm keeping well, though I must say that you becoming a Mohammedan has really taken it out of me and I'd be telling you a lie if I said anything different.

Thank you for the books you sent me. However, Father McNally told me to put them in the bin and I did.

Your Loving Mother

Abdul Wahhab Higgins sighed and ejaculated in Arabic. Then he took his mother's letter and, one page at a time, tore it into tiny pieces. These he wrapped in a piece of air-mail A4 paper. He placed this paper in the breast pocket of his gown, making a mental note to deposit it down the lavatory on his next visit.

The other letter, from his superiors in Fadlabad, gave a breakdown for the activities of the Ministry for the Suppression of Vice and the Encouragement of Virtue for the month of Haj 1411.

Abdul Wahhab Higgins gazed at the statistic for Long or Absurd Hair and felt a quick thrill at the realization that one of the cases had been his, and that without his vigilance the number would read three and not four.

But then he recalled himself. All this was almost nothing. There was little in the memo that rebounded to his credit. His part was very small beer - dealcoholized beer - indeed. Still, that was going to change. With Sheikh Al Gaz absent - and Abdul Wahhab Higgins curled his lip in distaste at the memory of the fat, hawkish, hypocritical face of his absent boss - Abdul Wahhab Higgins knew that he could achieve something really spectacular for the spread of religious principles throughout Ras Al Surra. No more sorting through waste-paper baskets or steaming open the mail. He had set in motion something that would establish his credibility. Why, he had already informed King Fadl of his intentions. Sheikh Al Gaz had dismissed his idea out of hand. But Sheikh Al Gaz was abroad and would stay abroad for some time to come.

Now was his time. He, Abdul Wahhab Higgins, had been left in charge. He would leave his mark! He would be Savonarola with a happy ending! He would prove that a convert could enter totally into the spirit of his adopted religion. He would confound the cynics!

Having cheered himself up, Abdul Wahhab Higgins set about the holy work of the day.

3

Some hours later, in a very different world from the one inhabited by Abdul Wahhab Higgins, Sir Harry Pryke-Smith, Head of MI42 – a little known arm of British Intelligence – awaited the arrival of Charlie Hammond, one of his 'sniffer dogs', at a safe house on Highbury Fields in London.

He looked at his watch. 10.01 a.m. Hammond was late, and would, no doubt, be later. This, despite the fact that Pryke-Smith had stressed the urgency of the matter when he had called him in for the meeting over his car-phone while stuck in a traffic jam on the A2, two hours before. He knew exactly what Hammond would say when he finally arrived. 'Sorry, Herne Hill. Points Failure.'

Sir Harry stood up from his desk and strolled across his fifteen foot Kashan rug to the window. Across the road, kids were swarming over the obstacles, swinging from the trees, in the new adventure playground the council had built opposite the house. He watched them for a while, thinking what a bad show it was. When he had moved in there had been an uninterrupted view, across the leafy Fields, to some splendid houses. But not any more. The loony left council had seen to that. Adventure playgrounds indeed! Weren't the streets and the council flats adventure playground enough! The Great Unwashed were taking over. It would soon be time to move on.

The doorbell buzzed. Sir Harry Pryke-Smith flicked on the video screen and watched the back of Hammond's head. Hammond was watching the children at play – he would, no doubt, prefer to be playing with them. Sir Harry aimed daggers at the head and pressed the buzzer which admitted Hammond to the building.

Sir Harry reached into his pocket and took out an aerosol of breath freshener. He opened the top and released five times the recommended dose down his throat. Then he replaced the cap, and justifying his excess on the grounds that breath freshener was more or less his only vice, returned it to his pocket.

'Sorry I'm late!' exclaimed Hammond.

Sir Harry waited.

'Preposterous Presents!'

'Not Herne Hill?'

'Well, yes, Herne Hill too, but mainly Preposterous Presents. Look!' And Hammond fished inside a green bag and pulled out a folded piece of banana-yellow plastic. 'Good, eh?' he said.

'Doubtless, doubtless, but what is it?'

'Ah,' replied Hammond. 'Now if I show you you must promise not to tell a soul.'

Sir Harry looked at his name on the desk, facing inwards, to remind him, to console him: SIR HARRY PRYKE-SMITH CBE. DSO. MA he read. Yes, that was who he was. 'Look, Hammond, I've invited you here for a reason, you know. All is not well on your patch.'

But Hammond ignored him. 'Promise you won't tell? You know you never could keep a secret – you let slip about Miss Stone's present last year. I've got to make sure you've reformed.'

'There won't be any peace until I give in to you, I suppose. Go on, Hammond, let's see what you've bought. I won't tell a soul, I promise. Then perhaps we can get down to the business in hand.'

'Right you are!' exclaimed Hammond.

At once he unrolled the piece of plastic and started blowing down one end. The plastic reached down to his feet, then, as the air filled it, it slowly but surely began to tumesce until Sir Harry was faced by a five-foot banana with the puffing, puffy, florid face of Hammond on its summit. Hammond stoppered the banana and said quietly, but proudly, 'What do you think of *that*?'

'Very nice. Very nice. But what's it for?'

Hammond placed the banana against one of the Chippendale chairs across the desk from Sir Harry, then he sat down heavily in the other one, looking well-pleased with his work. 'Well, actually, this one is a present for Speedy Gonzalez. You know he's on leave from his stint in Honduras at the moment. We got his passport in and I saw that it's his birthday tomorrow. Good wheeze, eh?'

'You're such a consumer, Hammond. A kid really,' remarked Sir Harry, almost kindly.

'It's true, I am,' confessed Hammond, adopting his fifty-year-old hangdog expression. Then he brightened. 'I almost bought you one too!'

'Whatever for?'

'Well, I thought you could hang it prominently in the front window. That would put Boris off the scent. What safe house would have a five-foot plastic Chiquita banana in the window?'

Sir Harry looked doubtful, like a dull day that might turn into a stormy one.

'They have others. A whole range. They have a pair of bright red lips. Just lips. Nothing else. That would be good too. The main thing is that people passing and nosey-parkers think that ordinary people live here.'

'What ordinary people of your acquaintance have bananas and red lips in their front windows?'

'Several in Herne Hill do,' replied Hammond.

'I think, perhaps, you should move out of Herne Hill.'

Hammond looked suddenly sombre and stubborn. 'Out of the question, old boy. The window boxes are just reaching maturity.'

Sir Harry did not attempt an answer to that. 'To business,' he said.

'Ah, yes, business,' said Hammond and he gave the banana across from him a smile of regret.

'I got a fax in from GCHQ this morning. Quite a disturbing memo. During routine surveillance of communication satellites over the Middle East, one of the Arabic-speaking wallies found himself listening to a conversation between King Fadl of Ras Al Surra and Sultan Nabil of Zibda.'

'Didn't know they were on speaking terms.'

'I have the text of their conversation here,' continued Sir Harry, ignoring the interruption. He passed two sheets of grey paper embossed with Top Secret throughout.

'Snazz new paper,' observed Hammond, holding the paper to the light.

'Quite so. Read it, Hammond.'

Hammond read. Then he finished reading and read the memo again. At last he placed it on Sir Harry's desk and leaned back in his chair. 'Some joke, surely?' he said.

'No joke, Hammond. Deadly serious, I'm afraid.'

'Are you absolutely positive, Sir Harry? Could it not be one of those disaffected deviants at GCHQ – one who has failed positive vetting and is waiting for his heave-ho to come down the bowels of the firm grinding exceeding slow – and all that? You know the Arabic section at GCHQ is full of them. That letter is just the sort of whingeing revenge that type would take to get us bed-wetting.'

'No, Hammond. I checked with our boys at GCHQ before I called you. A good, red-blooded heterosexual of sterling virtue caught the information. Dexter, in fact.'

Hammond frowned. 'They don't come any loyaller than Dexter and that's a fact. Still, Nabil hasn't consented to sell Al Bustan to Ras Al Surra. Sounds to me like he's dismissed the idea out of hand. I can't see what we have to worry about. It would only be worrying if Nabil were interested.' Then a thought occurred to him. 'I say, you don't think that Fadl *knows* about Al Bustan, do you? I hadn't thought of that!'

'Hard to say,' replied Sir Harry. 'He may have just

taken a shine to the place. He's a bit like you in that respect.'

'A bit of an impulse buyer, you mean?'

'Yes, except he's got kingly tastes and you've got the taste of a temp.'

'Thanks. However, I would not describe Fadl's tastes as kingly. Have you heard about what he buys at Aspreys and Garrards? He just gets his bananas hand-crafted in solid gold, that's the only difference.'

'Well, that's as maybe. But back to the matter in hand. Fadl offered Nabil four billion jumpas. That's no mean sum, especially as far as Nabil is concerned. Now it may be that he just glanced at a map of Ras Al Surra and decided it would look a good deal more symmetrical with the addition of Al Bustan. Al Bustan should by rights belong to Ras Al Surra anyway. We managed to deflect the boundary line just in time before giving them independence. And thank God we did! Fadl has been going his own sweet way since. Hasn't left a stone unturned, a sand dune unlevelled, in his search for unearned income. Much better to have Al Bustan under the control of a deluded visionary like Sultan Nabil.'

'But you could not say that Nabil is exactly in our pocket?'

'No, far from it. But he's such a trusting cove. Remember how he never questioned the results of the Barefoot Geologists scheme we sent out there, of which you were one of the early stars? You told him there was no mineral wealth of any sort under Al Bustan and he believed you. Didn't even think to get a second opinion. I wish there were a few more world leaders like Nabil.'

Hammond smiled. Any reference to the Barefoot Geologists made him smile. It had been a merry jape. He missed those days. Twenty-odd years later he still looked back on the two jobs he had done with the Barefoot Geologists as the highpoint of his career. It had been all downhill after that. He was still living off the reputation that successful piece of deception had earned him with the Firm.

'So you will appreciate why I am so concerned that Al Bustan should remain in the hands of the Sultan of Zibda,' continued Sir Harry. 'If Fadl got his hands on it he'd have a team of geologists from RASONGRO digging around before you could say Mercedes Benz and then the Geiger counters would buzz and all hell would be let loose. Britain would lose control of her single most valuable and untapped access to uranium. You know how the Boss likes to keep the pantry well stocked. She'd never forgive us.' Sir Harry looked hard at Hammond.

'You don't need to tell me all this. I do know it already, Sir Harry!'

'Yes, I know you know but do you *know*, Hammond?' asked Sir Harry in a tone of the utmost seriousness.

Hammond glanced over at the five-foot banana. It seemed to belong to a different world, a world of play and Christmas and window-shopping – a world he felt comfortable in. Now he was in that different, distinctly uncomfortable world, that gave him his living. 'I'll keep a close eye on the situation, Sir Harry,' he said soberly.

Sir Harry nodded. 'Not only your eyes, Hammond. Every available orifice. Apart from everything else, if the Barefoot Geologists were ever revealed as a sham, I would be totally discredited. And don't forget the Barefoot Geologists are still active. Don't forget that!'

'I won't, Sir Harry. Leave it with me.'

Sir Harry nodded. 'One last thing, Hammond . . .'

'Sir?'

'I think they have sold you a dud banana. Correct me if I'm wrong, but doesn't it seem to have deflated rather?'

Hammond looked at the wrinkled banana with sad eyes and a clown's downward-pulled mouth. 'Yes, you're right. I'll have to take it back.'

'Hammond!' barked Sir Harry Pryke-Smith, 'you don't have time to take it back! You have work to do!'

Hammond, a very different man from the one who had entered the safe house on Highbury Fields a few minutes before, nodded and left Sir Harry's office without another word.

4

Sultan Nabil of Zibda, who had unwittingly ruined Charlie Hammond's afternoon in overcast London, was walking with his wife Zarina, along the waterfront of Al Rahman that same day, two hours after sunset.

Zarina had noticed that her husband had been preoccupied with something all day – something which he was unable to bring himself to broach with her. He had gone about his normal daily tasks in his usual dogged manner: meeting people with complaints and problems in the majilis of their home; studying and then signing papers sent to him from the various ministries; visiting a couple of schools. But all the time he had seemed to Zarina to be far from his usual open self. Something was worrying him, she knew, and she wanted to find out what.

In the late afternoon she summoned her two eldest daughters, Latifa and Aziza, asking them to do their best to make sure that the other children did not fall on their father that evening, pleading for time and attention. There was something the matter with Daddy and she wanted him to have a rest that night. The two of them needed to have some time to themselves.

The girls promised that they would do their best and succeeded in calming the rest of the family. After the evening meal all of the children miraculously disappeared, leaving Sultan Nabil and Zarina alone in the quiet dining-room.

'That's odd,' Nabil had said, suddenly looking up from a rapt contemplation of the carpet on which he was sitting.

'What's odd, Nabil?'

'Oh, nothing. It just seems a bit quiet. I can hear the ocean.'

'Yes, it is quiet. It is a beautiful night, too. There is a cool breeze blowing. Would you come for a walk with me?'

'But what about the children?'

Then he looked at his wife and nodded, 'You have arranged everything, I suppose.'

Zarina said nothing, but, smiling, took Nabil's hand and gently lifted him up.

They walked along the beach in the dark. The phosphorescence in the breaking waves laid down a path on their right to guide them. The lights from the shops and old merchants' houses above the high water mark did not impinge on the dark. Out in the harbour pinpricks of light marked the spots where dhows had moored. As they walked they could hear, in between the crash of breakers, snatches of a song sung by a deep-voiced crewman aboard one of the havened dhows.

Nabil stopped half-way along the length of the crescent-moon beach.

'Do you remember what we used to plan before my father died?'

Zarina searched for her husband's hand in the dark, but could not find it. 'Yes, I remember well, Nabil.'

'We never did sail away, did we?'

'No, we never did.'

'And now it is too late, I suppose.'

'Well,' Zarina found the hand and pressed it gently, 'it is late, but, perhaps, not too late. However, the children—'

'The children are not the problem. This . . .' Nabil turned away from the sea and gestured towards the lights of Al Rahman, '. . . is the problem.' He sighed and dropped his arms to his sides. 'Wouldn't it be wonderful to be able to just sail away and leave the problems to somebody else?'

Zarina moved herself between Nabil and his capital city. 'What's wrong, Nabil?' she asked.

'Nothing. Everything,' he replied.

'Yes, but something has happened. Tell me what has happened to make you so unhappy today. Do not think that it has escaped me. I can read you like one of the children's story-books. You know that.'

'I know that,' answered Nabil quietly.

They continued walking, but still Nabil was not telling Zarina what was on his mind. She waited patiently.

At last he said, 'Didn't the children tell you that I had a call from Fadl yesterday?'

'They told me. Is that the problem?'

'Partly . . . mainly. Fadl offered me four billion jumpas for Al Bustan.'

For a long moment Zarina said nothing. She hardly needed to, for she knew well enough what a conflict the offer would set up in her husband's mind. Every night she heard him talking in his sleep, debating with invisible jinn on how to earn enough money to provide the people of Zibda with the things they needed. She knew what a temptation Fadl had put in front of Nabil. She could imagine Fadl talking to Nabil from behind his desk with its bank of multi-coloured, superfluous telephones. Perhaps his dreadful wife, Noof, had been at his elbow, egging him on. She knew what she would have told Fadl to do with his four billion jumpas. She felt she knew what Nabil had told him to do with his four billion jumpas too. But, having told him, he was still left with nagging doubts.

'I told him that I could not consider such a thing,' Nabil said.

'But the call has left you unhappy and unsure. Well, I can understand that. It was a cruel thing for him to do to you. Typical of Fadl. Now you are thinking what you could do with such a sum, wondering if you should sell Al Bustan after all?'

'That's about it, Zarina. It is a pretty valueless piece of land for us. Why, even after good rains, there's no grazing for livestock there. The soil is sour and there isn't a well to speak of. Fadl says he wants it to make Ras Al Surra look "right", and I suppose he does have a point. The British should never have diverted the border in that way to give us Al Bustan. Father always said that he thought they just wanted to rub in the fact that we had been stuck with every last piece of oil-less land in a peninsula floating on the stuff. He was probably right, but I have always put it down to some British surveyor's hangover.'

'Are you positive that Fadl doesn't have some other reason for wanting Al Bustan? Perhaps he wants control of the beds of desert roses. I know they have desert roses on the Ras Al Surran side of the border, but they have let people dig them up. I hear they are completely ruined. Maybe he wants a new and untouched field of them.'

Nabil laughed wryly. 'I would doubt if desert roses would interest Fadl in the least. I just can't see him getting excited about pieces of crystallized sand that resemble rose petals, can you? He would rather have the real thing flown in from Holland or a few dozen crafted in platinum. As regards mineral wealth, I'm sure there is none of any sort. You surely haven't forgotten how that volunteer British team searched for weeks on end in Al Bustan, looking for something of value. We in Zibda took a year out of their lives. I've never seen people work harder – but all to no avail. What was to be found in Zibda, the Barefoot Geologists found. I am happy that we have the five wells they discovered in the north – if only to give them some thanks for all their work.' And Nabil named each of the wells discovered in the course of the Barefoot Geologists scheme, 'Iain's Well, Tony's Well, Robert's Well, Charlie's Well, and Livia's Well. God, they worked! I loved that lot, Zarina! Sometimes I think that I keep myself so busy over national affairs so that I won't let them down. Are you still in touch with Livia, by the way?'

'Yes,' replied Zarina, 'I heard from her only last week. She's in Northern Nigeria now, near the Chad border. Still doing the same thing. Tony and Robert are with her, but she says that Iain has "sold out", as she puts it. He's gone into some government job back in Britain apparently.'

'What happened to Charlie?' Nabil asked.

'Shame on you, Nabil! You're getting old. After he left here he joined the others on a similar volunteer programme surveying in Southern Sudan. He got a bad case of jaundice and had to be sent home. We were still writing to them quite frequently then. Don't you remember how we went to Fadlabad airport with a huge basket of dates and got a passenger going to London to hand-carry them for us to his bedside?'

'Ah, yes. But we never heard much from him after that, did we?'

'A thank you note and a couple of records, but I have no idea what happened to him. Livia never mentions him in her letters.'

'Give her my regards when you write, will you? Ask her when she's coming back for a visit. My God, I would love to see them again!'

'Me too,' sighed Zarina. 'Remember how Livia loved Joan Baez and Bob Dylan? She said they were "inspirational". Sometimes I still imagine that I can hear Joan Baez songs coming from that old ruined merchant house we put them up in.'

'It's Charlie playing his harmonica that I remember,' said Nabil. 'You know, I don't recall him even once getting through a tune without making a mistake.'

'He came close a number of times. I think I liked him best. He was so funny – though I'm not sure he knew it – and he never minded when we laughed at him.'

'We laughed all the time in those days. Didn't Livia send you some tapes?'

'You know she did, but the tape recorder needs mending. It has needed mending for a year, Nabil.'

'If I sold Al Bustan to Fadl I could buy you a new one, Zarina.'

Zarina smiled. 'I know all those songs by heart, Nabil.' And at once she began to sing:

'You soy un hombre sincero
De la tierra de las palmas.'

'I too remember Guantanamera.'

'You ought to, Nabil. You've been living it for the last twenty years.'

Nabil sighed, stopped and looked out at the ocean, 'But the times have changed. Only Zibda has not changed.'

'No, we haven't changed. We are not like Ras Al Surra.'

'There's comfort in that, I suppose,' said Nabil, continuing to gaze out at the ocean.

Zarina tried to see Nabil's face, but it was too dark for her to do so. She felt her love for him enveloping her. Usually her love was like one of those songs, every rhythm and nuance of which was familiar and comfortable and could be sung, hummed, whistled, as part of the mundane round of days and tasks. But here, now, she was feeling a rekindling of a strange new song. No, it was not new. It was the song of their falling in love. It jangled and tingled like Jimmy Hendrix. It longed like Janis Joplin. It had been a song they had known well but which, though then they would never have thought they could ever forget it, had been forgotten, had been replaced by softer songs more easily sung around the children.

But now the old song pulsated through Zarina. She put her arms around her husband and whispered into his ear.

'We daren't, Zarina!'

'We always used to dare. When Livia and Charlie and the others were here, we dared.'

'But it would be no good example to the children of Zibda.'

'The children of Zibda should be tucked up in their beds by now, Nabil.'

She could tell that he was looking to left and right, like a guilty schoolboy about to smoke. Then she saw his robe rising above his head, the swishing sound of underwear being removed. Laughing, she removed her clothes too. Then the Sultan and Sultana of Zibda walked hand in hand into the ocean.

After their swim they made love on the beach and the forgotten song came back and sang itself to them throughout their slow and tender brawl.

'I don't know what to do about Al Bustan,' Nabil confessed in the midst of everything.

And she thought. That is it. Just that. He is stuck. My sincere man from the land of the palm trees is on the rack.

'We'll think about it later, my husband. We'll work it out together.'

'We can work it out,' he sang.

'Of course we can, my dear. Of course we can. Of course,' murmured Zarina.

5

The following morning, Armitage stood in front of five Ras Al Surran Fire and Safety Officers of the Naffa industrial port, a map of their place of work behind him. He looked with some distaste at the slouching firemen. Then, with even more distaste, he turned his attention to the map of the port. He pointed to the port with his teacher's pointer.

'This is the port,' Armitage said.

Silence.

'This is the port,' he repeated.

Silence.

'What is it?' he asked.

Silence.

'This is the port,' he said, answering his own question, as no-one else would.

Silence.

'This is the port,' he said once again, only louder.

'This is the bort,' they repeated.

He smiled, 'Good,' he said.

'Good,' they repeated.

'Hmm, not so good,' he said.

'Hmm, not so good,' they repeated, feeling they were getting the hang of it now.

'This is the port. What is it?' Armitage asked.

'This is the bort. What is it?' they replied.

Armitage frowned and turned his left hand into a 'question puppet' and his right hand into an 'answer puppet'.

'What is it?' asked the question puppet.

'It's the port,' answered the answer puppet.

The question puppet turned towards Mahmoud, who wore a smile which said that he was enjoying the show.

'What is it?' the question puppet asked Mahmoud.

'Hand you,' replied Mahmoud.

Armitage was barely able to restrain his question puppet from turning itself into a rampant fist and imparting a straight left into Mahmoud's over-ripe stomach. But instead he made the question puppet say, 'Yes, but . . .' between clenched fingers and then had it move on huffily to Salim.

'What is it?' asked the question puppet.

'It's the bort,' answered Salim.

'Good,' said Armitage. 'It's the p-port!'

Then he practised the question and answer around the class.

'Now,' continued Armitage, 'how many ports are there in Naffa?'

'Two,' replied Salim, unasked.

'Please put your hand up!' exclaimed Armitage teacherishly.

'I sorry!' said Salim.

'Well, you're always sorry but you just keep on doing it, Salim. It really is highly irritating. It really is. You just don't have any consideration for the other students – none at all. Has it ever occurred to you that they might want to answer? Has it? No, I don't suppose for one minute that it has. As long as *Salim* knows, he'll just go ahead and shout out the answer. Well, I call that selfish and where I come from selfishness is . . .' said Armitage, forgetting, as he often did, that his students could not understand a single word he was saying.

He closed his eyes momentarily and then moved his hands rapidly back and forth, as if he were cleaning a blackboard. It was a signal that communicated, to Armitage at least, that a new start was being made, a new page about to be turned.

He gestured to the map of the port once again.

'There are two ports in Naffa, the industrial port and the commercial port. Repeat!'

'Ports . . . Naffa . . . Indus . . . and . . . Comm . . . Sorry!' repeated the class. Armitage gave them his coldest look and pursed his lips.

'You knew this yesterday,' he told them in his most hurt tones.

'It's the bort!' exclaimed Hassan.

'No, it isn't!' corrected Armitage, still huffy.

'What is?' asked Hassan.

'What indeed?' asked Armitage of the ceiling.

Then he rubbed at the invisible blackboard again.

'There are two ports. Repeat!' he said.

'There are two borts,' they repeated.

'Two ports!' repeated Armitage, emphasizing the p.

'Two borts!' repeated the class, emphasizing the b.

'Ports!' exploded Armitage.

'Borts!' shouted the class, ever obliging.

'No, ports!'

'No, borts!'

'No! Not "No borts!" P-p-p-ports!' popped Armitage.

'Borts.'

Armitage was down but not quite out. He looked around in his bag for his box of tissues. He offered one to each student, practising.

Armitage: Here you are.

Student: Thank you.

Armitage: You're more than welcome.

as he did so. Then he took a tissue for himself from the box, a pink one, he noted with distaste. Theatrically, he raised the tissue to his face, holding it by one corner. He held the corner at eye-level so that the tissue drooped down in front of his mouth. Then he turned side-on to the class:

'Port! P-p-p-p-port!' exclaimed Armitage, sending his tissue blowing like a lace curtain in a gale from his unvoiced bi-labial plosive.

Pleased with himself, he said, 'Salim, you try.'

'Bort!' said Salim, 'bort, bort, bort!' The tissue remained flaccid. 'Bort bort bort bort bort bort!' The tissue was still unmoved.

'No, Salim! It must come out with force. P-p-p-port!'

Salim managed to make his green tissue ripple slightly, but, to balance this advance, a particularly dull student called Abdul was in the middle of eating his tissue, and opened his mouth to shock Armitage at the sight of the yellow cud on his tongue.

'Really, Abdul! That is not good. I am most displeased!'

'No, no. Very good, teacher. Nice.'

'Yes, but . . .' began Armitage.

But Mahmoud stretched and yawned. Hassan kicked Abdul in the groin. It was time for a change. Armitage was well aware that one always had to be sensitive to the attention span of students. His philosophy of Education came from AN Whitehead's notion of making every class a balance between Structure and Romance. Now it was time for Romance.

'Scrabble time!' exclaimed Armitage.

At once the class woke up and Abdul stopped telling Hassan what he thought his mother had been before she became a she-goat.

Armitage fetched his five-times-larger-than-life Scrabble board – drawn across several large pieces of white card in his own time. He distributed seven letters to each fireman.

'Right! You start, Hassan,' enthused Armitage.

'No can,' said Hassan.

'Try Hassan!'

'No good letter,' mourned Hassan.

Armitage moved behind Hassan's chair. From that vantage point he saw a C, an A and a T. 'You have a word, Hassan! Here's a hint: Miaaaoooow!'

Hassan looked over his shoulder at Armitage with alarm.

'What is?' he asked.

'Miaaaooow!' repeated Armitage helpfully.

Hassan stared at his letters and giggled to his friends.

Armitage pointed to Hassan's C,A,T, and Hassan placed them on the board.

'Good, Hassan! That's five points to Hassan!' beamed Armitage.

Everyone clapped Hassan and Hassan held his hands, joined above his head, in a victory salute.

'Now it's your turn, Abdul!'

'Nobody good!' said Abdul, referring to the letters.

'Come on, Abdul. Think!' commanded Armitage. But Abdul was stumped. Once again Armitage had to sidle up to assist, pointing out P,P,L,E in Abdul's collection.

The game continued thus for three rounds, until the firemen had tired and Salim had started writing 'Allah' in beautiful Arabic calligraphy on his T.

'Right! That's it for today.'

The class bolted for the door. Armitage was left alone in the classroom to pick up the scattered Scrabble cards and replace them and the board behind the teacher's desk.

While doing so, he wondered how he could possibly continue this charade for another day, let alone the year of his contract. 'The English language. Teaching the English language. Dear God!' exclaimed Armitage to the strip lighting. And he wondered, as he had often wondered before, what George Bernard Shaw would have said.

Down the years Shaw's adage: 'Those who can, do. Those who can't, teach,' had followed him like a demanding stray cat. Shaw, as he was portrayed behind a cloud on the LP cover of *My Fair Lady* pulling the strings of Rex Harrison and Julie Andrews, shook his head in wry contemplation of the career that was Armitage's. This image had chased Armitage up the garden path of his twenties, into the potting shed of his thirties and on to the compost heap of his forties where everything went to creating the fertile soil of regret.

Not that it had been all doom and gloom. It hadn't. He had enjoyed great chunks of his working life and had often found teaching not only pleasurable but almost ecstatic. On those occasions when he had had a responsive class, when language sank in like water into a sponge, he had been left by his class – as now – in an empty room and felt that God, whom he imagined looking rather like George Bernard Shaw on the aforementioned LP cover, was looking down on him and saying: 'Though thou be lacking in many things, though thou beest a trifle on the whimpish side and dost lack the greater manly virtues thou art – nonetheless – a smashing teacher!'

But not today and not on any day since his arrival in Ras Al Surra.

He looked at his watch. Ten-thirty. That meant it would be seven-thirty in Herne Bay. People would be having breakfast, kissing their wives – or, if they were Peter or Tom or Patrick, kissing their lovers – goodbye and heading off to the railway station to catch their trains to London. If he were there, he would be getting out of his lumpy bed at Mrs Polletto's guest house, looking across the sea outside his window towards France and wondering what the day would bring at the Quick School of Languages.

The Quick School of Languages had been Armitage's life since leaving university. He had been the first teacher employed by Arthur and Henry when they had set up the school in the late sixties. Armitage had not intended to stay in Herne Bay for so long, but the years had crumbled away at amazing speed – as chalk sticks crumble against a blackboard – and Armitage had lacked the energy to move on. He had moved into Mrs Polletto's guest house almost right away and her bacon-and-egg breakfasts and her treatment of him – the stern but loving mother – served to keep him in a state of dithery indecision that just went on and on.

He had never made a decision to stay on at 'Quickies', as Arthur and Henry affectionately and affectedly called the school which had allowed them to buy a large house at the top of the town and swan around Kent and the Continent in a Jaguar, while Armitage did everything that was expected of the senior teacher. He assigned classes, taught them, smoothed ruffled feathers of temperamental teachers and played father and mother to an endless stream of foreign students. And perhaps it had been this aspect of his job that had held him in thrall for so long. Armitage loved people to get on, hated anybody to be uncomfortable. He would spend many hours every week sorting out the problems of his students, liaising between them and the sometimes miserable families to which the students were assigned around the town. A student complained that her sheets were not being changed weekly. Armitage would turn up on the doorstep of the erring family and read the riot act. An Arab student was, a mother informed him, creating pools of water in the bathroom. Armitage would go and explain the muslim way of bathroom hygiene. He felt that over the years he had played his part at cross-cultural clarification. He had taught both students and Herne Bay residents alike a little about the differences that made the world – and Herne Bay – a more interesting place.

All the time he had wanted to tell the householders who took in foreign students that they were privileged to have an exotic part of the world staying with them to widen their horizons. The money was not the point. Think what an education it was for their children to have a living, breathing piece of 'abroad' staying with them! But such appeals would have fallen on deaf ears. Increasingly the families who took students did so only for help with the housekeeping. Armitage found himself battling for extra blankets for a shivering Indonesian; appealing for a diet other than fish fingers and chips for an unwillingly-anorexic Argentinian; demanding that the stone-cold radiators come to life for a coughing Catalonian. He tried to be patient and balanced. He tried to explain the queer unfriendliness of many of the families to the bewildered students.

But, if Armitage was able to explain the queerness of folk to one another, he seemed constitutionally unable to explain his own queerness to himself.

Often he would return from a day at the Quick School of Languages to his single room at Mrs Polletto's, sit at his desk in front of the window that looked out on the brown sea and let his thoughts beat him down. And as he had negative dialogues with himself about why he was where he was and not somewhere else sharing his life with someone nice, he would constantly wonder that this nervous, ageing English teacher, who could not find himself a friend, who could not even pluck up the required courage to go into a pub where he might have the possibility of meeting somebody, could contain Armitage the senior teacher who mothered overseas students and sang old Seekers songs at Quick School parties. He inspected classes ruthlessly and struck Herne Bay families off the register and consigned them to the outer darkness inside his filing cabinet; in every way he was the life and soul of the school, yet he would come back alone to Mrs Polletto's and sit biting his nails – fearful of the loneliness he was living and would always live, unless he could bring himself to *do* something.

But then last year hooligans had started beating up his students. He got telephone calls late at night from Italians and Arabs and Africans in the casualty department of the hospital. He found it harder to explain to his bloodied charges the reason for the unprovoked attacks that were being made on them than he had when their families acted up or acted mean. 'There are good and bad everywhere,' he had tried, but that had not seemed enough and was not enough. These incidents of thuggery wrought a seachange in Armitage. The thugs that beat up his students would beat him up too if his difference were as obvious as a black face or a foreign accent. Herne Bay began to scare him. Also, Arthur and Henry, once chums, were less and less in evidence, having bought themselves a villa in Marrakesh to which they had never invited him.

One evening, Armitage – almost a quarter of a century after everyone else – saw *Lawrence of Arabia* at the Herne Bay Odeon. He left the cinema in a daze.

When the conductress on the bus back to Mrs Polletto's had said that there was a council ordinance in writing which stated that she did not have to take the five pound note he proffered her, Armitage had replied, 'Nothing is written.' As he lit a cigarette on the top deck, he snuffed out the match slowly between thumb and forefinger and observed, as Lawrence had observed, 'Of course it hurts. The trick is not to care that it hurts.' And he had not cared either, for the pain of the match on his thumb had given him an idea, emptied his mind of all worries and considerations except for that one idea: Leave!

Well, he had left, but he had brought himself – as a snail carries its shell – with him to Ras Al Surra.

With a sigh, Armitage finished picking up the Scrabble set.

It was hard to make sense of it all. He tried to tell himself that here in Ras Al Surra he was merely experiencing the culture shock that he had kept telling his students about in Herne Bay. Yes, perhaps that was it. Ras Al Surra just wasn't what he had imagined it would be. Just as no smiling Queen Elizabeth greeted members of the Commonwealth off their planes, so no Omar Sharif had whisked him through passport control and on to the back of a camel. And nothing magical had happened since.

Armitage sat down in his teacher's chair and looked at the door. If he conjured up a visualization of the Friend coming through that door, perhaps it would happen. He closed his eyes and conjured up such a vision, but when he opened them again the door was still closed. Still, he told himself, you have to do the visualizations for ages. If I can just keep it up, then something will turn up.

He screwed up his eyes tight and concentrated on conjuring up a vision of the Friend who would make everything work out all right.

6

'I'll take six of those, my friend!' said Charlie Hammond. 'No, make it nine.'

He reached into his pocket and gazed along Oxford Street, noticing that the dense crowds of shoppers, from his perspective at any rate, seemed to be doing a bobbing dance.

He handed over a five pound note and four one pound coins to the cockney sparrow who had set up his stall outside the South African Airlines office on the corner of Regent and Oxford Street. There he had been selling little worm-like creatures in primary colours. One sat at the bottom of a jam jar, placed on a little collapsible stool, no doubt recovering from its exertions. For the salesman had just completed a show involving the violet, smiling worm. First the worm had been coaxed out of its glass on to the salesman's hand where it moved in paroxysms of pleasure when stroked by an eager Hammond, who was at the front of a large crowd of onlookers. Then quick as a flash, the worm had climbed up the front of the salesman's mackintosh, up his face and down his right arm. There it had paused, seeming to look at the crowd, appealing, aching, demanding cutely to be bought. It had then darted straight away back into the jam jar.

Hammond had decided all this must have been achieved as a result of the friction he had created with his finger when stroking the worm's violet, nylon fur. He had at once seen infinite possibilities for the clever little worm: the faces of neglected nephews and nieces lighting up at being presented with one for Christmas; Miss Glover melting towards him as one climbed up his pin-striped jacket at the Firm's Curzon Street office; himself in his person-empty, possession-full, flat entertaining and being entertained by this lively little creature, a creature he knew to be inanimate but did not care, so animated did it seem – and so mysterious. A steal for a quid, he thought.

'Want a bag for 'em, do you, squire?' asked the salesman.

'No, that's all right. Just put them into my briefcase, will you?' He opened up his briefcase while the salesman poured nine of the little worms, in their own round plastic boxes, into the briefcase which Hammond held open.

'Top Secret, eh?' remarked the man, looking at the folders in the briefcase.

'What?' asked Hammond, suddenly on his guard and thinking fast. 'Oh, no! Just another novelty item. I'm partial to novelties, you know.'

'Well, hope you get a buzz from those little fellows, guv. They've been selling like hot cakes. Not surprising really, when you think what they can do, and how reasonably priced too.'

'Look,' said Hammond, frowning, putting down his briefcase and fishing around in his pocket for more money, 'give us three more, would you?'

'A pleasure. There are full instructions included,' said the salesman.

Hammond weaved his way along Oxford Street towards Mayfair. He resisted the blandishments of the shop windows, having had his fix of spending for the day, and postponed his planned, dreaded trip to Zwemmer's in Charing Cross Road, where he lusted and longed to buy Robert Mapplethorpe's *Black Book*, but had so far lacked the necessary courage. Don't need it, he informed himself, not fooling himself for a moment.

Instead, he concentrated on assigning the little worms to those recipients who would most appreciate them. He wondered if he should keep back two for himself. After all one might get lonely. Perhaps he should keep three and have one for the office, but then he thought he should have four so that the one in the office would not get lonely. His gargantuan appetite for nylon novelty worms – a longing he could not even have imagined a mere ten minutes before – ate him up outside the Oxford Street Boots and he swivelled around, facing Oxford Circus, determined to go back to the man and buy more. But then, confused and disoriented, he found himself facing Marble Arch again before the thought of his saner side – the side of Charlie Hammond which almost never won an argument – could be articulated, 'You have got enough! You don't need any more!' But a further melancholic ninety degrees had him half-way round, facing H Samuels, towards retracing his steps yet again. He searched in his pocket for any forgotten one pound coins. What saved him was a collision with a passer-by who had been the bemused, then irritated, witness of his consumer dance in the middle of the pavement.

'Do you *mind*!'

'Er . . . sorry! Sorry. Thought I'd forgotten to forget something,' he told the fast-disappearing back, unable to admit that he was having a shopping fit. In a panic, appalled that the stranger had been privy to his nonsensical utterance, he corrected himself loudly to the back that had already forgotten him, 'I've forgotten to *remember* something, sorry!' he told it.

Charlie Hammond commenced walking again, seeing his life forever changed by his purchase. I could go around orphanages and Cheshire Homes, entertaining poor unfortunates with my little worms! God, I should have bought more! he thought as he walked. Then he stopped again, the Devil of Desire having planted the thought in his brain that his purchases could, in fact, contribute to the betterment of the human condition. Wondering if, after all, he should go back and purchase a couple of extra worms, he decided that common sense must prevail. I'm sure one at home and one at the office is sufficient. I can always take the one in the office home at weekends. This notion satisfied him.

Then the thought struck him that he had not given enough thought to the Crisis. What had he achieved in the twenty-four hours since his meeting with Sir Harry? Well, he had got in touch with GCHQ and urged extra vigilance on Dexter and his cronies. All ears would be glued to each and every call bouncing off the Ibn Batuta satellite. What else? He had checked up on everyone at GCHQ who was remotely connected with monitoring and passed the word along that all translation work was to be done straight from tape and double-checked. That should take care of the poofter problem. 'The poofter problem' hmm, and he thought of the Charlie Hammond standing in his mackintosh outside Zwemmer's. Then that thought was gone the way it always went. Anything else? No, he felt like he had done his bit.

Hammond turned into South Molton Street feeling well satisfied. An aroma of roasting coffee reached his nostrils and he decided to reward himself for his sterling efforts for Queen and Country with a pound of Kenya Peaberry. He usually used Sainsbury's French Blend in the digital alarm-clock-radio-coffee-maker he had bought some weeks before at John Lewis. Might as well give the coffee machine a treat. He had more than satisfied his own lust to buy, but why not let the coffee machine in on his pleasure? How happily it would purr and puff and give forth sweetness as he opened his eyes to the first flush of a Herne Hill dawn!

As he watched the bald assistant wrap his pound of coffee, tying the package with string, Hammond saw himself alone with his worm in his flat in Herne Hill, drinking a cup of fresh Kenya Peaberry. The worm climbed all over him and smiled at him affectionately. It perched on the edge of his coffee cup and took little dolly-sips. Then it looked up at its master.

He left the shop and wondered absently if that scene of domestic bliss would be heightened by a new compact disc for his Denon player. The window boxes were definitely responding to the quality stereo achieved from that machine. That new *Merry Widow*, he thought. But he chided himself: Enough! Tomorrow is another day! and quickened his pace towards Curzon Street.

Half an hour later Hammond sat at his desk, looking disconsolate, a blue, nylon worm on the desk in front of him – very still, very, very still.

'Why can't people be honest? Why can't they be decent? Such deception and corruption at the very heart of this once-great country – the very epicentre of this throne of kings! I am shocked! I am scandalized! The evil little salesman should have pointed out that the worm was attached to a piece of nylon and that it would take years and years of assiduous practice to develop the necessary sleight of hand to be able to operate it with the least fluency!'

The active little worms were not, it turned out, moved by friction and a touch of magic, but by a nearly-invisible piece of nylon thread attached to the head and then looped about the operator's person. The salesman had pulled the string at the right moment and made the worm move. The deceitful wretch! There ought to be a law! thought Hammond. Indeed, there probably *is* a law. What there isn't is *respect* for law. Oh, yes, there were instructions inside all right and the box had even included a long piece of nylon thread, but it was a trick and a sham all the same. How dare he! This, for sure, thought Hammond, was the unacceptable two faces of capitalism if ever there was one! Hammond had bought his automatic coffee machine because he had the distinct impression that it made coffee automatically. Had he got it home and found that he had been mistaken in that impression then he could have gone straight back to John Lewis (as he had gone back to Preposterous Presents and succeeded in obtaining an air-tight banana) and demanded his money back. But with the twelve *twelve!* boxed nylon worms! He knew that the rogue would long since have left his spot in front of South

African Airways, pocketing his ill-gotten gains. Wouldn't have paid a penny in rates either. Nor taxes!

Hammond looked down at the worm and decided to give it one last try. He took one end of the nylon thread and pulled it up his jacket sleeve, round his neck and down the other jacket sleeve. Then he placed the worm in the bottom of his water-glass. He pulled, his left hand holding the end of the nylon. It cut into his neck. The worm moved an inch up the glass, like a worm on a fishing line, but it did not wriggle as it had outside the South African Airways office. It did not spring to life. It was hopeless.

The telephone rang on his desk. He sat down and answered it.

'Come and see me straight away and bring the Zibda file with you.'

'Right away!' said Hammond to Miss Glover, his immediate superior, and he replaced the receiver.

He opened his briefcase and was met by the sight of a pound of Kenya Peaberry and worms in round plastic boxes. He seethed again momentarily, but forced himself to be calm and sort through his papers.

'Funny!' observed Charlie Hammond, feeling his face reddening, tingling and then going suddenly cold. 'My God, they're gone!'

He poured the contents of his briefcase over his desk, frantically seeking out the Zibda file. Coffee fumes reached his nostrils, reminding him of days of innocence before disgrace. The worms in their round boxes rolled across the desk and dived, lemming-like, away from him. 'Don't go now!' he told them. 'I have to face Miss Glover! Help me find the Zibda file, worms!' He leafed through all his files and as he searched he remembered the scene at Oxford Circus when the worms had entered his life and realized that it must have been then that the Zibda file had left it. Everything was in that file. The whole history of the Barefoot Geologists. If it got into the wrong hands, then it would all come out. But maybe it was there. Maybe in some part of the briefcase that he had never before located. He rooted further. The end of a paper-clip pushed itself down the nail of his right index finger and Charlie Hammond yelped and kicked the side of his desk. He sucked on his finger and looked into the briefcase morosely. No, there could be no mistake. The Zibda file had gone. He made one last frantic, hopeless, feel along the lining of the briefcase and found a Nuttall's Minto, sticky and softened, caught in copulation with the lost top of a long-forgotten Bic. He had bought a half pound a month ago and given everyone in the office one. Briefly he wondered whether Miss Glover would take a Nuttall's Minto instead of the Zibda file. He saw himself knocking at her door in the moral equivalent of short trousers with a pee stain on the front and offering her a Nuttall's Minto.

'It's my last!' he pleaded to the no-nonsense, unforgiving eyes of Miss Glover.

Charlie Hammond shook himself and surveyed the wreckage on his desk, aware as he watched it that he could well be watching the wreckage of his life.

Then, a condemned man, he made his way to Miss Glover's office. As he mounted the staircase he could recall every item that littered his desk top. If they were items in 'Remember the Tray', he would win hands down. He knocked at Miss Glover's door, feeling his life had come to an end. He saw in the near-future, himself, pilloried and persecuted for betrayal, his sins the talk of gentlemen's clubs and corridors of power . . .

'Of course he was a poofter. Knew Blunt apparently.'

'Yes, but at least Blunt betrayed his country for a cause. Charlie Hammond did it for the sake of a bargain!'

'Miss Glover, I have something terrible to tell you,' began Charlie Hammond.

Miss Glover listened, staring at Charlie Hammond and pressing the end of her nose with her right index finger. She was wearing her Aran cardigan, her Friday, ready-for-the country ensemble.

When he had finished his sorry tale, Miss Glover motioned him to sit down.

'And did you think to retrace your steps?' she asked him, her mouth scarcely moving as she spoke. Her lips, a horizontal pair of parallel lines held a rigid two centimetres apart.

'Well, no. I thought I should come and tell you straight away, Miss Glover.'

'Probably too late now. God, you're such an idiot, Hammond. As soon as we give you a chance to earn your keep for a change instead of being a rather expensive drone, you have to *fuck it up*!'

Hammond blanched, not so much from what Miss Glover had said, but because of her sudden coarseness. Such an expression must be virgin territory for Miss Glover, he thought. God, things were bad!

Miss Glover continued, 'You know, Hammond, I often think you enjoy being a failure. What have you done for the firm in the last decade and a half? Sniffed out a couple of deviants at GCHQ, that's what. Not what one would call sterling service, is it, Hammond?'

Hammond murmured towards the floor that perhaps Miss Glover was right.

'Well, Hammond, this should do for you. I think I can confidently say this will spell the end of your lacklustre career with MI42.'

She picked up the telephone and Charlie Hammond heard his case being discussed with the department whose men all looked like they were auditioning for *Strand* advertisements. He tried to distract himself by looking out of the window, heard the traffic of London passing in the street below and imagined he could hear a slow, low bell tolling sadly somewhere in the distance.

7

King Fadl sat in his rumpus room listening to a compact disc, watching a compendium of *EastEnders* recorded for him by the London embassy on video-cassette and flown out twice a month, and reading through dispatches from embassies around the world.

Usually moderately content when doing three things at the same time, King Fadl could not think of a fourth item that would complete him, fill him up, occupy the last iota of uncatered for sensation. A Thai massage? A gin and tonic? The lady gardener from Japan raking gravel in the garden outside? A tray of Turkish Delight? No, he didn't think so. But he lay on, his face drawn into a dark frown, wondering what the matter was. He wanted *something* but he could not for the life of him decide what.

He sighed and tried to become calm. The thought of the F15 and the 747 and the B51, always kept fuelled and fail-safe to respond to his every whim, helped his mood momentarily. It was comforting to know that in the space of time it took to lever up Jeeves, who was lying on the carpet in front of *EastEnders*, and get him on the phone, the whole might of the Ras Al Surran King's flight could be mobilized by klaxon to obtaining his whim – whether he decided on a Daimler, the company of an Egyptian film-actress, a bunch of grapes plucked fresh from one of his own vines on his estate outside Bordeaux – all were within his power to obtain in a matter of hours. The trouble was that he did not want any of these things. He wanted something else but he could not remember what. Perhaps old age was setting in. Would a face-lift help? A draught of some rare Chinese root? A Swedish physical culture expert? No, probably not.

'Anyway,' he decided, 'I've had enough of damned dispatches for today.' He had read the ones from Thailand and the Philippines, which were usually the best. The King enjoyed the embassies' accounts of the doings of the pure Ras Al Surran youth in Bangkok and Manila. Truly they were a credit to the Nation, an example to the less well-endowed of the vitality and potency of the thrusting Semite! Surely not since the last zenith of Arab power had so many nations quaked at the sight of lateen sails, or their twentieth century equivalent: Surreal Airlines flight 0069.

He closed the case of dispatches and concentrated on the music for a moment. But then he tired of that too and shut if off.

There only remained *EastEnders*. He would watch it later.

'Jeeves, would you mind watching the programme on your own equipment?' asked the King.

Jeeves looked round, lifted his eyes to heaven and pulled himself up from the carpet noisily. He ejected the video-cassette and plodded from the room, leaving King Fadl's television on.

The King got up and turned off the television.

He mused that crème de menthe had caused Jeeves. King Fadl had been feeling depressed that day in London. The sight of the crème de menthe had moved him somehow, reminding him of the flag of Ras Al Surra. It had seemed to slip down harmlessly enough. He hardly remembered taking the Rolls to Soho. He definitely did not remember what the photographs had shown him two days later. Well, he was paying for it now.

King Fadl removed himself to a recently-purchased vibrating armchair and watched a kinetic work of art on the wall for a long moment. The canvas changed constantly before his eyes as lights and mirrors projected an endless variety of coloured shapes on to it. The armchair jiggled under him and made his tummy fat move about like a turbulent sea.

'Well, this is it,' King Fadl told himself, referring to the present moment, which, the Californian Primal Scream therapist had told him, was all there was. 'Yes, this is it, all right,' but he could not gather together the energy to utter the required scream. Then the lights on the kinetic painting moved themselves into a configuration which was familiar. 'That's the exact shape of Ras Al Surra!' he exclaimed out loud, but as he spoke, the light patterns moved on and the shape was gone. King Fadl got up and grabbed his video remote, trying to rewind the kinetic painting to the point it had been five seconds earlier. Then he remembered: the remote did not work for the kinetic painting.

But he found himself smiling nevertheless. That was it! Ras Al Surra. Al Bustan. He wanted Al Bustan!

Sultan Nabil picked up the telephone. As he did so he turned down the portable cassette player he had bought Zarina that morning, smiling across the room to her as he did so.

'Is there hope for the future?' sang Joan Baez. He made sure the voice could still be heard.

'Nabil speaking.'

'Fadl. How are you, my brother?'

'I am well, and you?'

'Fine. And your family?'

'Well too, praise be to God.'

'And your country?'

'Managing.'

'Ah yes,' sighed King Fadl. 'Do you know why I am ringing?'

'I have a shrewd idea, Fadl,' replied Sultan Nabil.

'Do you keep cats, Nabil?'

'No, why?'

'Do I not hear a cat behind you as we speak?'

'No, it isn't a cat, Fadl. It's music. You do know what

music is, don't you? Or have your religious policemen succeeded in banning it? Listen!'

And Sultan Nabil moved the receiver in front of the tape recorder and was pleased when Joan sang out: ' "Throw the vandals in court!" cried the Bells of Newport,' feeling he could always rely on her for an apt line.

'Yes, charming,' said King Fadl when he was back in contact with Nabil. Then his tone changed suddenly, 'And have you decided?'

'The answer is "No".'

There was a long silence at the other end of the line.

Nabil waited.

Then King Fadl said, 'Isn't five billion jumpas enough for you, Nabil?'

'But when you phoned last time it was four billion jumpas!'

'Yes, I do recall. But I think an extra billion would be in order. You have the status of "most favoured nation" as far as I am concerned, dear Nabil. What do you say now?'

'The answer's still "No", Fadl. I've given it careful thought and, believe me, I've been sorely tempted. In my mind I had already spent the money several times over. But I do not feel I can say "Yes".'

' "I do not feel", eh? You sound doubtful, Nabil!'

'Of course I sound doubtful! What do you expect?'

'Look, Nabil. This is my last offer. Five billion jumpas and free access for all your people to the shrine of the Footprints of Aisha.'

Nabil laughed, 'But we already have free access to the shrine of the Footprints of Aisha!'

'Not any more, you don't. Not if you won't sell me Al Bustan.'

'But that's not fair, Fadl! You know what a devotion Zibdans have to that shrine. You also know how it helps the Zibdan economy by the pilgrims being able to bring back your cheap consumer goods tariff-free. If you stop us going to the shrine we'll be in the poor house.'

'Who said anything about stopping you? I would merely make sure that Zibdans have to pay the shrine tax like everyone else. Perhaps you have been having it too easy for too long!'

Nabil wanted to scream down the telephone, to blow up the royal ear-drum at the other end. He glanced over at Zarina who was looking at him anxiously and shaking her head. He tried to calm down before replying. 'You well know, Fadl, that we in Zibda do not have it easy. We do not have it easy with free passage to the shrine of the Footprints of Aisha; we still would not have it easy with an extra five billion jumpas in our coffers. But if you cut people from free passage to the shrine and, more importantly, to your consumer goods, we would have it a great deal more difficult and the Arab Nation would have a lot to say about it I should think.'

There was a sound of loud laughter from the Ras Al Surran end, 'The Arab Nation, dear Nabil, knows on which side its camel is cooked! You surely do not think that the Arab Nation looks to impoverished Zibda as some kind of beacon. Far from it! Few tears would be shed if you were ousted tomorrow, I can assure you. Your eccentric policies smack of a Godless liberalism to the Arab Nation. I, on the other hand, do feel a certain attachment towards you. You are an eccentric neighbour, it is true, but there could be worse. Now, Nabil, like a good neighbour, sell me Al Bustan.'

Nabil was chastened. 'Tell me why you want it, Fadl? Tell me that.'

'A whim, my dear. It is a matter of aesthetics. With the addition of Al Bustan, Ras Al Surra would look less like a rampant rude appendage and more like an ingot of gold. I know there is no value to Al Bustan, but a King must be allowed his way occasionally.'

'We must meet, Fadl,' conceded Nabil after a long pause.

'Good idea! I'll send you a plane right away.'

'That's no good. We're having a bring-and-buy sale and football tournament on the airport runway tomorrow.

Everything has already been set up. I've just come back from organizing it.'

'What's a bring-and-buy sale, Nabil?'

Nabil told him.

'Nabil, your quaintness never fails to bring a tear to the eye. You have your bring-and-buy sale. Do you think you can clear everything up before Monday?'

'I suppose so.'

'Very well. A plane will arrive to bring you to Fadlabad on Monday at nine in the morning. Is that all right?'

'That is all right.'

'Goodbye Nabil.'

Sultan Nabil put down the phone and joined Zarina on the sofa.

'Who was that?' she asked innocently.

Nabil told Zarina everything that had transpired. Then, with tears of anger and frustration in his eyes, he asked, 'What do we do?'

'It looks as if we may have to sell Al Bustan, Nabil. At present I cannot think of any alternative.'

'Neither can I. But what will the people say?'

'They will understand.'

'I am not so sure. They can forgive almost everything, but weakness they cannot forgive. I know them.'

'But you will tell them the reasons, surely!' exclaimed Zarina.

'If I can. If Fadl will let me.'

'How can he stop you?'

'How can he make me even consider selling part of our country?' asked Sultan Nabil, watching as his wife unravelled a child's pullover he had seen her knit the year before.

'Daud's grown out of it,' she explained when she saw his glance.

'That little pullover is Zibda,' said Sultan Nabil.

'It seems to me, your Majesty,' said Abdul Wahhab to King Fadl that evening, 'that insisting on circumcision for all non-Muslim employees in the kingdom would not only be a major contribution to religious hygiene but might also serve to encourage the benighted infidels, who wallow in a cess-pit of their own creation, to embrace the True Faith.'

King Fadl twiddled his tiger's eye worry beads, cocked his head and asked, 'And what, pray, brings you to that conclusion?'

'Well, your Majesty, it would remove one of the impediments that stands between the infidel and the True Religion.'

'But might they not go off and become Zionists?' asked the King.

Abdul Wahhab smiled serenely. 'Our screening for Zionists is second-to-none, your Majesty. You know that we investigate all our expatriate workers for Zionist blood as far back as their great grandparents. Conversion to Judaism would be an automatic reason for their deportation from the Holy Land of Ras Al Surra.'

'I didn't quite mean that,' replied King Fadl irritably. 'What I meant was, don't you think that compulsory circumcision of foreigners would be a certain way of driving them into the other camp? Don't you think that it would fuel resentment against us in the outside world?'

'Of course, you may be right, your Majesty, but what need has Ras Al Surra to seek the applause of infidel nations? We must hold rectitude above all other considerations. Do I not speak truth?'

King Fadl nodded without enthusiasm.

'Also,' continued Abdul Wahhab Higgins, pressing home his advantage, 'Ras Al Surra would be the first to issue such an edict. It cannot have escaped your attention that we have, up until now, always been the second to take progressive measures. We were the second to open an airport with state-of-the-art people movers; to build a corniche; to install closed-circuit, infra-red cameras on all streets, alleys and in public shopping malls and conveniences; to forbid women to drive; to incorporate double-tier classrooms to segregate the sexes in all educational institutions. It would be nice, for once, to be first. Don't you think so?'

Abdul Wahhab Higgins saw as he watched for the King's reaction that he had struck the correct tone at last.

'It might, it might,' conceded King Fadl. 'Be sure, I shall give the matter much consideration and shall notify the Ministry for the Suppression of Vice and the Encouragement of Virtue of my decision in due course. But, tell me, Mr Higgins, what brings you to our shores? You are, you must admit, an intriguing religious policeman.'

'I was, until a mere five years ago, a flailing infidel, your Majesty,' replied Abdul Wahhab Higgins.

'And what was it that caused you to cease . . . flailing?'

'Well, I had long been dissatisfied with the Church of Rome. The honour given to graven images and the unfortunate results of the Vatican Council . . .'

But King Fadl, as soon as Abdul Wahhab Higgins had started on an exegesis of his trip from Rome to Mecca, regretted having asked the question. For King Fadl did not have a religious bone in his body and could find no point of contact with Abdul Wahhab. For King Fadl, religion was something which entered into the chess game of political life. One could not imagine chess without the bishop, so one could not imagine Ras Al Surran politics without the Ministry for the Suppression of Vice and the Encouragement of Virtue. He looked at his loyal religious policeman blankly, letting his eyes ease out of focus, merely nodding on occasions.

It was with feelings of some relief that King Fadl heard the call to prayer above the drone of Abdul Wahhab's journal of a soul. He piously interrupted him in mid-sentence and, saying he must pray, sighed out of the room.

As King Fadl made his way back to his private apartments he thought about what Abdul Wahhab Higgins had said. He had been right in a way. Ras Al Surra always tended to be second to do everything.

King Fadl settled down in his rumpus room and thought for a while about how statesman-like he would be in the face of worldwide criticism to the circumcision policy. He saw himself addressing the United Nations. He could not for the time being think of what he would say, but that would be taken care of by the group of Egyptian novelists he kept in a basement room at the Fadlabad palace for that purpose. Yes, the United Nations would be no problem. There were many nations who would back him. If he said everyone had to wear pink on Tuesdays there were many nations who would back him. If they did not, he would simply turn off the tap.

King Fadl was feeling quite jovial when half an hour later Jeeves crept into the room and started asking for things in exchange for information to the King's advantage.

The purveyor of worms by appointment to Her Majesty's Secret Service had packed up his pitch after removing Charlie Hammond's file, an action which had employed the same sleight of hand he had used to sell his worms.

Off the man had scuttled into the bowels of Soho where, finding his way to the quiet corner of a pub, he set about reading the files.

They had not made much sense to him, truth to tell. However, the frequent mentions of Ras Al Surra throughout the pages of the file jogged the man's memory concerning Stan of *The Dancing Palms* nightclub. It had been the talk of the Soho cognoscenti some months back how Stan had shifted his wayward, wanted-for-questioning, brother on to the King of Ras Al Surra.

The man had drunk down his pint and made his way down Old Compton Street with his secret booty.

Stan looked through the papers with feigned indifference. They reminded him of his brother, and while he did not relish the reminder greatly, a certain sentimental feeling had leaked into him from emotional recesses he had not known he had and which he wondered if he should see a doctor about.

'I'll give you a hundred for 'em,' he told the man.

'They're worth more than that, squire.'

'Take it or I'll call the law.'

The worms salesman took the money with a shrug and a smile and left.

Stan, alone in his office, read the files from cover to cover. He could see that the files were important, that all hell might break loose were the contents to get out. He also saw the value of the file and itched to contact the newspapers.

He was in the act of lifting the telephone on his desk, when a counselling voice in his head commanded: Leave it! He nodded and let the receiver drop with a clatter back into its cradle.

For a long five minutes, Stan gazed down at the Top Secret file. Yes, it was too hot. Still, he might be able to throw something sweet to his brother. Sometimes his conscience pricked him when he thought of Len – turned into Jeeves – all done up in a monkey suit delivering drinks to tents in the desert, his black shoes hot as hell and full of sand.

Yes, he would give his brother the information. He might be able to wring something nice out of King Fadl with it. It seemed a bit of a pity to waste it like that, but it was too hot . . . far too hot.

Stan set fire to the file in the grate in his office. Then he called his brother in Ras Al Surra.

My goodness, thought King Fadl as he ordered the lights turned out later that night, what an interesting day it's been! Fancy Nabil having uranium on his land! He smiled to himself, then frowned at the thought of Jeeves riding around Fadlabad in the King's favourite Porsche. Still, it was a small price to pay for the information. How perfidious of the British to conceal from Nabil the massive wealth under his land. In fact, how perfidious the British were generally. There was *Sun*-reading Jeeves prepared to sell his country's secrets for a second-hand Porsche and Jeeves himself had been betrayed by his brother, Stan. There were, King Fadl knew, adulterers in the British cabinet. What a crew.

Before falling asleep, King Fadl mentally conjured up the map of Ras Al Surra on the wall of his rumpus room. He concentrated his mind on Al Bustan until he saw it covered in gold like the rest of his country. He made a mental note to have a team of RASONGRO geologists smuggled into the area to check on the information given him by Jeeves. Then, still thinking dark thoughts about the British, he decided that Abdul Wahhab Higgins should be given his head.

8

As a relic of his carefree golden-haired youth, Hammond had a king-sized bed. It came in useful that night, providing an extra pillow where he placed his twelve nylon worms in a row, drawing up the sheet as far as their necks.

Grasping his Honey Bear tightly on his side of the bed, he said good-night to his worms and turned out the bedside lamp.

But sleep would not come and he turned on the bedside light, closed his eyes against the third-degree glare and wondered what to do. He looked over at the worms. Their lack of utility, so irritating earlier in the day, was somehow warming now. They were a bit like him, full of unfulfilled promise. He reached over behind the headboard and pulled out a Sainsbury bag full of male nude magazines. He knew every model in his collection intimately. They were old friends. He consumed page after page, book after book, until the discarded ones lay higgledy-piggledy across the length and breadth of his candlewick bedspread. As the faces and bodies, big and small, smiling and sulky, passed through his leafing hands, his flaccid heart ached to catch sight of one which would send a thrill of novelty through him. But he came to the end of his by no means inconsiderable collection and found nothing that fitted the bill. No, what he wanted was the *Black Book*, imprisoned in Zwemmer's. He lay back, surrounded by the magazines, exhausted by his attempts to conjure up a thrill and his thoughts took him to Charing Cross Road. There

Hammond broke the window of the shop and seized the book he wanted. Cradling it in his arms, he gunned his Fiat back to Herne Hill and the king-sized bed.

Then he remembered that he had not charged his coffee maker with Kenya Peaberry.

Suddenly, with a reason for living again, Charlie Hammond got up and set off for the kitchen.

But in the hall, near the front door, Charlie Hammond recalled the day he had spent. He had tried to blot it out by thinking nice thoughts and doing what he enjoyed doing, but now it all came back to him like the draught under the door, reminding him that it was cold outside.

When Miss Glover was sure that Charlie Hammond was safely in the clutches of the men in raincoats, she had picked up her weekend suitcase, put on her tweed coat, and left the office.

He had told everything to the men in raincoats. They had not cross-examined him and had seemed to take everything he had said at face value. If they thought Charlie Hammond was a fool – and of course they did – then they did not let on. At the end of the interview they stood up and left, saying only that Hammond would be hearing from them again in due course.

'I'm free to go?' he had asked the men.

'Yes. Carry on as usual, for the time being.'

The men closed the door of Miss Glover's office with a dull thud and Hammond had sat on feeling relieved. But then he had realized that he was alone in Miss Glover's office and that things were not over. Not by a long chalk. The heavy wheels of investigation – which would run him over and crush his life and deprive his window boxes of water, his coffee machine of coffee, his Sainsbury bag of pornography, his worms of tricks – had begun its inexorable roll towards him.

The telephone rang, Charlie Hammond picked it up.

'More on the Zibda affair. We'll be faxing it to you in an hour,' said the voice of Dexter at GCHQ.

'Right you are!' said Hammond, though he wanted to say, 'Are you sure you mean me? You don't want me, do you?' But then he thought that they must mean him. If they didn't want him they would not have called. Perhaps they were not taking such a dim view of the matter as he thought.

It was only as he drove across Vauxhall Bridge that he recalled that all the magazines were still strewn over the bed. What if he died? What if the call to return to the office had only come in order to get him out of the flat?

Charlie Hammond mused how easily one little slip had undone the Gordian knot of his life. His little weakness for novelties which over the years had reduced to the occasional pang his great weakness for men, now threatened to completely undo him and leave him exposed.

Over the years he had gone to great lengths to make sure he remained hidden, had undertaken the weeding out of intelligence operatives suspected of being gay by dropping his façade for a moment, just long enough so that the suspect would relax, sigh and say, 'So *you*'re one too!' If comely, then Hammond might slake his frustration, telling himself that he was proving the matter beyond all reasonable doubt. Then betray. And as Hammond betrayed, he was in one part of his make-up, shocked and appalled too. 'Poofters in the Secret Service! Ought not to be allowed!'

However, he wondered as he drove along Ebury Street, whether there was not, after all, a price to be paid.

What came through the machine had been disturbing. King Fadl was putting the heat on Nabil and no mistake. He tried to put himself in Nabil's shoes but found it too much of a jump in imagination. In his year in Zibda as a Barefoot Geologist he remembered a young, handsome man who had worked hard but talked an awful lot of idealistic twaddle. The Barefoot Geologists had all pretended to go along with his visionary notions. It had been part of the masquerade. That year had taught him everything he needed to know about smiling deception and had stood him in good stead since. Still, he couldn't help having a soft spot for Sultan Nabil. For all his wetness, he was a decent cove and had never been anything less than the perfect host. Nevertheless, he remained beyond Hammond's comprehension. For the young Charlie Hammond, and now for the much older Charlie Hammond whose cynicism had hardened into a creed, Sultan Nabil, with his peculiar mixture of A.S. Neill, Krishnamurti, Solon, Jesus, Joan Baez and Marcus Aurelius, was a leap in imagination too much even to contemplate.

Would he say 'Yes' to the sale? It was beginning to look highly likely. Could it be that his lost file had already found its way to Ras Al Surra and that King Fadl was privy to its contents?

Hammond was back in bed an hour later. Nothing had been disturbed in his flat as far as he could judge. The magazines fanned across the bed and his innocent worms lay asleep on the pillow.

Ahead of Hammond stretched the weekend, a narrow, unpromising path which led straight to the sheer cliffs of Monday morning.

9

The following day, Saturday, was the first day of the working week at the Naffa industrial port.

The expatriate employees of the port made their way to work with the heavy hearts of schoolboys and workslaves the whole world round. Friday had been spent aimlessly in the main: reading pulp-fiction; swimming at Celibates' Beach; watching videos or RASONGRO television – and sneering at what had been christened the 'Rasongro Kiss', whereby in all films the couple approached one another as to kiss and were then seen moving away again in an instant, the stars' contact having been excised by devout scissors at the Ministry for the Suppression of Vice and the Encouragement of Virtue.

Captain Pooley and McGregor, his office-mate, had used their Friday to better effect, however. They had gone out to the desert rose fields with their spades. There, in the company of hordes of Koreans – for Koreans loved to dig for the sandy quartz formations and carry away great slabs – Pooley and McGregor had wandered around like florid vultures with knotted handkerchiefs on their heads, only taking what the Koreans rejected. They were after little pieces that would fit between socks and underwear in their baggage. They returned home in the evening tanned and cheerful, though that emotion alloyed by the approach of an impending Saturday and the knowledge that for friends and family at home it was a Friday night, with a weekend ahead to look forward to.

Unlike the other expatriates, however, Abdul Wahhab Higgins made his way to his office on the first floor of the administration building, happy to have its peace to escape to after a Friday spent with his wife and her family.

Marriage had been one of the more difficult things that Abdul Wahhab Higgins had had to embrace as a result of his conversion. It was incumbent on all Muslims to be married. There was just no place for bachelors. Abdul Wahhab Higgins had resisted for a year or more. He felt strongly that as he no longer felt strongly one way or the other about the pleasures of the flesh, he should be allowed to continue in his accustomed celibate state. He had even dared to argue the point with Sheikh Al Gaz when the pious chief of religious police had dropped hints and offered ready relatives as candidates for his bed. Surely, Abdul Wahhab Higgins had argued, he would be able to give more attention to the spreading of religion, to the eradication of vice and the encouragement of virtue, if he were not encumbered by a wife and family?

But Sheikh Al Gaz had told him that he was dangerously mired in the false doctrines of his pre-Islamic past and had insisted that he marry one of his own second-cousins. Seeing how the land lay, Abdul Wahhab Higgins had relented. But it had come hard.

He thought of all the years he had struggled with his flesh while a young man in the seminary. Many had been the nights spent in mortification, beating himself into the chaste state that the priesthood required. It just seemed so unfair that now, with desire daily ebbing, he should be saddled with a hungry wife and told to gallop for all he was worth.

He had managed to do the necessary and had hoped that his wife would leave him alone with his books for much of the time. But it seemed a crime to be alone in an Arab household. Somehow it was felt that he would be up to no good if left to study his Islamic texts in the air-conditioned study. His wife kept coming in and talking about what she would buy if allowed to go on a shopping trip to Marks & Spencers. She tried to sweeten him up with an endless supply of condensed milked tea and sweet-as-sin biscuits and stultifying chatter about the doings of their neighbours in Naffa. And she insisted on bringing round to the house a succession of tiresome women and their husbands. The women would go into the women's room and he would have to take care of the men in the majilis. All this stole time from his studies. There was so much to do. Almost half his life had been spent mired in a foolish heresy. There was still so much to learn and so very much to forget.

And Fridays were the worst. On Fridays they went to see his wife's family and the whole day was eaten up in pointless conversation about worldly things; a vapid waste of time with the television blaring. Fridays were a sore test of Abdul Wahhab Higgins's new faith.

He sat down in the office and surveyed the mail as usual. Another letter from his mother. One letter from the Ministry for the Suppression of Vice and the Encouragement of Virtue.

He did not feel that he could face his mother's letter. He wished that he could just tear it up and consign it to the waste-paper basket unread, but, thus far, he had been unable to do this. Only when he could would he be truly free.

He laid the letter aside and opened the one from the Ministry for the Suppression of Vice and the Encouragement of Virtue. He read:

To: All Religious Policemen
From: The Ministry for the Suppression of Vice and the Encouragement of Virtue.
Date: 1 SAFAR, 1411
Subject: Circumcision
It has come to the attention of this Ministry that many of the unbelievers at present employed in the kingdom are uncircumcised. Be it known that this is an abomination and must immediately be remedied.
The Ministry requests and requires that all

uncircumcised unbelievers be given the choice of either submitting to the operation in one of the hospitals of the kingdom or of facing immediate deportation to their countries of origin.

It is the responsibility of the loyal and righteous religious policemen throughout the kingdom to take steps to ensure that this matter is dealt with immediately – as it is abhorrent for the Holy Land of Ras Al Surra, on whom falls God's bounty, to play host to the uncircumcised. May God give you the strength.

Abdul Wahhab Higgins read the memo a second time. His habitually stern features melted into a seraphic smile. King Fadl had taken his advice. The memo which he had just read would at this moment be being read by all religious policemen the whole length and breadth of Ras Al Surra. He stood up and started pacing the office. Truly he had reached the zenith of his career. All the religious policing he had done up until this moment had been leading to this.

Straight away he left his office to inform the port's Director General. As he walked along the sandalwood-scented corridors, Abdul Wahhab Higgins felt, once again, reborn.

Alfredo de Madriaga Jr, the factotum of the port's Director General, knocked at the door of Armitage's classroom.

He heard Armitage call, 'Come in!', smirked and entered.

'Director General want see you chop-chop,' he said.

'Who, me?' asked Armitage, looking glum.

Armitage at once regretted his response. He was failing to control his 'self-talk' again and his book on self-assertiveness, *How to Feel OK about being Top of the Heap when the Times Bottom Out*, had told him that 'Who, me?' was one of those phrases that had to disappear from his linguistic repertoire if he were ever to attain his full potential.

'Right! Straight away!' Armitage added assertively.

Alfredo de Madriago Jr smirked again and left the room.

Armitage stood up and fluttered his hand over himself, patted his hair nervously and wished he had a mirror with which he could check his appearance. What could Al Tundra possibly want with him now? he wondered as he fluttered. Since his arrival at the port, Armitage had met Al Tundra on two occasions, neither of which had been pleasant experiences.

On their first meeting, Al Tundra had asserted that he was a hard man who demanded results; on the second he had chided Armitage for not producing results. Had he not, he had asserted, addressed some Ras Al Surran employees in English and had they not been unable to reply? At neither meeting had Armitage been given a chance to respond, or even utter a few incoherent phrases of self-justification.

In the footsteps of Lawrence of Arabia, Armitage had wanted to lead the Arab Nation to the English Language as Lawrence had led them to Damascus. He had wanted to experience wild places, to be reborn and shrug off his forty tepid summers. The interviewer at Marine Helping Hands International, like a dentist, had said that life in Ras Al Surra might hurt a bit at first. But the interviewer, like every dentist in Armitage's experience, had been economical with the truth, nay, had lied to his backmost filling. If Lawrence of Arabia had landed at Ras Al Surra's international airport, been speeded to the terminal by a computer-operated car, seen through the acres of plate-glass Arabs languidly sipping Pepsis with umbrellas inserted in the top of the glasses; if he had then been whisked along freeways that made the M25 look like a country track, past modern apartment blocks and mosques with aluminium domes under yellow sodium lighting that stretched endlessly on into the distance – then he would have wanted to turn around and say, 'This just isn't what I wanted! This isn't *me* at all! There's been most *frightful* mistake! Get me out of here!'

Armitage walked along the marble corridor, noticing that with each step the saliva was drying up in his mouth. He passed Abdul Wahhab Higgins on his way to the lavatory and greeted him in his Linguaphone Arabic. Abdul Wahhab Higgins, as was his custom, did not reply.

Too soon he found himself knocking on the door of the Director General. He went in and saw Al Tundra, still some distance away, sitting behind a vast desk. Mouth dry, Armitage walked towards the unsmiling figure. Pictures of members of Ras Al Surra's royal family glared down at him.

The Director General was speaking in Arabic to someone on the telephone. He did not acknowledge Armitage's presence and Armitage sat down and took the opportunity offered by the telephone conversation to calm himself. He breathed deeply, tried to relax, but it did little good. He was terrified and there was nothing he could do about it.

The Great Man put down the telephone at last and directed his attention to an area of air about a yard above Armitage's head. It was an arrogant look, a look that made a meal of life, a look full of oil revenues, white Mercedes cars, suites at Claridges and paradise for Afters.

'It has been coming to my attention that you are to teach the grammar to your students,' said Turki Al Tundra.

'Well, I—'

'This is not the wish I am entertain. There is no excite in grammar. It is the dead wind. You are to bringing the fresh wind into your classroom – wind that is to excite the pure Ras Al Surran youths and make grow the Flame of Education. Nothing stale, please. No grammar, Mr Archer.'

'Well, actually, my name's er . . . and it seems to me that before—'

'Before all, this is not school. This is bort . . . bort.' He paused between the two words, then closed his eyes, entwined his fingers and looked at the ceiling, 'You must to excite the pure Ras Al Surran employees with your class. Must I suggest that you are using stimulate materials ravished from sources such like the RASONGRO *Monthly* and *Bukra*, the on-board magazine of Surreal Airlines? Subjects like to, "The Contribution of Islam to Computer Programming", "The Legacy of Islamic Navigation", "The Arts of Eastern Ras Al Surra". These topics will to excite.'

'Yes, of course. But the trouble is, with respect, that—'

'Do not speak me of troubles. We are hiring the foreigners for solve the troubles. This is your function.'

'Yes, I agree and, of course, I'm doing my best, but—'

'You may go, Mr Archer.'

'Well, actually, my name's er . . .'

But Al Tundra had already turned his attention to some documents lying on his desk.

Armitage retreated from the Presence.

On his way back to his empty classroom, he answered Al Tundra's queries, 'Well, one has to teach grammar in *some* form or other! Your pure Ras Al Surran employees don't give a hoot about the contribution of Islam to personal hygiene – far more interested about where to go in Bangkok!'

Armitage went off to find Captain Pooley. Relating the interview to him might help him make sense of it all. But, on entering Pooley's office, he found him poring over blueprints with his office-mate, McGregor, the port statistician.

'Not now, Armitage. There's a good boy,' said Captain Pooley.

Fuming and forlorn, Armitage made his way back to his classroom – there to plot ways of escape.

Abdul Wahhab Higgins frowned as he pushed his mother's postcard of The Sacred Heart to the back of his top, left-hand drawer and set about composing a memo to the expatriate staff of the port.

A seraphic smile played about his grey face as he wrote the memo. He felt himself to be an instrument of the divine will whenever the duty fell to him of knocking the stuffing out of the unbelievers. And nothing inspired him more than putting the Holy boot into the British. He was still Irish enough to remember stories of the 'Black and Tans' and to seethe whenever he saw the ungodly British troops in Northern Ireland.

He finished the memo and buzzed for a messenger, who would have it typed and distributed to all the non-Muslim employees immediately.

Then he looked at his watch which told him that soon it would be time to proceed to the port's mosque and summon the faithful to prayer. After leading the prayers, he decided, he would stay around the mosque for an hour or two to give time for the memo to percolate through to all the godless in the port.

'Captain Suleiman's going to Bangkok,' said Captain Pooley's office companion, McGregor.

Pooley looked up from *The Times* crossword. 'Can't place him.'

'The one with 'RAS AL SURRA'S A THRILL A MINUTE' on his sunhat.'

'Oh, yes, him!'

Captain Pooley was silent for a moment. 'Six letters. Begins with B,' he said.

'What's the clue?'

'Sans everything.'

'Bereft.'

'Maybe,' said Pooley, writing the word in the spaces. He was never able to give McGregor any credit for help received with the crossword. 'Off to Bangkok, is he?' he asked, adjusting his spectacles and looking over at his companion.

'Yes. I expect he's doing a survey on Buddhist architecture,' replied McGregor drily.

Pooley frowned. 'You know it really amazes me how the Ras Al Surrans have managed to develop a world view that sees "abroad" as one big knocking shop.'

'Yes, I expect so,' replied McGregor in a bored tone, having heard Pooley's world view on more than one occasion before.

'Expect nothing!' snapped back Pooley vehemently. 'It cannot have escaped your attention, McGregor, that the Ras Al Surran for all his wealth and outward sophistication only manages to imbibe the very worst of what the world has to offer, while completely missing the best. The richer ones go off to London where they guzzle, lech and gamble their way through a city which has taken Man a thousand years to build. I can only surmise what goes on in Bangkok, but I suspect it is not a pretty sight.'

'Go to any good concerts in London on your last leave, did you?' asked McGregor, tying up his shoelace.

Pooley looked puzzled.

Just then a Philippino messenger entered the office without knocking. Both McGregor and Pooley were startled, thinking that it might be Al Tundra or some other bogeyman. Relieved, Pooley said, 'Oh, it's only you, Sebastian. What do you have for us today?'

'Memo from Mr Higgins.'

'O Lor! Has somebody been failing to flush the loos again?'

Sebastian placed a copy of the memo on each desk and departed.

'What is it this time?' asked Captain Pooley.

He read the memo.

He looked up, eyes wide, and stared at the wall for a moment. Then he looked down and re-read the memo. At last he addressed McGregor in a quiet voice which, on each word, rose in volume and pitch, 'This must be some kind of joke!' he said.

'Must be,' agreed McGregor.

Both, eyes down, read the memo yet again.

'Pretty poor taste, though, don't you think?' observed Pooley.

'Yes. Pretty poor taste,' agreed McGregor.

'Who do you think could have done it?'

Both were about to say 'Pontin' when Pontin – the expert in roll-on/roll-off infrastructure – walked into the office.

'Seen the memo from that re-frocked, ex-Papist, Higgins?' he asked.

Captain Pooley fixed Pontin with one of his steady, steely looks. 'I suppose you find this highly entertaining,' he said coldly.

'Doesn't bother me. Been clipped already. How about you?' asked Pontin, lighting a cigarette. Pooley's frown deepened.

'Look here Pontin,' he said, '. . . and I do wish you wouldn't smoke in this office. It has been declared a smoke-free zone.'

'Just like Ras Al Surra's been declared a foreskin-free zone. And not before time if you ask me,' shot back Pontin, puffing away.

'You're behind this memo, aren't you, Pontin?' said McGregor.

' 'Fraid not, old son. It's the real McCoy, as they say in your northerly climes. How do you stand on this issue, McGregor?'

McGregor pursed his lips and looked across at Captain Pooley. 'You mean this memo *is* genuine?'

'Looks like it, Cap'n,' leered Pontin. 'And quite right too. Everyone ought to be snipped at birth. You should be grateful for the chance to have the op on the Ras Al Surran government. No waiting lists for you like there would be in old blighty. However, I have observed in the course of my travels that the Brits are not the only nation who are upset. I've already seen a couple of weeping Thais in the utility room, weighing the pain in their pricks against the pain to their pockets of repatriation. Mucho weeping and gnashing of teeth throughout the industrial port!'

'Well, if it is genuine,' said Captain Pooley.

'It is,' repeated Pontin. He looked around for somewhere to deposit the ash from his cigarette and finding nowhere, let it drop on the carpet. 'You'll notice in the memo,' he continued, 'that we are given a choice. We can either have it done or accept repatriation within two weeks. Seems quite fair to me. At least they're not going to violate our so-called human rights by dragging us – or rather *you* – kicking and screaming into the Naffa general hospital.'

'It's incredible! Just incredible!' fumed McGregor.

Captain Pooley, his face the colour of beetroot, inhaled deeply and said, 'You know what really pisses me off about this sort of thing is the damned unfairness of it. There they are, a know-nothing, do-nothing crowd in their damned angel outfits, hot-footing it off to London for heave-hos and hair-transplants and Playboy clubs and orgies with the flower of English womanhood, with a beautiful Mosque to go to of a Friday – while we poor buggers come here trying to earn an honest crust and are treated like slaves and denied our most basic human rights! It ought not to be allowed.'

'But you have to admit, Pooley,' replied Pontin as he rolled up his cigarette end in a piece of Captain Pooley's stationery, squeezing the flame out of it prior to depositing it into the waste-paper basket, 'there is a certain poetic justice to all this. Until thirty years ago we were strutting round the world in pith helmets putting shirts on naked natives, outlawing so called barbaric practices, lecturing on the evils of opium to one lot while we sold it to another lot, replacing favoured totems with pictures of our own dear royals, forbidding weeping wives from burning on the pyre after husbands had snuffed it, drawing lines up and down Africa and Asia, dividing tribe from tribe, pushing groups together that loathed each other, pinching raw materials for next to nothing and being haughty to boot! Like it or not, what has happened here is a superb case of poetic justice.'

'I will admit nothing of the kind, Pontin!' replied Captain Pooley in dangerously low tones. 'The English had a civilizing mission and we were doing it damned well. If it hadn't been for a loss of will by a few misguided do-gooders, we'd still be doing it today. And the world, if you want my opinion, would be a far better place than the absolute charade we are currently witnessing.'

Pontin shrugged.

'Well, if this memo is genuine,' said McGregor, 'I think the sooner we have a meeting with the rest of the company the better!'

'That should be interesting,' remarked Pontin and he lit another cigarette.

Captain Pooley also fumed on.

Pontin had been correct about the two Thais. They were weeping in the utility room.

Both had heard the terrible news via Alfredo de Madriaga Jr. He had told them, using a mixture of English, Thai, smirk and sign language. Knowing the word for 'penis' in Thai (as did most employees at the port) Alfredo had repeated the word again and again, while making a sawing motion with his hands. He followed this by slapping his hands together, as if he were removing dust or genitalia from them. This conveyed to Thinkarjan and Chulalonkorm that what was being asked of them, in return for their being able to stay and earn money in the kingdom, was rather more than circumcision. The two wept for their imminent loss of manhood.

It did not occur to either of them to question the accuracy of the Philippino's bizarre explanation. They had become used to a daily ration of strangeness in Ras Al Surra. More, even if it might seem to an outsider to be going over the brink into the realm of the ludicrous, to them it was a logical step. For did these people not cut off hands, drop rocks from dump-trucks on females who erred sexually, throw great quantities of food away, refuse to eat pork (that most delicious of meats), behead people in public and scowl at all softness and pleasure? If they could do all that, then they could also lop off the genitalia of Thai cleaners.

Alfredo de Madriaga Jr had managed to point out to them that they could opt for repatriation, rather than go through with castration, but this was no choice as far as the two Thais were concerned, for they were recent arrivals in the kingdom, and would spend much of the next year simply paying off the agent who had procured them their lucrative jobs in Ras Al Surra. It was unthinkable that they should return home now. Extended families were dependent on the savings they were able to remit each month, a pitifully poor amount when compared with the salaries of the European employees, but a king's ransom to them.

Thinkarjan, sitting on an upturned metal bucket, wiped his eyes. He looked over at his friend, Chulalonkorm.

'What are you going to do?' he asked.

Chulalonkorm did not look up as he replied, 'I must let them do it if they must.'

'It is all right for you, Chulalonkorm, you already have two babies. Your future is assured. I do not have any children as you know. What am I to do?'

'It is up to you, Thinkarjan. I cannot decide for you.'

'It is impossible for me to go home now. Too many people depend on me. And if I did, the agent would send his men to kill me. But why do you think they want to take our sex away from us, Chulalonkorm? Why do they want to do that?'

Chulalonkorm shook his head, 'I do not know. It is very strange. But I have seen many strange things here. You see how they cover their women all the time and worry about them like we worry about food for our children? Perhaps it is that which makes them wish to unman us. They are afraid that we will rape their women!'

Both laughed at this in spite of everything.

'The very idea!' laughed Thinkarjan. 'They're much too big!'

'The Philippino says they are going to do it to everyone. The English too.'

'The English will never allow it. They are proud people. They will send ships and planes.'

Chulalonkorm nodded his agreement. 'But what about

the Philippinos? They are very proud of their penises. They will never consent!'

'I am not so sure. They are poor, like us.'

The mention of poverty returned both Thinkarjan and Chulalonkorm to basics. Both were silent and then, at the same time, both began to weep again.

Sebastian had tried to give the memo to Armitage, but the door to his classroom being locked from the inside, he had pushed it half under the door. There it remained unnoticed and unread.

Armitage had other things on his mind. He had been expecting a group of Security officers from the port to grace his classroom that afternoon. Indeed he had prepared a stimulating role-play for them. He was to have taught:

Officer: Good Morning. May I see your security pass please?
Expatriate: Certainly. Here you are officer.
Officer: (*Looking at the pass carefully.*) Hmm. Everything seems to be in order. (*Passing the card back.*) That's fine. Drive carefully on the port, please. And have a good day.
Expatriate: And a good day to you too, officer.
Officer: Goodbye.
Expatriate: Goodbye and thank you.
Officer: Don't mention it!

Armitage had imagined that this piece of friendly conversation would, through his sweat and toil, replace the present, rather curt, exchange he had witnessed taking place at the gate of the port each day:

Officer: Pass?
Expatriate: Here.
Officer: (*Dismissive hand movement.*)

He hoped thereby to change the negative attitudes that had grown up between security and foreign port employees, break down the unfortunate barriers which marred the brief daily intercourse and somehow contribute to a better understanding between peoples on the port.

Why could everyone not be brothers, instead of adversaries? It was all so silly and Armitage had decided to change all that.

But Armitage was to be disappointed. Instead of the eight or ten Security Officers he had been expecting, only the Head of Security, Captain Sa'ad, had shown up.

Captain Sa'ad spoke some English and did not need the lesson Armitage had prepared. In fact it soon became clear that Captain Sa'ad did not want a lesson at all.

'I have come to see you,' he said, in a boisterous bass voice and, without being invited to do so, he sat in one of the desks, twiddling his moustache while his legs described 180 degree arcs under his gown.

'Well, that's nice, but I was expecting my class. Do you know where they are, Captain Sa'ad?'

'Busy,' replied Captain Sa'ad. 'Show me video!' he added, gesturing to the video and television monitor in the corner of the room.

'Everything is a bit easy for you, Captain Sa'ad!' managed Armitage, not liking Captain Sa'ad's tone at all.

'Show me!'

'Say "please",' said Armitage, out of habit.

'Please,' said Captain Sa'ad.

Feeling in charge, Armitage went over and the turned on the video and monitor. He popped in a language learning cassette.

Then Armitage sat back in his teacher's chair, holding the remote as the humdrum tune of the video-course started. He fast forwarded, feeling suave and in charge.

Jane and Peter wanted to go to Brighton.

'How far is it to Brighton?' Jane asked.

'It's about 100 kilometres from here to Brighton,' Peter replied.

'How shall we go? By bus? By taxi? By car? By train? On foot?' asked Jane, all at a loss.

'On foot!' exclaimed Peter. 'We can't go on foot. We'll have to go by car.'

Captain Sa'ad seized the remote from Armitage and expertly rewound the tape to a full-frame shot of Jane. Then he froze the picture.

'You like?' he asked, looking hard at Armitage.

'Yes, er . . . yes. She's very nice,' replied Armitage.

'Why you no married?' asked Captain Sa'ad.

'Well, er . . .' replied Armitage. He had been about to say that he was too young to be married. He had been saying that for years, but that explanation was becoming a very leaky bucket indeed. He decided to equivocate with Captain Sa'ad by taking him into his confidence. 'Well, you see, Captain Sa'ad, some people are made for marriage and some aren't.'

'Why you no made for marriage?' asked Captain Sa'ad, once again twiddling his moustache and describing arcs with his legs.

'Well, you see, I am married to my work,' tried Armitage.

Captain Sa'ad gave him a sideways glance of disbelief while redoubling the twiddling of his moustache and Armitage felt himself reddening.

'Look,' he said, a trifle quaveringly, 'I think you had better return to watching the video. You may damage the tape if you leave it on "freeze" too long.'

Captain Sa'ad leered at Armitage, a leer which made him feel most discomforted, and pressed the 'play' button.

Jane and Peter were riding down to Brighton in an open car. But Peter had got them lost. He stopped and asked for directions.

'Excuse me, can you tell me the way to Brighton?' he asked.

'What is this Brighton?' asked Captain Sa'ad.

'A town near the sea.'

'People swim in Brighton?'

'In summer they do, yes.'

'Men and ladies together?' he asked disingenuously.

'Well, yes.'

'This is very bad.'

Armitage did not reply. He looked at the video as if it were an interesting programme he did not want to miss.

Then Captain Sa'ad turned off the video, stretched and yawned.

'I was watching that, Captain Sa'ad!' cried Armitage. 'Why did you turn it off?'

'You are no marry so what you do?' asked Captain Sa'ad.

'I don't know to what you refer,' replied Armitage.

'I no marry too. I went Bangkok last year. Very nice Bangkok. Girls and boys and everything!'

'Really, Captain Sa'ad! I don't think you should be talking to me like this.'

Captain Sa'ad stood up and stretched himself and Armitage could tell that there was something not quite usual about the lay of his gown. He tried to ignore it but it was hard for him to ignore.

Then, without any warning, Captain Sa'ad darted to the door and turned the lock. He strode back to Armitage, lifting his robe high as he did so.

'You like?' he asked.

'How dare you!' exclaimed Armitage, his voice tremulous. The scene in *Lawrence of Arabia* where Mel Ferrer lusts and waits for Lawrence to submit to his wicked desires flashed before his eyes and he backed away from Captain Sa'ad.

'I know you. You are English,' said Captain Sa'ad, bearing down on Armitage, who made a bolt for it around the students' desks. 'Five minutes! Five minutes!' he called, following Armitage at speed.

'But I am your *teacher*!' exclaimed Armitage breathily, making a second circuit around the desks.

'Please! Please! Five minutes,' pleaded Captain Sa'ad.

Then Armitage in his confusion and excitement made a left where he should have made a right and ended up crashing head on against the visual aids cupboard. And

Captain Sa'ad was up against him, fumbling with his pants.

Armitage wanted to say, 'Be gentle with me!' but instead tried to reason with the rampant Captain Sa'ad, repeating that he was a teacher and that if Captain Sa'ad even now, at this late stage, did the decent thing and left him alone then no more need be said and he would never make reference to the unfortunate incident.

But Captain Sa'ad had already found his way through Armitage's Dunns' trousers and knew that his teacher was excited too.

'There you are!' he exclaimed. 'I know you English!'

Armitage, half-stripped and completely exposed stood before the strutting unreason that was Captain Sa'ad and said, quite cool suddenly, 'You won't tell anyone, will you? You must promise you won't tell anyone.'

Captain Sa'ad smiled and nodded.

Neither spoke much afterwards. Captain Sa'ad said he would come for his lesson at the same time the following day. He was brusque towards Armitage and quickly left the room. As he did so he picked up the memo that had been pushed under the door and threw it on to Armitage's desk.

Armitage sat down heavily in his teacher's desk, wishing he could call the Samaritans. Then he read the memo and buried his face in his hands.

10

Charlie Hammond spent the weekend on that ill-defined border between limbo and purgatory. He did not go out, unless the balcony of his flat counted, but stayed double-locked and chained inside its confines, as if seeking to get in some practice for the hefty period of imprisonment his imagination told him might lie in his near future.

But Miss Glover did not let the weekend slip by so unproductively. She telephoned Sir Harry Pryke-Smith on Friday and arranged to meet him for dinner at a restaurant back in London on Sunday night to discuss the situation. And the situation largely concerned the erring prisoner of Herne Hill.

'It's a bad show, a deuce bad show,' said Sir Harry Pryke-Smith to Miss Glover.

'It certainly is, Harry,' agreed Miss Glover, as she spooned down a rich chocolate dessert. 'Of course, I do not believe that Hammond is guilty of anything more than the most culpable carelessness. He's far too thick to be a spy or anything of that sort.'

'So what's to be done?'

Miss Glover worked her lips and frowned, 'Well, we can't just forget it,' she said. 'At the same time, I think we must make sure that Hammond's blunder does not leak beyond the walls of MI42. As to Hammond—'

Sir Harry interrupted, 'Yes, that is essential. Containment is the name of the game now, Janet. But let's look at the worst case scenario. Supposing whoever lifted the Zibda file knows exactly what it is all about and passes it across to the enemy. What then?' Sir Harry had spent the weekend with worst case scenarios plopping into his brain like ice into some boiling viscous fluid.

'That, if you'll excuse me for saying so, Harry, is not the worst case scenario.'

'Isn't it?' he asked mournfully. He was not at all sure he could take more than he had already conjured up while seated on the swing-seat in the conservatory of his detached house in Bexley.

'No,' insisted Miss Glover, 'the worst case scenario is if the recipient of the papers does the decent thing and hands them in at his local police station. For then, you see, MI42 would be exposed.'

'Yes, but—'

'Look, Harry, if Fadl or Nabil do find out about the uranium it isn't really *that* bad. I'm amazed that they have not double-checked the report of the Barefoot Geologists long before this. We've been able to keep it from them for a decade and a half – thereby avoiding God knows what geopolitical shifts in power and dangerous super-power chess-games. The Barefoot Geologists have given us sterling value for money. Were either Zibda or Ras Al Surra to announce a discovery of uranium – and, of course, I hope neither does – we could easily put it down to their having re-surveyed Al Bustan. It is unlikely that Nabil would admit that he had been duped by a few idealistic geologists, isn't it?'

Sir Harry nodded, though in truth, he was not so sure.

'And MI42 remains as white as the guests at an intimate gathering of the Monday Club,' concluded Miss Glover.

'So we must just pray that the papers get themselves into the wrong hands?'

'We must pray, Harry, that the papers disappear down a grid. That's what we really want, but if worse comes to worst, there are worse things that could happen than their getting into the hands of Fadl or Nabil.'

Sir Harry nodded, frowning at his treacle tart.

'Eat up, Harry! I've already finished mine,' said Miss Glover in her gym teacher voice.

He tucked into the treacle tart like a good boy.

'Any thoughts about what we do with Hammond?' she asked him strategically, just as the treacle had gummed his top and bottom set together.

'Mo, hab you?'

'Personally, I feel strongly that it is time we put Hammond out to grass.'

Sir Harry thought of Hammond's father and all he had done for Sir Harry's career. He swallowed, feeling the masticated tart going drily down his throat, like gratitude. 'I would be reluctant to be quite so er . . . draconian, Janet. Hammond has many years of sterling service behind him. His work during the first years of the Barefoot Geologists . . .'

Miss Glover gave Sir Harry one of her looks. 'It's not the first time, Harry.'

'No, that's true. It definitely isn't the first time. I'll admit that Charlie Hammond is not our sharpest operative but—'

'So get rid of him!'

'You're a hard woman, Janet.'

Miss Glover smiled sweetly and eased a foot out of her Clarks Polyveldt slip-on, sending it exploring under the restaurant table. It located Sir Harry's right shin and started to massage it.

'That's why you're so inordinately *fond* of me, Harry!'

Sir Harry looked to right and left and winked at Miss Glover.

'I am, Janet. *Inordinately* fond!' he replied.

Miss Glover was suddenly her usual self again.

'But what do we do now?' she asked.

Sir Harry was thinking of his pied-à-terre at Dolphin Square, but replied that he had not the foggiest. 'To tell you the truth, I've been thinking of taking early retirement.'

'Did you see the news this evening?' asked Miss Glover.

'Never watch it on Sundays. Anything of interest?'

'The Ras Al Surran government has decided that all expatriate workers have to be circumcised or leave the country.'

'Whatever for?'

'Religion, apparently.'

Sir Harry nodded. 'I don't know why I even asked. That area gets curiouser and curiouser.'

'I think what we have got to do is get somebody out there pronto for a nose around. King Fadl has never been so peculiarly perverse before. Who would you suggest?'

Sir Harry took a gulp of wine and gazed at Miss Glover who was wearing her most knowing look. 'How about Hammond?' he asked, and laughed.

'Yes, why don't we send Hammond?'

'Where to?'

'Ras Al Surra, of course.'

'Yes, but Hammond!'

'Better Hammond than nobody. If the Boss asks what we're doing we can at least say that we've got operatives working on it. Anyway, Hammond will be on his best behaviour. He might well surprise us.'

'You've changed your tune, Janet,' remarked Sir Harry with a smile.

'Not really, Harry. It's obvious you are not going to screw up your courage and get rid of Hammond. I am merely doing a bit of crisis management. I would be quite happy to get him out of my immediate vicinity if I can't get him out for good. Anyway, he's bound to see his posting abroad on a mission as getting off the hook. He'll be doing his best to impress. Also, despite what I have just said, I do have a soft spot for him. He has been rather good at weeding out the deviants. Seems to have a sixth sense for them.'

'Hammond's good at that, true. He can't do any harm in Ras Al Surra, I suppose.'

He had to hand it to Miss Glover. She was getting him off a very barbed hook. And not for the first time either. He smiled at her warmly, 'But how shall we place him there?'

Miss Glover smiled and moved her foot upwards until it came to rest between Sir Harry's nut-cracker thighs.

'I'll arrange everything,' she told him. And he believed her.

By Monday morning Hammond was stiffening with despair. By that time he had watched his reputation, his livelihood, his possessions, fall away from him – disowning him – screaming and running for the balcony of his flat in Herne Hill. Over the guardrail they jumped, telling the window boxes of his shame as they did so. His flowers heard and wilted and the window boxes became one tiny perspective of desert and whichever way Charlie Hammond turned, he saw deserts of bare skirting boards, uncharged coffee machines – their filters open, gasping – a desk top littered with dry, unpaid bills and crackling bailiffs' notices.

After an hour of knuckle-biting at his office desk, he was summoned to Miss Glover's office. Miss Glover smiled at him.

'Well, Hammond,' she began, 'I expect you are fearing the worst. You do, of course, deserve the worst. However, I have been talking to Sir Harry, and he and I are of the opinion that you may still have your uses. We are prepared to give you a chance to limit the damage you have caused. What do you think of that?'

'Well, of course I'm very pleased. I—'

'You are to go to Ras Al Surra to gather intelligence on the situation there. We will arrange for you to be a guest of the British Council. The British Council, as I am sure you know,'—and Miss Glover smiled her driest smile—-'is a cultural organization. Their representative in Ras Al Surra will not be made privy to the fact that you are there for reasons other than cultural ones.'

'So what shall I tell him, Miss Glover?'

'I'm coming to that, Hammond, if you'll give me a moment,' barked Miss Glover unkindly.

Hammond hung his head to atone for his impatience.

'Your reason for being in Ras Al Surra will be that you

are there to sow British culture on that country's starved earth. You are going to be a cultural missionary, Hammond. You will put on a show for the locals, a one-man-show. It really doesn't matter what the one-man-show is. Perhaps you could do an "Oscar Wilde Evening" or a recitation of "The Four Quartets". It really is not of the least relevance. Nobody except a few culture-starved Brit expatriates will come to it anyway. You think of something, but think of it quickly. Say by tomorrow?'

Hammond frowned, 'That's going it a bit, isn't it, Miss Glover?'

'Not at all, Charlie. It is a mere detail. You will be in Ras Al Surra to gather as much intelligence as you can about the situation and how we can minimize the damage. The one-man-show is, as I believe I have said, just a cover.'

'Yes, of course.'

'Be ready for the off day after tomorrow – a.m.'

'Yes, Miss Glover.'

'And Charlie?'

'Yes, Miss Glover?'

'Ras Al Surra is a very hot place, I'm told. You may regard your trip there as a way of burning off your sins. Do well there and you may make us forget your recent lapse.'

'Yes, Miss Glover.'

He left the office wondering how his window boxes would get on while he was away in Ras Al Surra. What on earth could he put on as a show? How in hell was he going to get information? Information about what? God! Still, a trip to Ras Al Surra was miles better than anything else he had been able to imagine for himself during the endless weekend.

Hammond wandered out into the noisy street, his mind befuddled by the future. He made straight for HMV in Oxford Street, on the way thinking of travel and himself tongue-tied on an empty stage. He treated himself to the new *Merry Widow* on CD and then also purchased the *I Pagliacci* for good measure.

He trotted over to John Lewis and, after much searching, found himself an automatic plant-waterer. He bought two. Next it occurred to him that he might not be able to boil his own water for coffee in Ras Al Surra and in the electrical department he found a small pot with a variety of plugs and voltages. Then there was a supply of coffee to be bought and down South Molton Street went Hammond and bought five pounds of Kenya Peaberry.

Ideas for wants and needs came to Hammond and, justifying his extravagance because he would shortly be away from civilization and there was no telling for how long he would be away, Hammond's feet took him up and down Oxford Street satisfying his lusts. In Boots he bought water purifying tablets and three tubes of toothpaste and a bottle of mouthwash. Then back he went to HMV and bought a pack of blank cassettes. He would record some music for himself to take away with him. But what would he play them on? In Dixons he bought a Sony Walkman which also had short wave so that he would be able to pick up the BBC World Service. Then to the Body Shop where he bought some perfume essences and, with some difficulty, a packet of Mates, just to be on the safe side, though, he thought ruefully, if the past decade was anything to go by, both he and his Mates would return from Ras Al Surra in virgin condition.

After that, Hammond was on automatic pilot. One thing led to another. The plastic bags grew around him like hopeful spring sprouts on a once-dead plant. The knowledge of the Walkman took him down Piccadilly, through Covent Garden, en route to the BBC shop on the Strand to buy a World Service world map so that he would be sure of the times of everything while abroad. He would also pick up a *London Calling*. But in Covent Garden he passed an oriental book store and bought a compilation of *Bedouin Poetry* and a *Teach Yourself Arabic*. Then remembering that he was quite handy for Chinatown and that a friend had recommended a Chinese brand of tea-bag for various mild malaises, he made his way across St Martin's Lane and the Charing Cross

Road to a Chinese food shop. He found the tea-bags and bought three boxes. Next door he browsed at the window of a novelty shop and saw some wind chimes. These, he felt, would be nice on his balcony. They would play while he was away and keep his plants company. Inside the shop, while the assistant was bagging his wind chimes, Hammond caught sight of a long Chinese harmonica in a stout cardboard box. It was then that the idea for a one-man cultural presentation struck him.

Hammond had once enjoyed playing the harmonica. He hadn't played since his days with the Barefoot Geologists, but there was no reason to think he could not pick it up again. He bought a harmonica and left the shop happy with his purchase and made for the BBC shop across Covent Garden. There he bought the map and the copy of *London Calling.* Then he saw a sweat-shirt which announced BBC WORLD SERVICE, and he saw himself being mistaken for Kate Adie, or, more likely, Frank Bough. He had to have it and shot it to the cash desk.

He stood outside Bush House and looked up at the building, thinking of all those voices going out from that building and around the whole wide world and wondering what else he needed. Zwemmer's came into his mind. He went suddenly cold.

Dare I? thought Charlie Hammond.

He turned towards Zwemmer's and ten minutes later, loaded down with purchases, was standing outside the window, looking in.

Come on, Hammond! You can do it! It's an art book, after all!

He pushed open the door and went up to the assistant.

'Have you Robert Mapplethorpe's *Black Book*?' asked Hammond, wondering as he spoke if it was Charlie Hammond speaking.

'I'm sorry, Sir. We're sold out. We could order it for you.'

'No, it was a present for someone,' lied Hammond.

He treated himself to a taxi home.

11

That day, Sultan Nabil, accompanied by Zarina, flew from Zibda to Fadlabad to meet King Fadl. Nabil had spent the weekend trying to come to terms with the likelihood that Al Bustan would have to be sold to Ras Al Surra. He had called an emergency session of Zibda's Democratic Council and told its representatives what King Fadl was trying to force him to do.

Many of the representatives of the Democratic Council had urged Nabil to resist all Fadl's blandishments, but after intensive debate a majority voted that, if absolutely necessary, he be empowered to sell Al Bustan – as long as certain assurances were agreed to by King Fadl as to the uses to which the area was to be put. So crucial to Zibda's viability as a state was free access to the shrine of the Footprints of Aisha that all but the most stubborn came round to the idea of the sale.

Sultan Nabil and King Fadl went into closed session at the Fadlabad Palace straight away.

Fadl had been surprised to see Sultana Zarina step off the plane with Nabil, but he quickly whispered to Jeeves, at his side in full butler uniform, the keys to his own Porsche in the pocket, 'Get Queen Noof!'

Noof was not at all pleased to be asked to entertain the Zibdan guests at such short notice, while Zarina, for her part, was scarcely able to conceal her dislike for the Chief Queen of Ras Al Surra. She was conducted to the Queen's drawing-room and served cakes and tea by a small army of Philippino maids dressed like waitresses in thirties films.

'And how are you?' Noof kept asking Zarina.

'Fine, thank you,' Zarina kept replying.

A cup of tea was offered and drunk, a cake eaten and the same exchange took place once again.

'And do you like my little sitting-room?' Noof asked Zarina, stretching her lips horizontally and thinking what a dreadful dress Zarina had on.

In truth Zarina hated the room. The heavy fake Louis Quinze furniture sat unhappily with the tubular steel sideboards on which Noof kept her Lladró figurines, a signed picture saying, 'Love and kisses from Imelda (your sentimental baby) XX', another picture of Noof sharing a joke with Barry Manilow, Garrards' silver objects and other rich baubles.

'Yes, it is sweet, isn't it?' said Noof, answering her own question. 'I like to retreat here away from the affairs of state, which are all too taxing. However,' she added, with more than a hint of pique in her voice, 'had I been given some notice about your arrival I would have been able to entertain you in the state rooms. They are much more grand.'

'Oh,' said Zarina, attempting to emulate Noof's hollow smile, 'this is grand enough for anybody, thank you.'

'More cake? It is from our Viennese pastry-cook. So very delicate, don't you think?'

'No, really. They are very rich,' said Zarina.

'Oh, my dear, one can never be too rich or too thin,' said Noof.

'Can't one?' asked Zarina. 'I think one very easily can. Anyway, I have had enough. Thank you.'

'Of course! Of course! Now what shall we do to fill in the time? How about a little tour of the palace. You may find it of interest.'

Zarina let herself be led by Noof from the room.

The two women walked down a long corridor. On the walls they passed several portraits of Fadl and Noof, sometimes together, sometimes alone. The artist, or so it seemed, had specialized in painting religious subjects, particularly spectacular versions of the Ascension. In each and every picture, the royal faces were surrounded by an invisible light. Their idealized bodies – in the case of Fadl, greatly idealized – stood against a background of angry far-eastern cloud formations through which the sun darted rays, fortuitously landing on the royal personages.

Zarina listened, nodding politely, as Noof told her the price of everything. She had been warned by Nabil not on any account to lose her temper and was determined to play the diplomat, though it seemed a boring and distasteful game. To every remark made by Noof a countering reply leapt into Zarina's mind. She started biting her tongue. By the end of the first endless corridor she could taste the blood in her mouth.

They turned into another corridor decorated with stucco cherubs. In fact the stucco seemed to be representing a world conference of cherubs. Noof pointed to one corner where a manikin had been set into a corner, eternally attempting to piss on the royals below.

'The artist's little joke,' she observed in a practised sort of way.

A door was opened by an invisible hand and they found themselves in a huge rectangular room with high ceilings. It was bare except for a magnificent silk Tabriz rug which covered the whole of the floor. The rug had woven into it a picture of King Fadl – standing in Ras Al Surra – shaking hands across the water with the Shah of Iran, who was standing on Western Asia.

'It took ten years to create,' asserted Queen Noof. 'It was delivered to us three months before the poor Shah's fall.'

'Making that must have worn many, many fingers to the bone,' said Zarina quietly.

'No doubt. No doubt,' replied Noof, smiling regally. 'However, please observe!'

Noof nodded and a servant Zarina had not noticed before pressed a button. At once the whole floor in front of them, including the carpet, slid back silently and disappeared into the skirting board to their left. What remained was a half-size olympic swimming pool.

Noof clapped her hands and doors at the far end of the room opened and a dozen pretty Philippino girls in bathing costumes dived into the water one after the other. A Richard Clayderman number filled the room and the girls began to swim around the pool in formation.

'This is our little bow in the direction of Hollywood. I am a great admirer of Busby Berkeley and dear Fadl got the idea for the pool from a James Bond film.'

Zarina's tongue felt as if it would shatter her clenched teeth if she did not allow it expression. Suddenly, hardly knowing what she was doing, she let rip with a torrent of abuse at Queen Noof. The Queen tried to face the barrage with a tolerant, if forced, equanimity for a while, but then her eyes hardened, her red lips fixed into a thick bloody cut.

'We are here as your guests,' said Zarina. 'Sultan Nabil, my husband, is the ruler of your neighbour, a poor country. We are not here because we want to be. I have had to have other teachers take my classes at the technical college in order to accompany my husband. He is here because your husband has taken a fancy to a piece of our country. I always knew you had appalling taste and indulged it until the hilt had buried itself deep into the rotten carcass your country has become. But what I want to know, Noof, is why you show me this endless rubbish? Why must you thrust your lusts for fripperies in my face? Do you think I am impressed to see a dozen wretched women kept in thrall so that they can dance like trained circus animals to your imperious command? Well, let me tell you, Noof, I am not impressed. What I think when I see all this nonsense and obscene consumption is what it all costs in wasted lives; what it represents in kilogrammes of rice that should be filling hungry bellies. That's what I think!'

Zarina's shouted outburst filled the room and caused the swimmers to cast worried glances towards the two women. They were not able to understand what was being said, but sensed that it had to do with them.

'They do not have such things in Zibda. So primitive! In Zibda they do not value the Arts,' Noof informed the swimming pool.

'The Arts! You call this the Arts!' screamed Zarina, louder now, drowning out the Richard Clayderman and causing the circling Philippino aquatic dancers to lose their formation and become ragged. You may be able to thrill the Bolkiahs and the Mobutus with this nonsense, but not me, Noof. It's common and vulgar – like everything else in your damned pampered little country.'

'This is just the sort of behaviour I would have expected from you, a fish wife of Zibda, a laughing stock among the whole Arab Nation.'

But Zarina was not to be stopped. She continued her tirade. And Noof continued to reply in kind. Then Zarina gave Noof a gentle push which sent Noof back a pace across the matching Tabriz runner bordering the pool. She tripped over the hem of her dress and with a scream fell backwards into the Hockney water.

A dozen Philippino aquatic dancers swam to rescue Noof. Zarina continued to hurl abuse at the monarch from the edge of the pool.

Then, as Noof emerged from the water, spluttering, her make-up running down her face, Zarina turned on her heel and strode out of the door.

After five minutes of walking down silent marbled corridors Zarina arrived at a glassed-in veranda which looked out over a Japanese garden and over a wall to the high-rise section of Fadlabad.

She sat on a sun lounger and slowly felt her anger subsiding, turning into a niggling regret. She knew that Nabil would shortly find out what had happened. It was what he had feared, what she had feared too. But Zarina felt the regret ebb. It had merely been the retreat of the wave of her anger and was replaced by a feeling which passed for calm. My, it had felt good to say what she thought, what Nabil at his meeting would have been unable to say. Was it not enough that Zibda be pushed around by the whims of a strong and arrogant neighbour without both she and Nabil lying down and taking it? She felt that Nabil, though he might make an outward show of being angry, would really be proud of her performance. In the future it might be the bright spot they homed in on, tried to press between the page of this day in the diary of their lives and keep fresh and colourful in order to expunge the hurtful reality of what the day had signified for them and for their small country.

Zarina sat on, contemplating the Japanese garden, and waited for whatever would happen next.

In another part of the palace Nabil stood up, upsetting the heavy chair he had been seated at opposite King Fadl. Ignoring the protestations of King Fadl he paced through the thick-piled carpet, out of the room and shouted to a sentry, 'Where is my wife? Find her.'

Zarina heard Nabil before she saw him. She heard her name shouted by a voice she knew to be Nabil's, a voice which echoed through the stuccoed corridors of the palace, giving the sound the resonance of a shout high on mountains.

'I'm here, Nabil!' Zarina shouted back.

He stood at the door to the veranda and then he was running to her and holding her in his arms, holding her fast.

'Come, we are leaving this infernal place, Zarina.'

'But what about Fadl? Have you finished everything? How have you managed it so quickly?'

'I'll tell you everything later, Zarina. Now we must go back to Zibda.'

Hand in hand they retraced their steps, only to be confronted by King Fadl, flanked by two of his bodyguards.

'There is still much to discuss,' said King Fadl quietly.

'There is nothing to discuss. Our meeting is at an end. After what you have said, how dare you presume that there is anything further to discuss!'

'Your wife grossly insulted Queen Noof,' asserted King Fadl.

'That is fortunate indeed. Now we wish to return to Zibda. Have someone take us back to the plane if you please.'

'If you leave without signing the Al Bustan treaty, Nabil, there will be a heavy price to pay. I am not mocked!'

'Are you going to have your servants take us to the plane or not?'

King Fadl aimed a look of great contempt at Nabil and Zarina, turned on his heel and strode away down the corridor, followed by his guards. Nabil and Zarina watched him go, then looked at one another.

'I don't think he will give us a plane, Nabil.'

'Then we shall hitch our way back to Zibda,' said Sultan Nabil.

In the event, however, Nabil and Zarina took a taxi to the shrine of the Footprints of Aisha, from where it was easy for them to find a Zibdan bus taking pilgrims loaded down with consumer goods back to Al Rahman.

They sat at the back of the bus and Nabil recounted to Zarina his reason for not selling Al Bustan to Fadl.

'I almost did, Zarina. He started the meeting by increasing the price he was willing to pay for Al Bustan from five to ten billion jumpas. I thought that strange, but went on with the negotiations, thinking that perhaps he was simply trying to ease his conscience. Of course, I should have known that Fadl does not have a conscience. The real conflict came about when I told him that the desert rose fields of Al Bustan must be left completely undisturbed in perpetuity. For some reason this angered him and he would not have it written into the contract of sale. I asked him, if he only wanted Al Bustan because of its position and for purely aesthetic reasons, why he should object to that condition. He said that, as he was paying us so much for the land, he was entitled to have it without any conditions. But by then I was really becoming convinced that there was more to his wish to purchase Al Bustan than he was prepared to reveal. I confronted him with this, saying that he knew something about Al Bustan that I did not know. He started making threats, and I walked out.'

'What sort of threats, Nabil?'

'War-like threats.'

'But he would not attack us, would he?'

'I am sure – I hope – it was just a ploy,' replied Nabil.

Zarina looked at Nabil, but he looked away, out of the open window at the passing desert. 'So what happens now?' she asked him.

He did not look back at his wife as he replied, 'We prepare for hard times; we get some geologists in to survey Al Bustan; we accept those offers of aid from Sweden. I'm going to have that radio station, Zarina. If Fadl does decide to attack us, there is precious little we can do. But I want to get our point of view to the outside world. And I want lots of other points of view which never get aired to get blown about too.'

Zarina did not know what to say. So many questions were piling up in her brain. She started at the top. 'But the Barefoot Geologists have already surveyed Al Bustan.'

'I know, Zarina, I know,' Nabil replied, still gazing out of the window at the stars hanging over the passing desert. So close they seemed, it was almost possible to believe that one could blow lightly and send them zooming off in all directions, like a mass of fireflies.

'And how shall we repay the aid money?' Zarina asked.

But Nabil did not hear her. He was thinking of all those nights under those same stars – nights of singing and good talk and world-changing dreams – with Iain and Tony and Robert and Charlie and Livia of the Barefoot Geologists.

Then, quite suddenly, he found that he was whistling one of their songs. He surprised himself. It must have been a decade since he had heard it. He whistled it again and again, trying to remember the words. They were there and the thought of them moved him, made him remember the best of times. But here and now, when he felt he had most need of them, they would not come back.

'I'm glad you're feeling cheerful in spite of everything,' remarked Zarina, snuggling up to him.

'No, Zarina. I was whistling rather a sad song.'

And Sultan Nabil returned to blowing away the fireflies from his eyes.

Part Two

Cleavings

12

At noon the following day at the Naffa industrial port, Abdul Wahhab Higgins was about to announce the call to prayer from atop the minaret next to the administration building.

He switched on the amplification system to maximum, coughed loudly two or three times and hearing the echo of his cough returning to him as a great thunder clap from all around, commenced noisily to wail into the microphone.

The expatriate employees of Marine Helping Hands International, at the first boom of coughing, fled for the safety of their air-conditioned Toyotas, turned on their tape recorders loud and headed off towards the town office and their meeting with Archie Brownlow, the manager of Marine Helping Hands International. Inside their cars they managed to block out ninety per cent of the surrounding din.

The meeting had been hurriedly arranged by Archie Brownlow, who, the night before, had been the recipient of an inundation of phone calls. Many of the callers had been abusive, a minority pleading, almost desperate. Archie, having heard the news only an hour or two before, had been unable to do anything except mutter something about a meeting, while wondering whether a meeting would go any way towards reconciling his men to the latest queer turn of events in Ras Al Surra.

Armitage sat beside a very taciturn Captain Pooley, who was listening to 'Jesu, Joy of Man's Desiring' played by an electric organ. He was elated in a way he had not been since his arrival in Ras Al Surra. This was partly due to the feeling that exceptional events were taking place, both around him, and, more importantly, to him. Anything at all in the sordid daily routine of his life that varied that routine – a visit to the doctor, a sandstorm, a power cut – buoyed him up.

And the nature of recent events was especially gratifying. It offered Armitage an honourable means of escape from the bondage in Ras Al Surra and a job that was quickly throttling his spirit. He could easily picture himself at future interviews answering queries about why he had stayed for such a short time at his previous post.

'They were attempting to force all expatriates to be circumcised. I just did not feel I could.'

The board would nod and understand and see that he had been through the mill.

Then Captain Pooley spoke.

'All hell's going to break loose at the meeting, Armitage.'

'Is it?' replied Armitage, sounding surprised.

Captain Pooley looked over at Armitage, who was gazing contentedly out of the window of the car at the thrusting smokestacks of the distant desalination plant.

'You don't sound too concerned, Armitage,' he said.

'Well – I am and I am not,' replied Armitage.

' "I am and I am not",' mimicked Captain Pooley. 'Well, aren't we the cool cucumber?'

'Not the happiest of metaphors, Captain Pooley,' breezed back Armitage, concentrating now on watching a silver-coloured methanol pipeline glint and flash with the movement of the car past it.

'Well, if you want my opinion, I think it's a bloody disgrace!'

'The royals at home have all been done,' stated Armitage.

'And how, may I ask, did you become privy to that sort of information?'

'Can't remember. Read it somewhere.'

Captain Pooley slowed down as they approached the port gate. A guard flagged them down and Captain Pooley wound down the window, wearing a smile that looked as if it had been tied on with string too tightly.

'How may I be of assistance to you, officer?' he asked the child-guard.

'Pass!'

Both showed their passes.

The guard hit the boot of the car with his hand. 'Open!'

Pooley released the catch of the boot and it sprung open. The guard rooted around inside then banged down the boot, motioning them on with a dismissive gesture.

'Little turd,' remarked Captain Pooley.

'He's only doing his job, Captain Pooley,' chided Armitage.

'That's what Eichmann said, Armitage.'

But Armitage for reply just smiled enigmatically.

'Well?' asked Captain Pooley after a long moment's silence.

'Well what?'

'Are you or aren't you?'

Armitage heard alarm bells ringing. 'Am I or aren't I what?'

'Now look here, Armitage. I take you to and from work each day as an act of kindness. I do not expect to be abused on my own ship, damn it!'

'I did not mean to abuse you, Captain Pooley. Nothing could have been further from my mind. You know that during the short time I have been here, I have come to value our friendship. However, I did not understand your question.'

'I was referring, Armitage, to your situation re circumcision. I had not thought I would be the recipient of such a fine speech. You're full of fine speeches, aren't you, Armitage? But when it comes to answering a plain man's plain question, you become suddenly dumb. You know, I wonder if you really fit in with this organization. You don't sometimes feel that you might be happier in a *school* or something?' Captain Pooley spat out *school* as if he were talking about something very seedy indeed.

Armitage felt his happiness ebbing out of him. He had already imagined several insults emanating from his companion and was angered at being so rudely forced back into the wasteland of depression after such a brief interval of cheeriness.

'How do you mean?' he asked unhappily.

'What I mean is that here at the port you are surrounded by a band of doers and movers who have little time for the airy-fairy notions that so often lard your attempts at metaphysical speculation. I should have thought that a refined soul such as yours, with more sensitivity than a Durex Featherlite, would have found it all a bit hearty and unsympathetic to your finely-tuned instrument.'

Armitage did not reply. He stared glumly at the passing desert, counting the empty Coke cans. When they reached the Marine Helping Hands International office, he said, 'Thank you for your lifts, Captain Pooley. However, I think it might be better if, from this day forward, I made other arrangements.'

'Suits me, sunshine! Suits me!' replied Captain Pooley.

Archie Brownlow shuffled his papers nervously and stared through the cigarette haze that was building up in the ping-pong room of the company offices in Naffa. In front of him thirty very stern British expatriates and a poster of Raquel Welch stared back at him.

'Is everybody here?' he asked.

'Let's get on with it!' shouted a voice from the back.

'Right you are,' said Archie. 'Right you are,' he repeated, in order to gain time and stop his voice from trembling. 'You are, no doubt, aware of the news that circumcision has become obligatory for all non-Muslims in the kingdom of Ras Al Surra.'

'Too right we've heard!' shouted the same voice from the back. It belonged to Eddie Blair, a berthing supervisor and maker of fine home-made spirits by appointment to anyone who had the equivalent of £30 to lay out on a bottle. 'But what we want to know is what the company is fucking well going to do about it. That's what we fucking well want to know.'

'That's what this meeting is about, Mr Blair,' Archie replied sternly. 'I'm sorry that Admiral Baker is unable to be with us today. He is, as you may know, on a fact-finding tour of the Eastern Region with Prince Azim Al Surra. However, I was in touch with him last night and he assures me that circumcision has many advantages.'

'Is that really what he said?' asked Captain Pooley.

'When you think about it, there is not much more that he could say. The law is the law after all and if you don't like it you do have the choice of leaving. You were well aware before you came out here that customs in Ras Al Surra can be a trifle eccentric.'

There were angry rumblings around the room. Archie looked up and thought that even Raquel Welch was looking daggers at him. He could not for the life of him imagine why she should worry.

Someone said that Ras Al Surrans in London should be force-fed black pudding. Someone else said that they should all be sent home. Another opined that every mosque in Britain should be closed. Then Eddie Blair said that hanging was too good for them.

Archie ignored these observations.

Pontin raised his hand and was called upon. 'It is all very clear. Either you get snipped or you get out. It's an accomplished fact. No use asking why or tearing your hair out. Look at it this way: is it worth your while to go through with a bit of pain and discomfort in return for a healthy bank-balance and a job? Good God, you have all been made eunuchs by coming to Ras Al Surra. I can't see why you should kick up a fuss about this! The moaning minnies had just better return to the UK and take their chances at the job centre. The rest should accept it and not get their knickers in a twist.'

Pontin sat down.

Pooley stood up.

'That's all very well for you to talk, Pontin. You've been done!' he exclaimed, pointing an accusing finger at Pontin.

Pontin smirked. 'That is completely irrelevant. The facts as I stated them remain valid.'

Pooley fumed and sat down.

'I think Mr Pontin is right, Captain Pooley. The choice is clear,' said Archie. 'The purpose of this meeting is not to discuss what action we can take. Clearly none can be taken. I have simply been instructed to pass on the facts to you and to inform you that the company will pay three months' salary to those who do not feel that they can go along with the instruction and who would rather leave Ras Al Surra. I do not see that we can go any further than that.'

Silence descended like smog over the group. Archie seized the opportunity to conclude. 'One more thing. You are all required to report to the Ministry for the Suppression of Vice and the Encouragement of Virtue on Thursday morning at 8.00 a.m. for an inspection of your parts.'

The men moaned. Archie searched around for his papers, planning a route to the door and thinking of whisky.

'I will go to the Ministry with you,' said Mustapha, the company's agent, whose job it was to lead the dumb expatriates around and lubricate their jumps through the many hoops of Ras Al Surran bureaucracy.

This offer did not serve to pour any oil on the troubled water, however. The meeting broke up to the accompaniment of a chorus of grumbles and choice expletives.

Archie Brownlow sat in his office five minutes later feeling dreadful. He badly wanted to finish work and hightail it back to Fadlabad, but knew that he should remain around the office for a while longer in order to minister to the employees who would need counselling. Counselling was one of Archie Brownlow's functions – it had even been mentioned in the job description.

He heard someone coming down the corridor towards

his office. He knew it was Captain Pooley from the sound of rubbing corduroy. The sound stopped and Archie waited in suspense for Captain Pooley's large fist to bang on his door.

'May I come in?' asked Captain Pooley.

'By all means,' said Archie, hoping that he sounded more welcoming than he felt.

They sat down and Archie lit a cigarette. Captain Pooley stiffened momentarily, then remembered whose office he was in.

'Well, what can I do for you?'

'I want to know if there is anything you can do to help me in this matter.'

'I don't quite know what you mean, Captain Pooley. You have already heard the company's policy. That is how things stand, I'm afraid.'

'Yes, I suppose I expected that. It's not that I really mind the pain of the operation or anything like that. It's being forced to have it which is so irksome. The last straw, so to speak. But I'm between the devil and the deep blue sea. There's nothing for me back home. It's a bugger, it really is. Just as I was settling down nicely too.'

'Well, if I were you, I would just grin and bear it. I'm in the same boat myself.'

Captain Pooley cheered up on hearing this. 'Are you?' he asked.

'Very much so.'

'Of course, I know exactly what Doris would say. She would say I should come home intact. She would say I have my honour and my manhood to consider. Yes, that is what Doris would say.'

Archie nodded. He wondered what his wife June would say, but thought he knew. June seemed quite happy to spend the money Archie earned abroad. Every time he suggested calling it a day she brought up one more item of expenditure. 'Just one more year,' she would say. And Archie saw his life dissolving in a succession of just-one-more-years. He had a country cottage and time shares in Spain and Scotland – but no time to share them.

Then Captain Pooley suddenly brought his right fist up to his mouth and let a tear fall from his eye. Archie got up, embarrassed. He put his hand for the shortest of moments on Captain Pooley's shoulder and squeezed.

Captain Pooley nodded and quickly recovered himself.

'Sorry about that. Sorry! It won't happen again. Sorry.' He reached for a Kleenex. He got up. 'Still it has to be done. Nothing for me back home. Too old. Far too old.'

A piece of polystyrene packing material tumbled across the rubbish-bedecked desert outside Armitage's window. Gossamer plastic bags in pastel shades, now given to wrap any purchases made in Ras Al Surra's shops, had wound themselves around each and every low desert bush. In the wind they would make a crushed leaf, sad, autumnal sound that would add to the double desolation of desert and dustbin waste. Two bedraggled camels, prophets without honour, grazed through the trash, flattening the soft-drinks cans with their hooves at each tread. Nearby, in an enclosure, thirty yellow dump trucks sat dust-covered and rusting. As he watched, the sun crept sullenly away towards the horizon, a yellow-brown ball in a sky as opaque as Pernod and water. It gave off no visible rays, no sign of a fantastic send-off. As Armitage watched, it began to redden with embarrassment for the searing sins of the day just done.

Armitage returned to his copy of *Time*, searching for something he might have missed on his two previous readings. A pop singer whom Armitage had never heard of was about to start a world tour; Liza Minelli was doing something for the cameras in a skyscraper with a view over St Patrick's cathedral; George Bush was talking to astronauts over the telephone; the world wagged on. But that world which reached him by mail each week seemed so far away now. He could scarcely persuade himself that it was all taking place on the same planet that he inhabited. Would the sun now setting be shining on Liza Minelli at this very moment? On George Bush? On Herne Bay? Leafing through the magazine, Armitage had a curious sense of reading fiction – and far-fetched fiction at that.

The sun had disappeared into the evening haze, leaving the pre-dusk landscape colourless. In ten minutes or so, the sky would explode with the memory of sun. But now the world from his window had taken on a grey, depressed appearance, which exactly matched his mood.

Following the meeting Armitage had gone out into the main street of Naffa and bought himself a Pepsi. As he drank it in the doorway of a shop, he saw the Toyotas of his fellow employees making their way back to the port. He would not be going with Captain Pooley; in fact, he told himself, he would not go at all. He had nothing to look forward to that afternoon except being chased around the classroom by Captain Sa'ad. Armitage deeply regretted that. that incident had occurred. It would probably be all over the port by now. People would be sniggering about him behind their backs. He was sure they would.

He had caught a taxi back to the block of flats in the compound on the edge of the desert the port employees called home. It had been nice to come into the cool, to lock the door, drink coffee and munch crisps while reading *Time*, then even nicer to lie down and let a glorious afternoon oblivion wash over him.

But two hours later he had woken up. Looking at his watch he saw that it was past four. He felt depressed. 'If I'd gone to work like a good boy, I'd be on my way home with a clear conscience by now.'

Armitage showered and wondered if, after all, he ought to leave Ras Al Surra. Even if they would take him back at the Quick School of Languages, did he really want to go? Might he not be standing in front of a class in a few weeks' time, the smell of cabbage from lunch pervading the room, as it pervaded every room, thinking of Ras Al Surra and the good time he had had there? Here he had a car, even though he had not plucked up the necessary courage to drive it yet. He would never be able to drive his own car in England. His wage there would not stretch to even a rusted wreck. Also he was accumulating leave and could go for a holiday to Bangkok or Manila in a few months. He might be able to find a job there. But if he returned to England all hope would die. He would be one of three or four frequenting the Odeon on week nights, then returning to his lonely room. Then it occurred to him that being circumcised might make a man of him. Maybe it would cut weakness from him, be a sort of baptism, a rite of passage and bring him out and away from his obscenely extended adolescence.

He switched on the colour television set and as he did so caught sight of his Walkman on top of it. I will jog in the desert this evening, he told himself. I will jog and listen to my Positive Thinking cassettes. I will heal my body as I heal my mind. Yes, that is what I'll do.

Cheered, he sat down in front of the television.

He always tried to catch the news in English. He did not usually emerge from it much the wiser about events in the outside world, but he had developed a fascination concerning the minds that produced it.

'Good evening. Here is the news from the television service of the Islamic kingdom of Ras Al Surra. First the main points: Today, his Majesty King Fadl bin Abdulla Al Surra sent a message of fraternal greeting to President Mitterrand on the occasion of the president overflying Ras Al Surran airspace on his way back from a state visit to the Caledonian Islands.

His Majesty King Fadl bin Abdulla Al Surra also met with his Majesty Nabil, Sultan of Zibda, at the Centre Palace in Fadlabad. Their talks were of a bi-lateral nature.

His Excellency the Minister of Sport and Acting Minister

of Female Problems, Sheikh Eisa Al Mukhtub, today had talks with the Libyan Minister of Education. In a communiqué after the meeting, the two ministers both emphasized the need for bi-lateral relations on the topics of Education, Sport and Female Problems.
And now to the World News.
A man in Tokyo jumped to his death from the twenty-third storey of an apartment block. Apparently his wife had destroyed his personal computer with a hammer only minutes prior to the fatal fall. We have dramatic film of that for you later in the bulletin.
Today, his Majesty King Fadl bin Abdulla Al Surra sent a message . . .'

Armitage changed channels. On the RASONGRO station, a thin and very elderly man was jogging backwards. An anodyne female commentator of intensely Californian gloss was telling the audience that Fred owed his longevity to backward jogging and that the sport was sweeping the country. Armitage changed channels.

An elderly Arab seated at a desk with artificial palms behind him was conducting an Islamic 'Agony Uncle' session. Viewers had written in to him and he was doing his best to answer their queries. 'After lying with your wife, total washing is necessary from the hair on your head to the soles of your feet. If water is not available a dust bath is permissible.'

Armitage turned off the television and got ready to go jogging. He decided to take the car and practise driving it across the rough and empty desert tracks. In the morning he would have to brave the traffic and get himself to work without the aid of Captain Pooley. He wondered for a moment if he should slip a note under Captain Pooley's door, apologizing. No, he thought, I won't. I won't. I shall go and drive my car and be independent.

But Armitage wished that he had a friend who would go out driving with him and help him – slap his wrist if necessary – just *be* there. But there was no-one he could think to ask. Captain Pooley was the nearest thing

Armitage had to a friend in Ras Al Surra and he did not want a friend like Captain Pooley. No, he wanted a different kind of friend altogether.

Armitage sighed out of the block of flats into the car-park and approached his unused company car gingerly, trying to think of a friendly name to give it.

13

On Wednesday morning Charlie Hammond arrived at Gatwick airport to take the Surreal Airlines flight 0012 to Fadlabad. His plane was not scheduled to take off until 10.00 a.m., but he had, as usual, allowed himself far too much time to get out to the airport.

Hammond was not a punctual person. He was often late for meetings and the theatre, but airports were an exception. Airports he not only arrived at in plenty of time, but with hours to spare: hours in which to worry and fret and pace and hope that they wouldn't charge him for the twenty-five kilogrammes he had calculated his luggage had weighed on the bathroom scales in Herne Hill. This still left plenty of time to consider how odd humanity-on-the-move appeared and what a frightful cup of coffee the airport café provided.

Charlie Hammond checked in, trying to look genial and poor at the same time. In a trice he had worked out that he was old enough to be the Surreal Airline girl's father and was acting out a familiar, familial role. He tutted to himself as the scales tipped thirty kilogrammes, telling the girl that he thought his wife must have added things. She was like that, he told her, just wouldn't be told that there was a maximum weight permitted. Probably she had inserted a fruit cake that weighed a ton to surprise him when he opened the cases a million miles from home. The girl smiled at him as she attached a label saying FAD to the handles of his luggage and pressed a lever which sent them tottering away on a conveyor belt. He knew he was not going to be charged excess then and strode away after giving the girl one last, fatherly beam.

Relieved, the front worry that had overpacked the bags of his brain now banished, he sat down, then lifted his feet to allow a lady in a sari to brush away the Coke can beneath his chair. He stood up, restless again, and made his way to the shops and bought socks and pens and a couple of plastic baggage labels with 'Gatwick' emblazoned on them, most of the day's newspapers, a dozen packets of Polo and a pound of tea in a fancy tin in the shape of an English cottage. Then, tiring of the crowds, he went through passport control, made the buzzer buzz in the metal detector and was intimately frisked, before finding himself faced with the sight of the duty free shop. But, before indulging himself there, Hammond took out flight insurance and went to the toilet. Then, armed with a basket, he pushed his way round the duty free shop.

He stood for long minutes contemplating the cigarette display, musing over the free offers and exotic brands he never saw anywhere else but at the airport. Charlie Hammond was always in the process of giving up the habit. Every packet was his last, every cigarette a memento mori. But in the duty free shop cigarettes became what they had been when Charlie had first taken up smoking. No longer did they threaten his health. Here – but nowhere else – they were literally international passports to smoking pleasure, each over-packaged brand an accessory statement. He seized a chunky box of Balkan Sobranie cocktail cigarettes, thinking they would cause a stir in dusty Ras Al Surra, but finally he chose a box of Harrods brand. Then he bought a Pringle sweater because there was a special offer on them, a bottle of Caron pour homme and a set of mini-speakers to make his Walkman audible.

Hammond, still with an hour to go before take off, found himself once again sprouting bags. His brain started to bulge again. He saw the notice: NO MORE THAN ONE CARRY-ON BAG ALLOWED ON BOARD AIRCRAFT and he worried about his, but blamed the British Airport Authority for encouraging people to accumulate at the airport. His reasoning satisfied him, but he worried about it nonetheless. He gobbled up the time by imagining himself arguing with cabin attendants at the door of his flight. He would be all sweet reasonableness at first – an absent-minded professor who is also everyone's favourite uncle – but if all that failed he would harden into the frequent flyer who had never before received such treatment.

Charlie Hammond sat down guiltily next to an ashtray in the departure lounge behind a sign which said 'Smoking Zone', lit a cigarette which he smoked while people's backs were turned and practised the future – just as he always had in the past – in order to make it, if not perfect, then at least unembarrassing.

Some hours later Hammond arrived at Fadlabad airport, there to be greeted by the representative of the British Council, Malcolm Plunkett, who was not privy to the fact that Hammond's cultural tour was a front for important intelligence gathering.

After greetings had been exchanged, the representative got straight down to business as he drove Hammond towards the British Council residence in the centre of Fadlabad.

'Hope you've brought out all your own publicity bumph,' he said.

'Rather!' replied Hammond.

'What are you doing, by the way?'

'Playing the harmonica,' announced Hammond, 'and doing a very spectacular sleight-of-hand show.'

'Hmm, sounds a bit down market from the usual stuff they send us. Still, you might get a local audience for conjuring tricks. The last cove they sent out caused no end of trouble. Perhaps you know him. Actor chappie. Somebody Something. Should remember the name. Fired off enough memos to London about the bugger. Anyway, he did an interminable rendering of what seemed like everything Wordsworth ever wrote. The audience consisted of yours truly, the Indian librarian and two English teachers who left during the interval. I was a wet rag by the end of the evening, but him – well he had enough energy left to chase the houseboy round the residence into the small hours. We sent him off to Borneo from here. Haven't heard what happened to him, have you?'

'Can't say I have,' replied Hammond. 'Get many cultural visits, do you?'

'Not many, thank God. Since Maggie got in all our energy is given over to money-spinning yarns. English for tycoons – that sort of thing. The problem with all this travelling culture is that only the expats come – and that's not really the point, is it? Me, I'm more comfortable with things as they are now. I can do without all those dipso thespians – and I know the houseboy feels the same way.'

Hammond thought he was being warned. 'I can assure you that you needn't worry—'

'No, of course not. Played the mouth organ long, have you?'

Hammond replied that he had. In a way it was true.

The idea for a filler utilizing his worms had come to him the day before he was due to leave for Ras Al Surra. He had tied the nylon cord to the head of one of the worms, secreted it about his person and tried to emulate the salesman. It had not worked at all well at first, but after an hour's frustrating practice – an hour during which he pulled the head off his test-worm (burying it reverently in the window box with the hyacinths and miniature conifers), he began to persuade the worm to dart and dance at his command.

'I will take you to Ras Al Surra with me, my dears,' he told the surviving worms.

Hammond was taken along the wide boulevards of Fadlabad.

'Quite modern, isn't it?' observed Hammond.

'Is it?' remarked Malcolm Plunkett absently.

In fact, Malcolm Plunkett's mind was far away from

the business in hand. He regarded Hammond's visit as a distraction, an unnecessary bit of frippery. This was typical of London. One wrote them an angry and distressed memo drawing their attention to the forthcoming chopping off of parts and what did they do? Send out a bloody conjurer to take one's mind off it. Plunkett thought he knew why there was absolutely no concern at the threat of circumcision – a threat to which he was vulnerable. He did not have diplomatic immunity. The embassy bods were not in any way affected. They could keep their damned foreskins – waggle 'em out of embassy windows for all anybody cared. But not the poor old British Council. Oh, no! Who cares about cultural organizations? Don't reply to memos. Just sent us some creep with a mouth organ.

Still, he told himself, it was perhaps a good thing in a way – the other matters apart. He had been growing extremely embarrassed at the British Council's lack of cultural events in Ras Al Surra. The Alliance Française and the Goethe Institute were running rings round the Brits culturally, as usual. Not to mention the United States Information Service with their Todd-Ao Retrospective. That had drawn crowds of curious locals and they had loved it. And what had the British Council done? What had been sent out for him by the cultural centre of the Western hemisphere? Well, precious little. Apart from this boring bod in the seat next to him, the only other thing that had occurred in the last year was Olivier's *Hamlet*. Well, that might have been all right. That might have done. Except that the buggers had sent him the first two reels of *Hamlet* and the last reel of *A Clockwork Orange*.

He slowed down the car and honked his horn three times. Hammond saw that they were in the midst of the business area of Fadlabad and could not understand why they were stopping. Mirror-sided buildings whizzed heavenward on all sides.

A gate opened, a noisy metal gate, and into a small lot between two enormous buildings, Hammond saw that they were entering a driveway fringed with palm trees. A garden. Through the oleanders he could make out a narrow, three storey, mud-brick house. It all looked very quaint to Hammond, strange too, considering the location.

He mentioned this to Plunkett.

'When I first came here, the seashore came up to the bottom of our garden. Then all the countries got their corniche craze. Everyone had to have a bleeding corniche. So they landfilled like mad and blocked the sea off half a mile away. Then they designated this area for business. The thing is that the land is owned by the British government. They could have sold it but somebody just couldn't be bothered to do the paperwork, so here we are, stuck in the middle of the new thrusting Fadlabad. We don't belong. We're from another era. Still, that's appropriate in a way, don't you think?'

'How?' asked Hammond.

The Council man sighed quietly. 'Well, if you don't know I can't possibly attempt to tell you, old chap,' he said.

A black servant appeared and took Hammond's luggage from the boot. Hammond greeted the man with a wide smile but the man frowned, as if he had been told to expect the worst.

Inside the residence Plunkett called, 'Charlotte!' and a tall, grey-haired, overtanned woman in a long, loose dress appeared from behind a Japanese screen.

Hammond was introduced to Malcolm Plunkett's wife.

'Right, I'm off to bed,' said Charlotte. 'Show him where everything is and tell him the rules.'

And with that, Charlotte made her way across a succession of identical Bakhtiari rugs to the stairs.

'Sorry about that, Mr Hammond,' said Malcolm Plunkett. 'Charlotte has had a hard day. One of our English teachers threw a wobbler this morning and had to be restrained.'

He gestured Hammond to sit down on a stuffed camel bag on the floor next to a carved Indian table.

'Does that often happen?' asked Hammond.

'What?'

'English teachers throwing wobblers.'

'Well, they're a temperamental bunch, these English teachers. They seem to think that because they are purveying the New World language to an eager populace, it somehow entitles them to live like kings. We have to disillusion them. The one this morning came into my office as calm as you like and asked for an electric toaster. Reckoned that his gas stove didn't have a grill and so the Council should provide him with one. Had the gall to quote his contract: "Suitable accommodation and a full range of furniture, fittings and fixtures will be supplied." Well, I told him straight that that was in no way intended to imply such things as toasters. They'll be wanting cars and business class tickets next.'

'And he threw a wobbler?' said Hammond shaking his head and wondering when a drink would be offered.

'Well, not then. Not really. You see there is also the situation.'

'What's that about?'

'Well, he's got to be circumcised, apparently. It's a very simple op, of course, but he's complaining that we didn't tell him in London. How did he expect us to know?'

'True. True. You know, I'm feeling very dry. I wonder if—'

'I said to him that he knew before he came out here that it was a hardship post. The bugger sat across the table from me in London at the interview and said he was after adventure. Adventure! And then two months later he is coming to me moaning about not having a bloody toaster and having to get circumcised!'

'National Service would have stopped all that sort of talk. Look I hope I'm not—'

'Just what I told him.' Plunkett was warming to his guest. 'Just what I told him. It was then that he threw a wobbler.'

'Was it?'

'Yes, and Charlotte had to intervene.'
'Did she? Look, I hate to be a bore but—'
'Yes.'
'I see.'
'So that's why she's gone to bed,' said Plunkett and yawned. He looked at his watch. 'And I think that's where I'd better be heading too. Got to be at the Ministry for the Suppression of Vice and the Encouragement of Virtue at eight.'
'Where?' asked Hammond.
'Bit of a mouthful, isn't it? Look, just to be on the safe side, I'd better take you along. Better safe than sorry.' He looked at his watch again. Pointedly. 'I'll show you to your room. You must be tired.'
'Yes, I was wondering—'
'Of course. This way.'
Malcolm Plunkett showed Hammond to a small white room with a wash-basin and an adjoining toilet. He left him, warning him not to drink the water.
Hammond surveyed the lavatory disapprovingly and watched the ceiling fan rotate, wondering if it would spin off and decapitate him during the night. He undressed, lay down and tried to sleep, but it was beastly hot and a great thirst was racking him.
At last he got up and went downstairs to look for water. In the kitchen the houseboy was spooning down a yoghurt from a plastic cup. When he saw Hammond his eyes grew big with fright and he made a bolt for the door.
'I say . . .' said Hammond.
Then, alone in the kitchen, he opened the fridge and helped himself to a can of Coke. He gulped it down in one draught and returned, burping and uncertain, feeling unloved, to his bedroom.
At five-thirty in the morning, after hardly any sleep, Hammond heard all the mosques in Fadlabad waking up the populace with a variety of amplified calls to prayer.
He went to his window, looked out at the skyscrapers all around him in the gloom, heard the screeches from every direction and thought: God.

He searched around for the main bathroom, found a shower nozzle all by itself in a completely tiled room and stood under the water for a long time. Then he dried himself, put on his clothes and went downstairs.

The houseboy had just completed his prayers when Hammond entered the kitchen.

'Morning!' said Hammond cheerily. 'Any chance of a cup of coffee?'

The houseboy retreated to the far corner of the kitchen, where he cowered by the pedal bin.

'God, you have been traumatized by these cultural visits, haven't you? No need to worry about me, old son.'

However, the houseboy did not believe Hammond and bolted out of the back door.

Hammond shrugged and set about making his own breakfast, then he fetched his harmonica from his suitcase and between sips of coffee, began to practise in the living-room. The rugs and Sarawak blow-pipes and Balinese paintings listened intently.

At seven he caught sight of Malcolm Plunkett heading for the kitchen.

'Morning!' called Hammond.

Plunkett popped his head into the sitting-room. 'Charlotte and I have been listening to your recital. Is that what you are going to put on for us?'

'Yes, that sort of thing,' replied Hammond, pleased that he had had an audience.

'Your "Bluebells of Scotland" needs a little more rehearsal.'

'Yes, I agree. I'm a bit shaky. Blow when I ought to suck. It's always been a problem. Still, it'll be all right on the night.'

'Got clean underwear on?' asked Plunkett.

'Course. Why? Am I going to get run over by a bus?'

Plunkett did not laugh. 'Well, I wouldn't like you to let the side down at the Ministry for the etc.'

'No, s'pose not.'

He started to vamp out 'Shall we Gather by the River?' wondering what Plunkett was on about. He realized of course that British Council bods were the twentieth century equivalent of second sons sent to the colonies. Instead of some seed-corn and five quid you gave them a set of English language books, the prospectus for the North London Polytechnic, a battery tape recorder and told them to piss off beyond the seas and spread culture. Normally, you never heard from them again. They got all involved in things foreign. He looked round at Plunkett's house. This one certainly had got involved. Everything that should have been on the floor was climbing the walls instead. Not a comfy chair in sight, just these busy-patterned saddle bags, arty books all over the place, back copies of *Punch* and *The Good Book Guide* and booking forms for the National Theatre circa 1978. It was a rum set-up.

At last Plunkett came in with a cup of Horlicks.

'We've got to be at the Ministry by eight.'

'What happens then?'

'Then we come home.'

'I see,' said Hammond. 'Any chance of a trip to the shops? I hear there are some real bargains to be had here.'

'Not another shopper!' said Plunkett.

14

At 6.30 a.m. a ragged convoy of white Toyotas could be seen making its way towards the office of the Ministry for the Suppression of Vice and the Encouragement of Virtue. In each car, tape recorders played the taste of the occupants, attempting that morning to do the impossible and calm down the anxious and angry port employees.

Captain Pooley, alone near the head of the convoy, was half listening to Heddle Nash singing the serenade from *The Fair Maid of Perth*. The other half of his depressed faculties was focused on the cottage he shared with his wife, Doris, between Devizes and Salisbury Plain. The music accompanied him on a tour of his property – into the cosy vestibule, through the black-beamed sitting-room to the modern kitchen he had built for Doris, on to the morning-room and pantry, then up the winding staircase to the upstairs landing – not forgetting to forbid Rudyard, their ageing black Labrador, from following him up the stairs as he was always inclined to do. He peeped into the bathroom – all his own work. The bidet had been a bugger to install, but Doris had always wanted a bidet. Then on to their bedroom with its high bed they had bought before the wedding, the mattress formed into a comfortable U-shaped valley, the big wardrobe which had only been got into the cottage by removing the window and the dressing table, the glass top covering doilies and those faded by a layer of Doris's dusting powder. Lastly, the spare bedroom, always kept ready and aired for the occasional visits of their daughter, Daphne, who did something in the City. At last he sighed as he gazed out at Salisbury Plain in the distance. The cottage was near enough to be able to view the old tracks that led on to the Plain, to discern the smokestacks of Westbury and to hear the train trundle towards London, but far enough away that only when a southerly wind blew could the firing on the army ranges be heard.

And as he toured and listened, Captain Pooley repeated to himself the reason why he was exposing himself to full-frontal inspection: It is necessary to go through this in order that Doris and myself be comfortable in our declining years. I do this for you, Doris, for the cottage and for Rudyard.

But Captain Pooley's lower lip quivered out of control.

Not having been able to pluck up enough courage to drive his own car, Armitage was sharing a car with Mike Taggart, a docking supervisor from Liverpool. Armitage, therefore, did not have any choice in the matter of music. He bore with Mike Taggart's choice of orchestral Beatles while listening to his companion moaning. At the same time, and with great difficulty, he was trying to entertain lascivious thoughts so that he would make a good showing in front of the examining officials. For, while he was still unsure whether to go through with the operation or not, vanity demanded that he put on a manly front.

'The circumcision's just an 'olyday of obligation where I come from,' stated Mike Taggart in his thick Liverpool accent which Armitage thought he ought to do something about.

'What's that?' asked Armitage.

'What's what?' asked Mike Taggart, who since making the observation, had passed on to thinking about other aspects of the problem.

'What you said. I can't remember the exact term you used.' Armitage was likewise distracted.

'If only they'd done it to me when I was a nipper,' said

Mike while the orchestra mulched its way through 'Eleanor Rigby', 'I wouldn't have to worry.'

'But they didn't,' Armitage completed the sentence for him unhelpfully. He did it out of habit, part of his training as an English teacher. Whenever he taught: 'I should have . . .' or 'If only I'd . . .' he found it helpful to add the funeral coda: 'But you didn't.'

They returned to their respective meditations.

Armitage was hoping against hope that, when he dropped his trousers, he would be able to impress the inspectors. The trouble was that it was such a delicate operation. Armitage had always found that his manhood, whose name was Moira – though he could not say how or why – was difficult, if not impossible, to control. At school medicals, in showers after games . . . in fact whenever it had to be displayed, Moira had stubbornly refused to co-operate. Either she would retreat into him and become a humiliatingly tiny nipple, or she would stiffen and elongate to a point where he would be sent out to cool off. Moira just could not get it right and seemed to take malicious pleasure in being in the wrong place and position at the wrong time.

How like a woman! Armitage told himself.

'You know I wouldn't mind having it off but the wife says it's me best feature,' Taggart said.

Armitage wondered about that for a moment. 'Well, maybe you shouldn't then.'

Mike Taggart looked over at Armitage. He took his right hand from the steering wheel and held his thumb and forefinger under Armitage's face. Then he rubbed the ends together.

Armitage nodded. 'Cash flow problems?' he asked.

Mike Taggart nodded and as he listened to a refined version of 'She Loves You', remembered where he had been when he had first heard it. Far from Ras Al Surra in the midst of a city which was soon to be the centre of the cultural universe and, as far as Mike Taggart was concerned, still was.

*

Abdul Wahhab Higgins was looking forward to the day ahead for it promised to contain all the ingredients that satisfied his requirements for a good time. Here he was about to see the British going through abject humiliation in order to keep their jobs. What was more, he had engineered the situation. He, a foreigner and a convert, was well on the way to becoming the top religious policeman in Ras Al Surra.

So, at six-fifty in the morning, Abdul Wahhab found himself seated happily next to Dr Ashraf Al Ashraf, whose main function as Medical Officer at the Ministry for the Suppression of Vice and the Encouragement of Virtue was to check virginity in prospective brides. Towards the ascertaining of evidence, Dr Ashraf Al Ashraf was seldom seen without a medical magnifying glass. This instrument was giving him some trouble as he drank the mint tea brought in by a very dispirited servant.

After greetings and polite conversation had been exchanged, Dr Ashraf Al Ashraf signalled his intention to get down to business by ejaculating piously. He took a grey folder out of his briefcase. 'The contents of this folder are highly immoral,' he told his companion, 'so I have taken the liberty of performing some censorship.'

He opened the folder and produced a line drawing of the male anatomy from the navel to the knee. A black felt-tipped marker had obliterated all of the loin area except for the very tip of the penis. An arrow pointed to this part, labelled, 'Foreskin'.

'This is the filthy part we must detect,' he said.

Abdul Wahhab Higgins eyed the picture with distaste. 'It is indeed a most repulsive thing, this foreskin,' he said. 'I know that it will be a major contribution to National Purity to eradicate them from the Holy Land of Ras Al Surra.'

'Indeed, indeed,' nodded Dr Ashraf Al Ashraf.

'We must be zealous in the enactment of our duty, my brother. Our examination must be thorough. Not a one who carries the badge of the infidel must be allowed past the sieve of our inquisition. It is a distasteful duty, I know, but one which will greatly contribute to the eradication of vice in Ras Al Surra. Take heart on that, believer!' said Abdul Wahhab Higgins.

Dr Ashraf Al Ashraf nodded. Then he put on a pair of surgical rubber gloves. He gave his magnifying glass a polish with a piece of tissue and nodded.

'Bring in the first!' commanded Abdul Wahhab Higgins.

The hapless group of expatriates sat in the unwelcoming waiting room of the offices of the Ministry for the Suppression of Vice and the Encouragement of Virtue. Nobody spoke. Mustapha, feeling his job as Marine Helping Hands Mr Fix It lying heavy on him, paced up and down the room, occasionally stopping in front of one of the mute expatriates and exchanging a word or two. But, given little encouragement, he kept moving on and eventually gave up his well-meant ministrations.

He wondered as he paced why the Ministry had demanded to see all the foreigners and not just those who claimed to be already circumcised. But he did not allow the thought to lodge too deeply because it would only upset him and Mustapha's doctor had told him on several occasions not to allow himself to get upset.

'Bring in the first!' a disembodied voice from behind a closed door shouted.

Mustapha nodded to the man nearest the door, who got up, hoisted his trousers manfully, and disappeared inside.

A minute later he came out, holding his hand up and gazing at the blue Arabic writing stamped upon it. He came up to Mustapha. 'What does it say?'

'It says you are uncircumcised.'

'That's charming, that is!'

'I don't know why they just don't go the whole hog and brand us all,' remarked Captain Pooley bitterly.

Silence settled again, only disturbed by the entrances and exits of the shamefaced men.

At last it was Captain Pooley's turn.

Looking neither to right nor left, he walked through the door and confronted Dr Ashraf Al Ashraf and Abdul Wahhab Higgins. He stood in front of them, lips pursed.

'Please show us your penis,' said Dr Ashraf Al Ashraf.

'Why?' asked Captain Pooley.

'We wish to ascertain whether you are circumcised or not.'

'I am not circumcised,' admitted Captain Pooley, a note of pride in his voice.

'Please show us!'

'I've told you that I'm not. Surely that is all you need to know?'

Abdul Wahhab Higgins spoke up. 'Please, Captain Pooley. Rules are rules, you know.'

Pooley pouted, then said, 'Very well then, but only a quick look, mind.'

Dr Ashraf Al Ashraf peered at Captain Pooley's member and then said quickly, 'This man is uncircumcised.'

'I did tell you,' said Captain Pooley, pushing himself back into his pants.

Abdul Wahhab Higgins nodded and made notes.

'And will you submit to circumcision or will you leave the kingdom?' asked Abdul Wahhab Higgins.

Captain Pooley, briskly pulling up his braces, said, 'Do with me what you will. I am yours to command.'

The irony was not lost on Abdul Wahhab Higgins.

'You will enter the Sayidnee hospital in due course,' he said. 'Next!'

Captain Pooley left the room muttering about grapes and Philippino nurses.

Armitage, now alone in the room, sat on, waiting to be called. He spent his time trying to visualize the Friend, but got stumped because nobody he visualized could he visualize visualizing him back. He sighed.

Tea was brought by the same dispirited servant and taken into the office. Evidently the inquisitors felt they had earned a break. Armitage now tried to conjure up imagery designed to make him appear more than adequate but less than overblown, but that was failing too, and when at last Mustapha interrupted his reverie of being chased by the entire Ras Al Surran security service with Captain Sa'ad leading the pursuit, the little match girl who froze and shivered just below his thin skin surfaced and sent Moira retreating into him, there to cower in the dark.

On his way in, he tried one last time to conjure up pictures of debauchery, but Moira was not moved and, shaking like a jelly, he stood in front of the determined duo and heard Dr Ashraf Al Ashraf say, 'Please show us your penis!'

Armitage fumbled with his flies obediently. As he did so, he remembered that he was wearing Marks & Spencers underpants – with the label uncut – and his panic rose. The zip stuck in his trousers and as he yanked at it, he could feel Moira retreating further.

The trousers fell about his ankles and he stood before the committee in his underpants.

'Show us!' repeated Dr Ashraf Al Ashraf.

Armitage pulled down his underpants and stood waiting for a reaction.

Dr Ashraf Al Ashraf approached Armitage and peered at him closely, then he announced that the man was uncircumcised.

'What is your decision?' asked Abdul Wahhab Higgins.

'Er . . .' replied Armitage.

'Come, Mr Armitage, we require an answer!' said Abdul Wahhab Higgins.

'Er . . .' repeated Armitage, close to tears.

Abdul Wahhab Higgins rose from his seat and came over to Armitage. He repeated the question and touched him lightly on the shoulder.

Armitage looked into the dark glasses of Abdul Wahhab Higgins. The touch on his shoulder tingled.

'Very well,' said Armitage, without quite knowing why, except that at that moment he desperately wanted someone to like and approve of him.

Abdul Wahhab Higgins smiled at him. And just then it seemed like enough.

Armitage fled from Abdul Wahhab Higgins and made for the front door of the Ministry building. Befuddled, but also greatly relieved to have got the unpleasant appointment behind him, he was not thinking in his usual lucid manner. He saw Charlie Hammond walking toward him and did not realize that the door – a glass construction – stood between him and Hammond. Armitage walked straight into the door.

'Ouch!' he cried and held his nose, which had received the full impact. He took two steps backwards and then sat down heavily on the marble floor. Soon the blood was gushing from his nose and dribbling down his front.

Hammond had seen what had happened, heard the bump and felt for its recipient. He stepped through the door in the usual manner and came over to where Armitage was sitting.

'Gosh, are you all right? You took a nasty bang.'

'Er . . . I think so, thank you very much,' replied Armitage, holding one hand cupped under his nose to catch the blood, while with the other he tried to find a handkerchief.

'It's a disgrace that a door like that doesn't have some sort of marking on it to show people it's there. Here, take this,' said Charlie Hammond, offering Armitage a snow-white handkerchief with CH embroidered on it in Tory blue.

'No, I couldn't possibly—' began Armitage.

'There are plenty more where that came from. I've got six at home. Go on, take it! You're an awful mess.'

Armitage took Charlie Hammond's handkerchief gratefully and pressed it against his nose. The flow of blood showed no sign of abating. He stood up unsteadily. A wave of nausea pushed through him and he sat down again on the floor.

Hammond helped him up and took him over to a bench. 'Here, sit down, old chap, and hold your head back.'

'Thanks awfully,' managed Armitage. 'It's very kind of you to help me. Did I bump into the door? It really is very kind—'

'Don't talk,' said Hammond and he took the handkerchief from Armitage and held it over Armitage's nose and tilted his head further back, holding it cupped in his hand. Armitage was reminded of a barber's hands adjusting his head during a haircut. He did as he was told, swallowed as he felt the blood passing over his epiglottis and down his throat.

'That's it,' said Hammond. 'You just stay like that. You got a bad bang there and you're going to have a bruise for a week or two. No, don't move. There's a good fellow.'

'Be careful of the blood,' said Armitage.

'A spot of blood never hurt anyone,' said Hammond confidently. 'My, you are a little worrier, aren't you? You're not the first nose-bleed I've had to look after, I can tell you. At school I sat next to a chap who had them as regular as clockwork before the maths lesson. Mind you, the maths teacher was a horrible little sadist, but he never could get used to it. Now *he* could *bleed*! What you're doing really doesn't measure up.'

'Yes, but you should be careful of blood. We live in er . . . troubled times.'

'Ah, yes,' said Charlie Hammond, 'I suppose we do. Still, you look like a healthy sort of chap to me.'

'Well, I think I am but I'm not sure. I mean, no one can be sure.'

'Yes, but you've got no reason not to be sure, have you?'

Armitage looked into Charlie Hammond's brown eyes and Charlie could see the uncertainty and worry and fear of exposure in his face. It was a look that had stared back at Charlie Hammond on occasions past counting in shaving mirrors, shop windows and in the glistening surfaces of his purchases. He also realized with a start that he had seen that look before on the faces of men who had thought he was their friend.

Armitage's blood was saturating the handkerchief and smudges of it flecked Hammond's fingers. If, he thought, there was a nick there, if his patient was infected, then death might be entering him here in the act of giving first aid, in his first act of kindness for a long time. The thought was a melancholy one indeed, but not without its own pathos – or was it irony? He thought of the mingling blood of schoolfriends and of Juliet sucking poison from Romeo's lips. There on a hard bench of the Ministry for the Suppression of Vice and the Encouragement of Virtue, Charlie Hammond began to think and feel things that he had not thought and felt for three decades.

'I'll risk it,' he said, in a confident, sensible voice that just came out like that. 'As I say, the blood flow can't compete with the chap at school I was talking about. Funny, I haven't thought of him in over thirty years.'

'Haven't you?' asked Armitage, addressing the ceiling. 'I really am sorry to cause you all this trouble.' He was feeling extremely happy there with his head held back, blood dripping through his nasal cavity and down his throat and the hand of a stranger caught over it, now more like an anaesthetist holding the thought-stopping mask. His recent humiliation at the hands of Abdul Wahhab Higgins was easy to forget now that the shock of the bang against the door and this public compassionate embrace by a stranger had enfolded him.

Hammond told Armitage to shut up and Armitage did so. For five minutes he stayed in contented thoughtlessness, almost in ecstasy, like a fed and changed baby being rocked to sleep, while Charlie Hammond ministered to him simply with his talk and his attention.

Plunkett and Percy, the English teacher who had accompanied them to the Ministry, came up and asked what had happened and Hammond told them to go away. It was wonderful to be of use. He had forgotten the feeling. Holding Armitage's head while people passed and stared gave Hammond the feeling of being other than himself. This was no new feeling, but this time he knew he was not playing the day's version of Hammond. He *was* the fireman who helps a suffocating child from the fumes; the St John's Ambulance volunteer comforting an injured person on the sidelines at a football match. He could remember many occasions in the distant past, at school mainly, when he had had this similar feeling. He had liked it then too, had wanted it to become all of him, but it had in adult life been forgotten, like a kid's penknife or scout's uniform. There had been no opportunities. And suddenly a voice was asking, 'And why did you not make those opportunities?'

'They're waiting for you, Hammond!' barked Plunkett.

'Then they'll just have to wait, won't they?' Hammond answered. He said to Armitage, 'Better now? Try coming forward a little, old son,' and he gently took Armitage's head in both hands and moved it forward, back to the vertical.

Again Armitage felt that joy in being ministered to, in cosy passivity. 'Thank you. I think I'm all right now.'

But Charlie Hammond held the handkerchief against his nose. 'Better make sure.'

After a couple of minutes, he carefully removed the handkerchief. No blood gushed.

'There. I think you're all right. A bit of a wash and you'll be OK. My, you're going to have a swollen nose, though.'

'I expect so,' said Armitage. 'It's throbbing like mad.'

Charlie Hammond made to put the bloody handkerchief back into his pocket, but Armitage grabbed it from him. 'No, I'll wash it for you!'

'That's not necessary. As I said, I've plenty more.'

Armitage shook his head. 'I insist! My name is Trevor Armitage, by the way.'

'Charlie Hammond.'

'Are you here to be er . . . looked at?'

'I'm not sure what I'm here for to tell you the truth. Do you work in Ras Al Surra?'

'Yes, I work on the King Fadl industrial port. I'm a teacher there. How about you?'

'I'm just visiting. I suppose you could say I'm a performer. I'm putting on a performance at the National Theatre here.'

'Are you?' asked Trevor. 'That sounds interesting. I must come and see you.'

Their conversation was interrupted by Plunkett. He and Percy had been checked and Hammond was the last remaining. Many were the rumblings of impatience coming from the devout inspectors in the inner office.

'Come on, Hammond! I'm sure your chum can manage.'

Charlie Hammond smiled at Armitage and stood up.

Trevor Armitage was beside himself. 'I must give you my address,' he said. Then he thought that he might sound odd and added, 'I mean, I must return your hanky . . . your handkerchief . . . when I've washed it.'

'Yes, I'd like to see you again.' Charlie gestured to where Plunkett and Percy stood. 'As you can see, I haven't many friends here.'

'Well, you have now,' said Trevor, surprising himself.

'You just go and wash that face of yours. I've got to go and see these people.'

'Best of luck!' said Trevor and he watched Charlie Hammond disappear into the office he had come out of a million years before. Then he realized that he had not given Charlie his address and telephone number.

Without shame, Armitage begged a pen from the dour man at reception and wrote down his name and address on a piece of paper which he ripped out of his diary without the least compunction. He gave the paper to Plunkett, telling him please to be sure to give it to Mr Hammond.

Then, carefully opening the glass door, frowning at it severely while feeling a certain affection for it at the same time, Trevor Armitage left the Ministry for the Suppression of Vice and the Encouragement of Virtue, his head full of visualizations of Charlie Hammond.

Earlier in the day, Hammond had expressed a desire to shop in the markets of Fadlabad, but now he did not feel like it.

'Why didn't you tell me?' he asked Plunkett in the car on the way home, while Percy the English teacher quietly sobbed in the back.

'Didn't I? I thought I had,' replied the Council man. He turned and addressed Percy, 'Come on! Snap out of it, Percy! We're all in the same boat, you know.'

'But my contract stated that—'

'Oh stop bloody whingeing! I cannot abide a whinger! Whingers are yesterday's men, you must realize that, Percy. Today we are all positive thinkers. You've got a class at eleven. English for Armaments Procurers, isn't it?'

Percy sniffed and nodded.

'Well,' said Hammond. 'I'll be well out of here before they get round to doing anything, shan't I?'

'That depends. You might be. Things tend to grind exceeding slow around here, but sometimes, when they've got a bee in their bonnet, it all happens in double quick time. It's hard to tell.'

'But I don't want to be circumcised,' moaned Hammond.

'Well you should have thought of that before you signed up,' answered Plunkett mechanically.

Hammond felt his heart go out to Percy in the back seat who was still sobbing quietly. Oh God! he thought, I must get in touch with London about this.

But London – in the stern form of Miss Glover – did not seem in the least interested. The gloat in her voice survived the bounce off the satellite as she said, 'Well, Charlie, one must pay for one's mistakes.'

Hammond sat despondent in Plunkett's house that evening, remembering the brief bright spot in a bleak day. He thought of the nice chap, Trevor, and how he had promised to give him his address. Must have forgotten, he thought.

Then, just as he was off to bed, Plunkett handed Hammond Armitage's piece of paper. 'From that queer fellow at the Ministry,' he said.

And Charlie Hammond's mood brightened a little.

15

'Wife, bring tea!' commanded Abdul Wahhab Higgins.

He was sitting on the carpet in his living-room, legs crossed reading a devotional text. The fan whirred overhead and the pink gloss paint on the walls glinted in the light from a single, halo-shaped phosphorescent bulb on the ceiling.

Abdul Wahhab Higgins was not at peace as he read, however. The letters from his mother were continuing on a daily basis and they were not only upsetting him but the Ras Al Surran post office, the customs department and the censors. Mrs Higgins seemed determined to ruin his reputation in his new country. He had tried to think of ways of stopping her constant meddling, to bring her round to an acceptance of the True Faith, pull her back from the papist precipice on which she teetered. But it had done no good. She, along with all the others in Castlebar, County Mayo, were not open to the Truth. That accursed dog, Father McNally, had made sure of that. Had he not duped his mother into consigning the three mind-opening pamphlets he had sent her—'The Zionist Plot Against Mohammed' (from *Contemporary Sources*); 'Jihad – War For All Seasons'; 'The Lie of the Crucifixion' – to the bin?

He wished he could have done with her. Surely he had done everything a man could to bring her round – to no avail! It was time to break off all connection.

He sighed at the impossibility of that. He had long ago ceased writing, but his lack of response to his mother's missives only seemed to increase their volume. He shuddered as he remembered the daily trips to the censors to be hauled over the coals for being the recipient of rosaries, immaculate medals, our Lady of Lourdes musical boxes, Pope John Paul T-shirts, a glass statuette of St Maria Goretti, which, when the top was screwed off, proved to contain Irish Mist, Mass cards, Padre Pio devotional material, shares in Knock airport, *True Stories of 1001 Deathbed Conversions*, postcards, holy pictures, scapulars, and cribs made from Holy Land olive wood – it went on and on, like eternity.

It was not easy to convince his pious brethren at the censorship office that his mother was waging war on him. They wore robes with splits in them – in the sleeves, chest and back. These splits could be fastened and unfastened with velcro. Thus it was easy for them to tear their garments – and they did so a hundred times a day – without having to replace them. Also, velcro made a piously loud ripping sound, almost better than the real thing.

The brethren at the censorship office had persuaded Sheikh Al Gaz to get a law put on to the statute books which made the recipient of any item of mail personally responsible for all mail received. No longer could the recipients of velcro-ripping videos say that they didn't know the video was velcro-ripping, had never asked for it, didn't want it. They had received it and therein lay their guilt. So far, the censors had accepted Abdul Wahhab's explanations, but, as he went in to their offices and saw them tortuously pressing the velcro of their gowns together or ripping it apart, he knew that their holy patience was wearing thin.

'Your tea, husband!'

Abdul Wahhab Higgins looked round, startled. There in the doorway stood the black shape of Mrs Higgins. Even in the house she wore her thick veil because Abdul Wahhab Higgins found her distracting without it.

She placed the tray on the carpet to her husband's right and poured him a glass of tea with her black-gloved hand. 'Do you desire anything else, O husband?' she asked flatly.

'No, wife. I will eat in one hour,' replied Abdul Wahhab Higgins, without looking up from his book.

His wife left the room. As she did so, she pulled tongues at Abdul Wahhab Higgins through her veil.

Back in the kitchen Faridah Higgins removed her veil and gloves, sighed and pulled another face at her sister, Amina, who was seated on the cool floor, her back against the fridge door.

'In truth, Amina, that foreigner is a beansprout of a man who thinks he is a cucumber of great flavour and refinement,' sighed Mrs Higgins.

'Did I not tell you, Faridah,' replied her sister, shaking a many-bangled arm at Faridah as she did so, 'that in marrying a converted foreigner you would be wedding sorrow?'

Faridah looked down at her plump sister and envied her. She had been happily married for years to a prosperous merchant who duplicated foreign videos and sold them in the market.

'Our father said that, though he was pious, he would surely take me to London to shop and treat me well,' Faridah observed, as she had observed on many occasions before. 'But as it is, I never even go to the suk and, if I do, I cannot see anything through that accursed veil he makes me wear. He must place my hand on the shopping trolley and lead me round the supermarket. I hear him dropping things in but I cannot see what. Why I cannot wear a nice, thin veil like everyone else, I do not know.'

'You are a badge of his piety, sister.'

Faridah nodded and gazed longingly at Amina's rich jewellery and gaudy dress. 'Just as you are a badge of your husband's prosperity,' she said sadly.

'But is he good when the lights are out?' asked Amina.

Faridah folded her bottom lip until it touched the tip of her chin. Then she spat into the stew which she was preparing for her husband's evening meal. Faridah ate different, spicier food.

'Of course, I am unable to compare, being a good and

virtuous wife. But all I can say is, if that is all there is to it, then it amazes me that people make such a great matter of it.'

'And are his parts adequate?'

'Well, naturally I have never seen them, but they feel adequate. It is merely that I feel them so seldom and when I do it is all so swift,' replied Faridah.

Amina held up her right hand, upon which a huge gold and diamond ring sparkled. 'Izaac bought me this yesterday. Ah, but he is generous!'

Faridah turned back to the brown stew and saw her own life in the tepid, flavourless mess. 'Abdul Wahhab,' she said, 'only finds satisfaction in making others unhappy.'

Amina shook her head sadly, then twiddled the ring on her finger. The strip light on the kitchen ceiling made it glitter and, as if by magic, Amina was smiling again.

King Fadl and Queen Noof were taking coffee in the Queen's private apartments that evening.

Jeeves had just served them, spilling coffee into Noof's saucer as he did so. Both eyed the cheeky, retreating back of Jeeves as he withdrew, whistling.

'You must rid yourself of the despicable, common fellow, Fadl,' observed Noof. 'Upon my word, he lowers the tone of the palace. Upon my word he does.'

'Jeeves has his uses,' replied King Fadl. 'Also, as I have told you before, dear Noof, he makes me laugh. Nobody else around here does.'

'Well at least make him bathe, Fadl. At least make him do that! His body odour is sometimes more than flesh and blood can bear. You know, of course, that it is highly carcinogenic.'

'What is, my dear?'

'BO. I heard a doctor talking about it on an American television show. He says that three inhalations of day-old sweat is equivalent to smoking a packet of cigarettes. So you see, Fadl, that precious Jeeves of yours is a health risk.'

Queen Noof drank a sip of coffee, her little finger crooked artistically. Then she asked her husband, 'To what do I owe this unaccustomed visit?'

King Fadl smiled sweetly, but his smile cut no ice with Noof. He replied, 'There are things to be discussed. You know I value your opinion highly. And, I thought, perhaps we might bill and coo later on.'

Queen Noof suddenly became agitated. 'Bill and coo!' she exclaimed. 'Bill and coo! What is this nonsense you are talking, Fadl? Why, I wouldn't bill and coo with you if you were the last man in the world!'

'Very well,' sighed King Fadl, quite relieved, 'then just a short discussion.'

'And what, pray, do you wish to discuss?'

'Politics.'

Queen Noof became suddenly interested. She lay her coffee cup aside and leaned forward in her seat to hear what Fadl would say.

'As you may know,' began the King with more than a hint of irony in his voice, for Noof had talked of little else since the whirlwind trip of Sultan Nabil and Zarina to Ras Al Surra, 'Ras Al Surra has recently been trying to acquire a piece of Zibda. I initially wanted the land because I . . . well . . . I wanted it. But Jeeves informed me, in return for a trifle, that there might be something to my advantage under the rather dull covering of the area; a rather large deposit of uranium. I have ascertained that this is, indeed, the truth. A team of geologists from RASONGRO found that Al Bustan is a very promising piece of real estate indeed. The British, apparently, were anxious that Ras Al Surra should not be allowed to acquire Al Bustan. Their actions betokened more than would be expected had Al Bustan been the useless wasteland I had thought it to be. Now, as you know, I have failed to buy Al Bustan. I destroyed my opportunity by offering to double the price. I had thought that my generous act would be appreciated and would speed Nabil to sign the contract. *Au contraire*, I fear. He smelled a rat straight away, baited a trap for it by demanding that the confounded desert rose fields remain undisturbed in perpetuity. I – I admit it – rose, so to speak, to the bait and foolishly refused to give this undertaking. And you know the rest.'

Queen Noof looked bored. She had started to count her gold bangles, pulling them up to her elbow one at a time, a habit which always communicated eloquently to her husband. 'So?' she asked.

'So, my Queen, I am wondering what to do.'

'Well, I know what I would do,' said Noof.

'And what is that?'

'Strike back! Bomb Al Rahman! Destroy Nabil and his whole shameful dynasty. Take the country over in the name of righteousness.'

'Well, yes, I did intimate to Nabil that there would be a price to pay. I am not sure that I had quite such a high price in mind, dear Noof,' replied King Fadl, making a mental note never to push Noof into a swimming pool.

'Oh, you men make me sick!' Noof replied. 'You do not have the slightest idea what is required. What have you done to Zibda? Charged for admission to the shrine of the Footprints of Aisha, that's what. By God, Fadl, that does not even make a start at responding to the great insult paid to us by Nabil and his woman.'

'But the implications of what you advocate—' began Fadl.

'There would be no implications. Were there implications for the British when they ventured across half the world to liberate those cold little islands from that nice Evita? Certainly not. Also, you and I well know that Nabil is seen by the Arab Nation as an apostate. We in Ras Al Surra, on the other hand, are seen as the Guardians of Islam in all its thrusting vigour. The Arab Nation would be pleased to see you take over Zibda. Those who might have some reservations can quickly be brought into line. We do, after all, finance most of them most generously. The merest hint that aid might be cut off would send them running back to our camp.'

'But what of the superpowers?'

'They do not like Zibda any more than we do. They would not be slow to see what economic advantages would be opened up for them, were Zibda to be developed. Think of the roads that would have to be built, the infrastructure for the exporting of the uranium and the rest. There are many profitable things for them to do to turn Zibda from its primitive ways. If I were you—'

Fadl felt it was time to assert his prerogative. 'Well, you are not me, Noof,' he said. 'You have given me much to think about it is true, but I still cannot help thinking you are being a little, well, draconian.'

'If I am it is because I see what weakness sires, Fadl. Look what happened to poor Ferdinand and Imelda! My heart bleeds whenever I contemplate their fate. And the Shah and Empress Farah! It was their lack of steel that caused their downfall, nothing else.'

King Fadl suddenly felt an urgent need to be alone. 'I shall think about what you have said, Noof,' he said. 'Now I will retire to my rumpus room.'

'Do that, Fadl!' said Queen Noof. 'But do not allow yourself to become sidetracked. There is, I detect, a peculiar mildness in your character which bodes little good.'

King Fadl smiled weakly and made his retreat.

Five minutes later he was lying on his vibrating armchair looking at the map of Ras Al Surra on the wall. He tried to envisage the whole area of Ras Al Surra and Zibda done in gold. Then he thought about his state-of-the-art armed forces. For the best part of two decades he had been footing the bill to have his forces trained and equipped. To date he had seen little return on that money. Perhaps it was time to test their metal. Zibda, he felt confident, would fall into his hand without much of a fight. But was Noof right about the reactions of outsiders? Did Zibda really have no friends who would rush to her defence?

He decided he would have to think about it further – and promptly fell asleep.

16

The following morning, Hammond was practising with his worms in the Plunketts' living-room. He had slept very badly, worrying about the future, regretting the past. Trevor Armitage kept coming to his mind, along with the small kindness he had been able to render.

'Shall I ring up that nice chap Trevor? What do you think of that?' Hammond asked the purple worm, prior to manipulating it into nodding its head and then darting mysteriously up his arm.

After he had been practising for an hour or so, Plunkett put in an appearance, wearing a dressing-gown with a Chinese character on the back.

'That's nice!' Hammond said, admiring the robe. 'Get it here, did you?'

Plunkett, downing a glass of orange-flavoured Eno, said, 'Yes, I did. But I prefer it unflavoured. Thought I'd give it a try but it's a mistake. The Eno people don't seem to have got the hang of orange.'

'I was referring to your dressing-gown, actually,' said Hammond.

'Oh, that! It's Charlotte's. She got it in Hong Kong, I believe.'

'They say Hong Kong is good for shopping,' said Hammond and he made his red worm nod and agree with him. 'Do you know what's written on the back?'

'Tell you the truth, I've never given it to a thought,' replied Plunkett. 'Prosperity or something like that, I should think.' He gazed at Hammond, thinking him a bit much on top of orange flavoured Eno first thing in the morning. He took his empty glass out to the kitchen, returning with a cup of coffee and a plate of All Bran. He watched Hammond's antics with the worms as he ate, musing on the state of the world.

'Fixed up a hall for me yet?' asked Hammond hopefully.

Plunkett replied through a mouthful of All Bran. 'They've promised us the National Theatre as soon as they've cleared up the mess left by Bulgarian Jam Week. But I wouldn't hold my breath if I were you.'

'But look, Plunkett, I've got to get this thing over with before they decide to chop me to ribbons. Ras Al Surra just isn't my idea of a good time. How do you stand it, by the way?'

'Usually I don't mind it too much,' replied Plunkett who, having finished the All Bran, was in process of drinking the milk direct from the bowl. 'But I'm always on the edge, if you get my meaning, and it doesn't take much to make me go over the edge.'

'Doesn't it?' asked Hammond.

'No, not much. Just the odd guest staying a bit too long, feeling up the houseboys, lecturing us on comparative shopping, talking to toy worms and playing simple tunes wrongly.'

'Steady on, old chap!' replied Hammond. 'I do not feel up houseboys.'

'I bet you would if he let you get close enough.'

'I would not!'

'Yes, you would!'

'Look,' pouted Hammond, holding on to his worms for dear life, 'I've told you, I would *not*. Anyway,' he continued. 'I can see you're unhinged.'

'How?' asked Plunkett.

'You have to be to let standards drop the way you have. Drinking your All Bran milk direct from the bowl. Come on, old man! That's just not *normal*!'

'Boys! Stop it at once!' cried Charlotte Plunkett.

She stood, dressed formidably in a powder-blue safari suit, holding a briefcase.

'Sorry, dear,' said Plunkett.

'Yes, sorry,' murmured Hammond.

Charlotte called for coffee. 'I'm late,' she said.

'Where are you going?' asked Hammond.

'Spot of visiting. Business,' replied Charlotte, looking towards the kitchen expectantly.

She scowled and came to sit down on the camel bag two away from Hammond.

'I didn't know you worked?' Hammond asked.

'Part-time.'

'What do you do?'

'Troubleshooting.'

Hammond grinned. 'Much trouble to shoot is there?'

'Enough.'

The houseboy brought Charlotte a cup of coffee and was given a split-second upward movement of the corners of Charlotte's downward-pulled lips by way of reward.

'Well, have a good time,' said Hammond amiably.

'I shan't,' said Charlotte Plunkett, 'but thank you for your good wishes. What are you going to do with your day, Mr Hammond?'

Hammond replied. 'Well, I'll practise with my instrument and with my worms. One soon gets rusty if one lets one's talent lie fallow.'

He saw the Plunketts exchange looks. Desperately, he searched around for something else to fill his day. 'Also,' he continued, 'I shall visit a friend.'

'Didn't know you had any friends here,' said Plunkett.

Hammond smiled. 'My patient at the Ministry. Trevor.'

'Oh, yes, *him*!' laughed Plunkett unkindly.

'That's right. Him,' said Hammond, suddenly feeling a hot anger rise up from his depths, sufficient to melt appearances. Plunkett's laugh reminded him of all the other laughs that echoed down the empty years, laughs that had driven him off the playing-field of life and on to the silly sidelines.

*

Armitage had only been back from work for ten minutes when the telephone rang. He picked it up and said, 'Good afternoon.'

'Remember me?' the voice on the other end of the line said.

'Of course I do, Mr Hammond! You're my ministering angel.'

Charlie Hammond coughed self-consciously. 'Well, I don't know about that,' he said.

'Oh, I do,' countered Trevor. 'In a funny way I think it was the best thing that has happened to me since I came to Ras Al Surra. I've been feeling marvellous since it happened.'

'Well, thank you for that—'

'I mean, I didn't enjoy bumping into the door, but meeting you and your kindness after that wretched inspection. That was lovely.'

'I suppose your nose is a mess, is it?' asked Charlie.

'Come and see for yourself. You know I have been cursing myself for not taking your address at the time. I thought you would just take your wings out and go straight back to heaven without getting in touch.'

'Oh, I haven't done that. Far from it. I'm still – well, I suppose you might say – a guest at the British Council in Fadlabad. My welcome here is wearing very thin indeed.'

'Why don't we meet?'

'That would be nice. Do you think we could? The trouble is, I don't have a vehicle.'

'I do!' said Trevor, not considering in his enthusiasm that, though he had a vehicle, he had still not plucked up the courage to operate it in Ras Al Surra.

'Then perhaps we could meet for dinner here in Fadlabad. Would that be convenient?'

'Yes. When?'

'Tonight?'

Charlie Hammond and Trevor Armitage arranged to meet at a small restaurant in the centre of Fadlabad.

Both smiled at the telephone after they put down the receiver.

Armitage got his ironing board out and fretted about the drive. At the Quick School of Languages he had driven the minibus the length and breadth of England year in and year out. He had negotiated spaghetti junctions and the roundabouts of Milton Keynes, the country lanes of Gloucestershire and the hills of Wales, singing simple songs to help his students' English, keeping an eye out for cultural clashes in the back while negotiating a safe route. He ironed his best white shirt and thought: If I did it then, I can damned well get a Toyota to the Bangla Desh Islamic Café in King Fadl Street, Fadlabad by seven-thirty. I need a night out.

He laid into his seersucker jacket with a will. 'I wonder if Charles Hammond *is*,' he mused. He had never been very good at spotting other gay people unless they came out and told him they were. His friends in Herne Bay had been quicker. 'That's one!' they'd say and Armitage would look and ask, 'Are you sure? How can you tell?' And they would give Armitage a look or say something trite like, 'Takes one to know one,' but that did not help at all. Armitage tended to think people were not, unless proved otherwise. It was part of his lack of self-esteem to be, in spite of himself, shocked to discover that someone was. The surprise never lessened with the passing of time. He had even found himself thinking to himself: No, he couldn't possibly be. Far too nice, only dimly aware that he was also speaking eloquently of his attitude to himself when he made such a statement.

'I don't care whether he is or not!' Armitage told his crisply ironed seersucker jacket. 'He's nice and he was kind to me.' He put the jacket on a hanger and filling the inside pocket with jumpas, set about ironing Hammond's handkerchief, happy that he had something to look forward to, other than an operation.

Two hours later Armitage had negotiated his Toyota on to the freeway to Fadlabad and was starting to relax. His drive through Naffa had almost convinced him that he would never make it. He had crashed the gears, jerked the car, and conked out at traffic lights and, despite the air-conditioning, had broken out in a sweat. He had only been saved from parking the car at the side of the road and leaving it by the thought of a friend waiting for him at the end of the journey.

But something had happened to him after he had pushed the car into the slow lane on the freeway. Confidence returned – a stranger he would have liked to know better – and he knew that as long as he kept the car between the white lines of the slow lane, no harm would come to him. Traffic whizzed past on the three lanes to his left and Armitage tutted disapproval and kept his eyes fixed resolutely on the straight road ahead. The lights on the chimneys of the desalination plant winked at him. In the distance he could see the illuminated causeway of the port and above all a near-full moon presided. He began to feel at home and wondered if, given time, he could become fond of Ras Al Surra.

He turned off the freeway and negotiated his way into the centre of Fadlabad. Anxiety returned then, but it was manageable. He had got the hang of the gears, stayed modestly in the slow lane of roads – giving faster drivers their head – and found himself a parking place only a block away from the Bangla Desh Islamic Café with ten minutes to spare before his appointment with Charlie Hammond.

He walked down the street, passing the usual United Nations of grass widowers who formed the majority of the visible population of Fadlabad: Koreans, Thais, Philippinos, British, American, Somalis, Sudanese, Palestinians walked in single sex, national groups along the pavement. Armitage, alone, but with company in prospect, felt happy to be a part of this strange manifestation of the twentieth century.

He arrived at the café before Hammond and took a table for two in sight of the door.

'I'm waiting for a friend,' he told the waiter, not without a hint of pride in his voice. He ordered a pitcher of Ras Al Surran champagne – a mixture of apple juice and

Perrier – so that he would have something to welcome Charlie Hammond with when he turned up.

The café was almost full. Armitage fiddled with his place setting and looked at his Seiko more times than was strictly necessary. When the Ras Al Surran champagne arrived he did not drink, rather he breathed deeply and waited for his friend.

Charlie Hammond arrived at a quarter to eight, just as the café proprietor was about to pull down the shutters for prayertime. This was the law in Ras Al Surra. All shops and businesses had to close up to allow the populace to pray without distraction. So, five minutes prior to the call to prayer one knew it was heading up by the sounds of thousands of metal shutters being banged down.

'I nearly didn't make it,' said Charlie Hammond as he took his seat next to Armitage. 'Sorry!'

'Think nothing of it, er . . . Charles. I'm glad you were able to come.'

The waiter took their order in the now half-full café. 'Now tell me exactly why you're in Ras Al Surra,' said Trevor.

Charlie told Trevor all about his harmonica performance, not mentioning the real reason why he had been sent – a reason he was in danger of forgetting so little did it impinge, so little idea did he have of the exact reason why Miss Glover had seen fit to send him.

'You must tell me when it's on and I'll buy lots of tickets,' said Trevor with enthusiasm. 'We're really starved of culture here.'

'Well, you may not get a chance at this rate. Bulgarian Jam Week seems to be the sticking point. It just goes on. Anyway, it looks like the circumcision thing may interrupt everything.'

'But it doesn't seem fair that you should have to go through with circumcision. You're not working here permanently after all,' said Trevor.

'Try telling that to the Council chap.'

'So you're not too happy staying where you're staying?'

'You can say that again, Trevor. They're not my type at all.'

Trevor stepped into the breach, though he reddened as he did so. 'Come and stay with me, Charles. I have plenty of room.'

'That's awfully kind of you.'

'Well, you were awfully kind to me. I wasn't feeling very good about anything before I bumped into the door – what with the inspection and everything – but since then I've been as happy as a lark.'

'Why?' asked Charlie Hammond.

'Well, do you mind if I'm frank?'

'No, of course not.'

'I was happy to meet you. You're just about the first person who has been kind to me since I came to Ras Al Surra. It's a funny place you know. It seems to bring out the worst in people.'

'Are you married yourself?'

'No, you?'

'No, not yet. I . . .' Hammond had been going to say that he had not found the right woman. He had even been about to pull out just the correct deep laugh from his prop cupboard, but recalling that Armitage had appended nothing to his bald statement of marital status, interrupted himself and, after a pause, during which he looked at his halo of rice with its steaming yellow vegetable curry in the middle, added, '. . . am not married.'

Trevor nodded. 'Do you think you will marry?'

Again Charlie wanted to say what he always said but, facing Trevor, he did not want to, did not think it necessary somehow. 'No, I doubt it. You?'

'No.'

Half-way through the meal the shutters of the café opened again and groups of new customers poured in and filled the empty tables.

The two smiled at one another yet again and had

enough of their smiles left over to look away and out to the groups at the tables nearby and through the windows to the pavement and the honking street.

After the meal they walked for a while and then Trevor asked Charlie if he would like to have a coffee in his flat. 'I can have you back here by eleven,' he said.

Charlie had coffee at Trevor's flat, but did not get back to Fadlabad that night.

When the coffee had been drunk, Charlie looked at his watch and slapped his knee, seeming to be about to make the effort to rise from his armchair.

'You want to go, don't you?' said Trevor, not even trying to disguise the disappointment in his voice.

'Well, perhaps I ought. You've got work in the morning.'

Trevor smiled wanly and shrugged. It would not be gentlemanly to proceed any further in hindering his guest's departure. And, if he did appeal, if he did make the suggestion that he wanted to make, then perhaps he would destroy his one stab at friendship in Ras Al Surra.

But Charlie did not move and Trevor relaxed again. He said suddenly, surprising himself, 'Charles, I think there's something I should tell you. I am gay.'

'I thought you might be, Trevor. I suppose I am too.' Charlie sounded tired, making his admission like a man admitting to being deaf after years of refusal to admit there was a problem.

They made love upon Trevor's single bed. Charlie said he did not want the light out. Trevor did not insist, though he would rather have been in darkness. For the first five minutes or so he kept arranging the bedsheet to cover what he considered to be his weak point: the place just above his waist where he had started to swell over the last year; his Rubens behind. But then Charlie pulled the sheet away and sent it across the room. 'We don't need that!'

'Don't we? You don't think you might not be better with a bit of covering? The draught from the air-conditioning will give you a chill.'

'What are you ashamed of, Trevor?'

'Nothing,' said Trevor, though he could have named ten items straight off.

'You're in better shape than I am.'

Trevor looked at Charlie and had to admit that it was probably true. For a moment a mean little thought came in to his mind: What am I doing here with this fat old man? But the reply came back as quick as a flash: What is this kind and distinguished gentleman doing here with me?

They spent great expanses of time hugging one another closely. They sighed a lot. Charlie Hammond worried about his erection holding up. Trevor constantly had to call a halt to proceedings to warn Charlie not to collide with his swollen nose. Both had trouble keeping out of the bed the easy ideal men of their fantasies who had for so long been their faithful companions in the world-wanking jerks into life. The reality each hugged would not have entered one another's purple dreams except as a barman, taxi-driver, or bath-attendant, to walk on and walk off, perhaps helping to establish the context in which the ideals would appear, rampant and lusting and aching for Charlie or Trevor as if each were an answer to the ideal's prayer, the only possible slaker for their enormous lusts. The past conjured itself up around their bed, but both willed it away, made a conscious effort to be aroused by the less-than-ideal present. Sighs were prayers for a non-wanking, non-wanting future.

Finally they came together and came together and lay, glued fast, snoring in one another's arms.

In the early morning Trevor drove his new friend back to Fadlabad, letting his right hand stray from the gear stick occasionally to rest easily on Charlie's knee.

'I'll come and collect you after work,' said Trevor. 'It will be lovely to have someone to stay with me. It's too big a place for one anyway.'

'I'll be ready for you,' said Charlie Hammond.

Trevor drove straight to work after dropping Charlie.

He felt full of energy and ready for anything that might befall. In class he sang 'I'm a Blue Toothbrush', 'A Four-Legged Friend', 'Getting to Know You' and 'The Rose of Tralee' for his class of firemen. They whooped and cheered and demanded that he write the words of 'I'm a Blue Toothbrush' on the board. Trevor did so with alacrity, singing the words as he wrote them, feeling like a teacher again.

17

The following evening Trevor drove to Fadlabad to pick up Charlie Hammond. He had hardly given a thought to the problem of the drive, only reproaching himself for not having plucked up the courage to do it earlier. But he was still a little anxious nevertheless, having received notification that he was required to enter the hospital the following morning.

Charlie was waiting for him outside the gate of the British Council residence. Trevor got out of the car to help him with the suitcases, packages and plastic bags that were sitting on the pavement beside him.

'My you've got a lot of luggage!'

Charlie looked glum and merely nodded.

'What's the matter with you?' Trevor asked, fearful that Charlie might be about to tell him he did not want to continue to be his friend.

'I've got to go into the hospital tomorrow. The news came today. I really thought I was going to be able to get away with it.'

'Is that all?' laughed Trevor. 'That's not so bad. Maybe they'll put us in the same room.'

'You mean you're going in too?'

'Yes.'

Charlie smiled. 'That's not so bad then,' he said.

'Perhaps it's fate. I'd like to think it was anyway. We'll go through a difficult experience together. When people do that it bonds them.'

'Does it?' asked Charlie, for whom bonds had up to

then been only nice, but somewhat confusing, things left him by dead aunts.

'Yes, I read it in one of my books. Of course, that is if you want it to bond us. I know I do.'

'Yes, I do, Trevor. But there are some things I'll have to tell you. I'm afraid that after—'

'No, Charles,' said Trevor firmly, 'I don't want to hear any confessions! I'm sure both of us have confessions to make. You don't get to middle age without regrets. But if you don't mind, I'd rather we saved them for another time. Tonight is special. I've made dinner.'

Charlie nodded and pointed out the Bangla Desh Islamic Café. They smiled at it affectionately. Then Trevor had to devote all his attention to finding the freeway entrance.

They ate baked fish and salad, followed by Trevor's speciality, All Bran bread-and-butter pudding. This was accompanied by a bottle of Pooley White which Trevor had obtained by making friends with Captain Pooley again. It had been easy. That day he had felt like a completely different person, breezing into Captain Pooley's office and apologizing for any misunderstanding. Captain Pooley accepted his apology and Trevor had then bounced out of the office, smiling at everyone he saw and refusing to be phased by the odd looks he got back. He even offered a cheery Arabic greeting to Abdul Wahhab Higgins.

As far as Trevor was concerned, everything in the garden was lovely. When the time came for he and Charlie to go to bed, Charlie was open mouthed when he saw the way Trevor had decorated the room. Brightly coloured sarongs, Arab head-dresses, a Brighton tea towel and another, placed directly on the ceiling over the bed, with 'If.' printed on it, billowed from the ceiling and fluttered in the draught coming from the air-conditioner. The room smelled of incense and little night-lights – at least a dozen of them – burned in saucers. New striped sheets, which Trevor had bought in the suk that afternoon, graced the bed. On the pillow lay two red roses.

Charlie Hammond said, 'It's a whole different world. How did you do it?'

'I am used to making a little place home, Charles. The basic tool of my interior decor is a staple gun. You should have seen my room in Herne Bay.'

'Are you from Herne Bay?'

'I lived there for almost twenty years. Still do, I suppose. Mrs Polletto is keeping my room for me. She thinks I'll be back.'

'I live in Herne Hill.'

'That's a coincidence, isn't it? The Herne Bay train to London goes through Herne Hill. Do you have a house in Herne Hill?'

'No, a flat.'

'All to yourself?'

'I live alone. But Trevor, there is something I need—'

'No!' said Trevor. 'Not tonight. We must savour tonight. It will be the last night for a long time. This operation is going to wreck us for lovemaking for quite some time, you do realize that, don't you? We shall have plenty of time for talk while we're recovering. Probably the more depressing it is the better. We'll be glad of anything that keeps us cool.'

'Yes, I suppose you're right, but—'

'I won't tell you again, Charles. Now you just get those clothes off. I've run a bath for you. I've put some Body Shop Woody Sandalwood perfume oil into it.'

'Oh, I went to the Body Shop just before I came out here.'

'What did you buy?'

'Well, er . . . Mates.'

'You are a rascal. Where are they?'

'In my suitcase.'

'Get them out, Charles,' said Trevor.

Their lovemaking reminded Trevor of a long-gone one-night-stand that had not seemed like that at the time. He recalled a night – *the* night – in Amsterdam in the late sixties at the end of a week which he had spent trying to find a club called the DOK. Somehow he had managed to miss the place each day and had not had the required courage to ask. Finally, on his last night, he had found it, gone in and for a few hours felt that he had been transported to wonderland, a world where he could be himself. A man asked him to dance, an American who was leaving for New York early the following morning. Trevor had returned with him to his hotel and with the man's bags packed by the bed in the small room, they had made love until they could hear the dawn chorus outside. He had helped the man carry his bags to the KLM bus station, swopped addresses which had proved to be forgettable but felt that the night had had crammed into it more passion and poignancy than most people gleaned from a long relationship. No doubt it was all in the mind, but on that night he had experienced feelings which he still recalled with gratitude. Quite simply it had been the highpoint of his life. It had not been shallow. Gays had to grab Mr Right whenever and however they could. The fact that geography or the outside world would quickly grab back the friend in a matter of hours in no way cheapened the experience. The man's name was Jimmy Zeigen and he had a mole on his left shoulder and completely straight pubic hair.

Trevor, twenty odd years later, lay under Charlie's bulk. Charlie laboured above him and Trevor could feel the perspiration on his back and the surprisingly cool drops as they fell on to him. Charlie's large bald patch glinted in the light from the night-lights. Wisps of hair hung down. When Trevor looked down he could see Charlie's paunch and the copious fat on his sides colliding with his own. Charlie was very far from being the ideal he had dreamed of, but then that cut both ways. The thing was that here he was. That seemed like a miracle in itself.

An hour later Trevor and Charlie were asleep, their hands on one another's shrunken, childlike cocks. A few miles away at the military airport an F15 took off to alarm the sleeping people of Zibda with the roar of its hellish engines. The noise of its take off rattled the windows where the friends lay, but it did not wake them.

In the morning they overslept. Trevor looked sleepily at the alarm clock, then picked it up and stared at it closely.

'Wake up, Charles! It's seven! Can't understand what happened to the alarm clock. It's never let me down before.'

'Let's see!' And Charlie reached for Trevor's old Little Ben. He frowned. 'Throw it away Trevor! Nobody's had one of these since the sixties. Get a nice Casio. Brauns are excellent too, but a bit on the pricey side. I've got one that you shout at and it stops.'

'I wonder if I can get this repaired. It probably just needs a good clean. It's not used to the dust.'

'Fadlabad is bursting with state-of-the-art alarm clocks, Trevor. Treat yourself.'

'Come on, Charles! We have to get a move on.'

'Of course, you could get one that makes a pot of coffee,' said Charles on the way to the hospital.

Trevor ignored him. 'What ward are you in?'

'It says R1.'

'You R1 definitely!' He waited for Charlie to see the joke, but Charlie didn't. 'I'm R3. Maybe we'll be close.'

'If it's like street numbers in England we may be next door to one another.'

'That would be nice.'

Trevor and Charlie checked in at reception and were sent up to the third floor. They walked along pink and grey painted corridors past identical rooms with three beds in each. Finally they came to 'R'.

There, lying in the middle bed of three, was Captain Pooley drinking milky coffee from a battered Thermos flask. He looked up when he saw Charlie and Trevor in the doorway.

'You two with me?' he asked.

'It looks like it. Is that all right, Captain Pooley?'

'Nothing is "all right" as you put it, Armitage. I left

"all right" behind somewhere between Victoria Air Terminal and Gatwick. But if you mean is it all right if the two of you bunk down with me, then I suppose the answer is "I suppose so". I'm sorry I can't be more enthusiastic, gentlemen, but that's how it is.'

'This is my friend, Charles. Charles, this is Captain Pooley.'

Captain Pooley nodded and watched as Trevor went over to the window which looked out over an old part of Fadlabad.

'It's a nice view, Captain Pooley,' he enthused. 'I'm surprised you did not choose the bed near the window.'

'I did consider it, but having surveyed the view, I decided I would prefer to be a rose between two thorns.'

Trevor glanced sheepishly at Charlie. They undressed and put on hospital smocks, placing their street clothes in the narrow closets provided.

'It's nicer than the National Health, isn't it?' said Trevor.

Captain Pooley grunted.

'When I was in for my grumbling appendix I was in a ward with thirty beds in it,' said Trevor.

'I'm on BUPA,' said Charlie, climbing into the bed nearest the door.

'A good move,' remarked Captain Pooley. 'Doris and I are on BUPA. Doris is my better half. Are you married, Mr Hammond?'

'Er . . . no.'

Captain Pooley pursed his lips and frowned. 'Ah,' he said. 'Armitage isn't married either.'

'I had my medical for my job with Marine Helping Hands at the Lister, though,' said Trevor hurriedly. 'I expect it would have cost the company a packet. They gave me a lovely thick towelling dressing-gown to wear.'

But Captain Pooley ignored Trevor. 'How have you managed to avoid matrimony, Mr Hammond? How old are you, forty-six? Forty-eight?'

'Fifty-one, actually. Well, of course I've considered it

many times. Been pretty close to the altar rails on more than one occasion.'

Captain Pooley nodded, but seemed to want more. Charlie wondered which line to take. Either he could say that he valued his freedom too much ever to encumber himself – that might go down all right with someone like Captain Pooley – or he could try the sob story. He usually kept that one for female inquisitors. However, he had not brought it out for a while. He might be able to present it with a certain freshness.

'Well,' Charlie began, looking solemnly at the Arabic writing on the counterpane, 'I was engaged once to a wonderful woman, Angela. We had named the date. Unfortunately she had a riding accident a fortnight before the wedding. She lingered awhile but died on the day we were to have been married. I suppose you could say I've been mourning her ever since.'

Captain Pooley nodded sympathetically.

'Nonsense!' barked Trevor from his bed near the window. 'The reason Charles never married is because he is as gay as I am, Captain Pooley.'

Both Captain Pooley and Charlie looked at Trevor in amazement. He looked back at them, blinked, and said to Charlie, 'No more lies, Charles! Don't forget last night. For all we know we could die under the anaesthetic. Captain Pooley's seen the world, haven't you, Captain Pooley?'

'Not certain I've seen the bit to which you refer,' he mumbled.

'Oh, come on, Captain Pooley! Two decades with the Blue Funnel line.'

Captain Pooley placed his Thermos cup on the bedside table and gazed at a print of a kitten being held by a weeping child gracing the wall opposite. 'The Fates,' he sighed.

'How do you mean the Fates, Captain Pooley?' asked Trevor looking at Charlie and trying to make him buck up by pulling funny faces at him.

'The Fates have really got it in for me,' replied Captain

Pooley after a long pause. 'Thought when I became a Captain with the Blue Funnel line I had it made, but no. The Fates had decreed that Blue Funnels were no longer the thing and shoved me into a dreadful desk job in London. Then the Fates saw me getting a little too cosy on the four-forty London-Devizes choo-choo each day and got me the heave-ho from that and a period of ignominious unemployment. The job here seemed like a bit of a nice gesture on the part of the Fates, but then this circumcision business came along and I knew that they still had it in for me. They do. Here I am in a spanking modern hospital with lovely oriental nurses admiring me like mad and what do the Fates decree? I'll tell you what they decree: they decree that I be a Dutch Wife, a bolster, between two rampant homos.'

'We don't like that word. We're gay for your information, aren't we, Charles?'

Charlie nodded at the counterpane, wishing he could crawl underneath it and suck his thumb.

'However,' continued Captain Pooley, ignoring Trevor, 'you are quite correct. I have bumped up against this little problem before. Had to develop quite a Nelson touch when dealing with certain stewards. I say to you what I said to them: Just don't frighten the horses. You may regard me as a horse, by the way. I would also say, Trevor, that your bombshell has not really hit me completely unawares. I have suspected on many occasions that you were er . . . gay.'

'How?' asked Trevor.

'Certain remarks you have made in unguarded moments. Also, your walk. You do tend to walk from the hip.'

'Do I?' He looked over to Charlie. 'Do I, Charles?'

Charlie nodded.

'I will make one final observation and then I shall put on my headset and become an inert Dutch Wife, a destiny I cannot shrink from. I am glad, Armitage, that you have decided to admit to yourself where you stand. Honesty is always the best policy in my experience.'

And Captain Pooley put on his headset, folded his hands over his stomach and closed his eyes.

'Why did you have to tell him?' whispered Charlie.

'I had to tell him because I wanted him to know. It wasn't easy for me either. But both of us have been cowardly for far too long. When I heard you going on about that woman falling off the horse I was reminded of myself doing the exact same thing – except my intended was killed in Uganda on VSO. Am I forgiven?'

Charlie nodded.

Some minutes later a Philippino nurse came in with cloths, aerosol shaving cream and a clump of disposable razors.

'Who first?' she asked.

'Now it starts,' said Trevor.

Charlie thought of Miss Glover, though he was not sure why.

18

Abdul Wahhab Higgins, safe in the knowledge that the circumcision ruling was being put into effect and wanting a location that might provide him with inspiration to both further his career at the Ministry for the Suppression of Vice and the Encouragement of Virtue and make of Ras Al Surra a truly religious country, went to Fadlabad airport that night. There he sat in the Oasis coffee lounge and ate a crème caramel and drank a cup of unsweetened Turkish coffee.

The Oasis coffee lounge served as a gathering place for the affluent but bored young men of Ras Al Surra. There they would sit and ogle the stewardesses from Singapore Airlines daintily pulling their little suitcases on trollies and smiling their Singapore Airlines smiles, seemingly oblivious to stares of abject desire aimed in their direction by the affluent and bored young men.

For these young men the airport departure area was a haven, a cool place with an international flavour. The roar of departing jets sent the adrenalin flowing to their brains and those who had been abroad would tell their less fortunate brethren how good it had felt. These cognoscenti whispered about how, once the seat belt sign had been switched off, the veiled women gave a collective sigh of relief and shed their veils; how black-clad females, the shape and opaqueness of Guinness bottles, ran to the toilets and emerged five minutes later as painted dolls; how the stewardesses, smiling sweetly, rushed around getting anyone and everyone, regardless of nationality or religion, a succession of little bottles of strong liquor. On a plane, they said, you could be sitting next to some pious religious policeman and he would not, could not, complain, when he saw you quaffing, desperate to be on the outside of three or four miniatures of Johnnie Walker. Why, intoxicated by the ambience, the zealot might even join you.

Planes had to be outside Ras Al Surran airspace before they could turn their cabins from dour plastic rows of seats into Shangri-La. Of course, no alcohol could be served while overflying the Holy Land.

These travellers did not talk about planes landing in Ras Al Surra. They also knew the feeling and the feeling, even here in the sweet Oasis café, momentarily depressed them. The warnings about importation of alcohol, the fear about whether they could get through customs in one piece while carrying the massive quantities imbibed over India, Austria, or Ethiopia; the painted dolls running to the toilets and emerging five minutes later as opaque Guinness bottles; the general nuance that they should be feeling guilty and uncomfortable about what they were – and this feeling so very distasteful and hard to take after the time away, where they had learnt a terrible truth: that an easy, voluptuous world existed where, within reason, they could follow their inclinations . . . like birds and fishes and flowers.

Abdul Wahhab Higgins witnessed these goings-on whenever he came to partake of his sweet and coffee. He missed nothing behind his dark glasses and meditated on ways in which the youth of Ras Al Surra could somehow be excluded from the corrupting ambience of Fadlabad International Airport.

He had once written a memo to the Ministry for the Suppression of Vice and the Encouragement of Virtue suggesting that the airport departure area be closed to all except departing travellers. This idea had been rejected. The King would not hear of it. The King, Abdul Wahhab Higgins was told, wanted the international ambience kept intact. Abdul Wahhab Higgins had not given up, however. He had fired back a second memo, suggesting that all females, including air stewardesses, be veiled while they were in Ras Al Surran airspace and particularly while they passed through the airport building. This suggestion had also been rejected out-of-hand. It might discourage planes from coming to Ras Al Surra. It might interfere with the wish of Ras Al Surra to become the Japan of the Middle East in a decade.

All this rejection of his wise suggestions irked Abdul Wahhab Higgins. Here he was, ready and able to be a strict and righteous religious policeman – ready to beat and bash the unrighteous into a shape more pleasing – but all his wise suggestions went unheeded. Well, not all. He thought of the infidels in their hospital beds and wondered why, at the very high point of his career as a religious policeman, he should be feeling unfulfilled. Why, he was poised to take over! Intelligence reports were reaching him from Thailand intimating that Sheikh Al Gaz was misbehaving himself. It would only be a matter of time before he was caught red-handed. Then no one would stand between him and the Chief of Police's job. Then Ras Al Surra would feel his presence! He would go on the television and harangue the masses. He would have the undivided attention of King Fadl. He would create God's own country in Ras Al Surra!

But Abdul Wahhab Higgins recalled that many were the religious policemen seeking to take on the mantle of Sheikh Al Gaz. Daily he heard of schemes for new religious laws emanating from the Fadlabad office. He had often been outdone! The circumcision edict had been a major coup but he had to follow it up with something, something really big.

He finished his second coffee and was about to leave when the loud noise of a taxiing plane made him look out of the window. He saw a 747 of Surreal Airlines coming to a stop outside. He gazed at it, reading the stylized Arabic calligraphy which proclaimed the airline's name. It was square, modern – the invention of a London advertising agency which specialized in Middle-East accounts. But Abdul Wahhab Higgins noticed that the writing concealed, in the gap between lines and words, a cross. He looked again, wondering if he were mistaken, but there was no mistake. Between the words was a clear cross.

He stood up, shocked, appalled and excited. In a daze he paid for his snack and wandered out into the concourse, ignoring the presence of the unveiled female passengers. He saw the check-in desks and all had a cross above them as clear as day with writing around the cross. But now Abdul Wahhab Higgins was incapable of seeing the message, like a man who has tumbled to a visual perception puzzle and can no longer comprehend his ignorance of a few moments ago.

How had nobody seen what he had just seen? How was it possible that such an abomination could be tolerated in a land that forbade the wearing of the cross, the importation of any book which showed a cross? Was it merely an oversight? It was hard to believe, but then, he reasoned, he was the first to see it. The streets of Fadlabad intersected at an angle of 120 degrees and sixty degrees in order to avoid the formation of crossroads; the design of windows was under the strictest supervision for the same reason. How could Surreal Airlines have slipped up so badly?

Abdul Wahhab Higgins licked his lips as he drove home, his fingers itching to write the memo which would, once and for all he was sure, establish his mosque credibility.

He was surprised upon entering his living-room to find his wife, Faridah, sprawled on the sofa in a state of total undress, being massaged by the Thai maid they employed.

Abdul Wahhab Higgins at once began to tear his garments and ordered the Thai maid from his house. She, proving reluctant to go, he bodily thrust out of the front door, prior to dealing with his wife.

'You realize, of course, that, by God, I shall have to divorce you, O Wicked One!' he cried, and continued, 'I divorce you! I divorce you! I divorce you!'

He felt suddenly as if a great weight had been lifted from his back. It was wonderful to be a bachelor again.

Faridah put a towel around her and said, 'I was only being given some Thai massage. It was very nice.'

'Leave my sight, O Daughter of Shame!' exclaimed Abdul Wahhab Higgins.

'Does that mean I can go home to mother?' Faridah asked.

'Not so fast!' shouted Abdul Wahhab Higgins. 'You must know that I will have to inform the authorities about your conduct. Such perversions as I have just witnessed merit the most severe punishment. And, though it grieves me deeply to have to take such a step, I must do my duty – may God give me the strength – O wicked woman. It will mean a stoning for you, for only by your death can my honour be restored!'

And Abdul Wahhab Higgins thought of his brand-new Sandhurst Stone'em, a product of the new enterprise culture of the cursed British, but, nevertheless, remarkably efficient. An enterprising salesman had sold five to the Ministry for the Suppression of Vice and the Encouragement of Virtue a year previously. They had lain unused in the basement of the Ministry. Now, he thought, he would have a chance to test its effectiveness.

The Sandhurst Stone'em was merely an adapted clay-pigeon shooter, with the refinement of sights and an auto-loading magazine that could be charged with fifty stones of the prescribed dimensions. Sheikh Al Gaz had decided on the purchase because of the enormous success of the Anderton Lash'em which had already proved its effectiveness and was a great crowd puller with its four severity settings: 1. Mild rebuke. 2. Severe rebuke. 3. Severe pain and rebuke. 4. Abject humiliation and unbearable anguish.

Faridah, Abdul Wahhab Higgins's ex-wife, interrupted his reverie, 'And where, O husband, are your witnesses?'

Abdul Wahhab Higgins's jaw dropped. He had not thought of that. Three witnesses were required for such an act. So, unless he could obtain a confession from the participating parties, there was nothing he could do.

He paced the pink gloss-painted room, his gown and his composure in tatters. As he paced he thought dark thoughts of revenge taken in the old bedouin way: a knife drawn across the throat of the wicked creature who had committed abominations beneath his roof. It would surely be fitting.

His brooding was interrupted by the pathetic knocking on the front door by the Thai maid. She whimpered, her mouth pressed close to the door, that she was hot and unhappy.

'Come not between the lion and his wrath!' shouted Abdul Wahhab Higgins. But the Thai maid did not understand and bleated inconsolably.

In response to the Thai maid's weeping, Faridah commenced a fit of hysteria. She lay on the floor and began writhing and ululating wildly. Abdul Wahhab Higgins stood astride her and commanded her to cease immediately. When this failed, he asked her if she had not already brought enough shame on him for one day without disturbing the holy peace of the whole neighbourhood, thereby causing unholy scandal? By God, he continued, a white-hot poker was already being heated in hell ready for insertion into her sensitive, sinning orifices; bubbling cauldrons of lead were, even as he spoke, being prepared by the Evil One, to be poured over her polluted body; white hot morsels of steel were sizzling on a hellish frying-pan to provide her with searing sustenance for all eternity. And what was eternity? Eternity was endless pain for the likes of her; eternity was a billion nights of agonizing torture. A mere millisecond of eternity was the time it takes for a bird to rub away with its beak a mountain as high as the sea is wide until the mountain is as flat as a piece of bread . . .

Abdul Wahhab Higgins's words flowed from him and down to the prone, now-quiet body of his wife. She lay there as, years before, faces had sat gazing up at Father Patrick Higgins delivering a perception of the life to come which would accompany them away from church into the workaday world, making them shiver and find life that much more difficult now that any sweetness it might have had had been adulterated by the poison of graphic and sadistic miseries hereafter.

He finished at last and stood over his wife – Wrath in a garden-spade-beard, dark glasses and a night-dress – panting.

Faridah looked up at him quizzically.

'But birds don't live that long! That's foolishness,' she said.

The Thai maid, hearing the commotion inside, redoubled her wails and then outdid the ruckus inside by starting a Buddhist lament coupled with a rhythmical knocking at the door in time to her wail.

'Well, this bird does,' Abdul Wahhab Higgins told Faridah.

'Take me back to mother immediately!'

Abdul Wahhab Higgins saw a knife drawn across the woman's throat, but he knew it was not to be, and visibly crumpled.

'And I'm taking Niramon with me,' added his ex-wife, not slow to take advantage of her husband's deflation.

Abdul Wahhab Higgins sat down heavily on the sofa.

'And the gold. And the Noritake dinner service. And the Sony Trinitron. And the Goblin Teasmade,' concluded Faridah.

Her ex-husband said nothing.

With a brisk nod of triumph the ex-Mrs Higgins set about gathering her trophies.

19

Armitage dreamed that the world lay at his feet. He sat on the great gold throne and emissaries from all over the unknown world came to him in their most exotic outfits, and said: 'Please rule us, O Great One! O Container of the Great Moira and of the Wise Book of Life! Unite this poor fractured world with the power of Moira and the teaching of your Great Language!'

A beautiful oriental youth unwrapped a Quality Street – the one in the purple paper – and popped it between Armitage's lips.

Armitage spoke and the great hall quaked. 'I must decline, I fear! For my heart lies elsewhere – in the desert vastnesses. All your lush kingdoms I must refuse. My people, the Hawks of the Desert, require a great leader and I, Armitage, shall lead them.'

Much was the sorrowing and unhappy rhubarbing in the great hall. Then, having had another Quality Street popped in, Armitage disappeared . . .

In Arabia, among desert sands, Armitage paraded before his bedouin troups in his white gown and gold agal and headcloth.

'ARMY-TAJ! ARMY-TAJ! ARMY-TAJ!' the thousands of men shouted, as Armitage strutted, blond and tanned and magnetically blue-eyed before them.

Then he took a solid gold scimitar from its solid silver and lapis lazuli-encrusted scabbard and held it above his head.

'AQABA!' shouted Armitage.

Then he was leading his army across the Devil's

Anvil. His best friend had fallen off his camel and been left behind. 'I shall go and retrieve him!' And retrieve him he did, though everyone thought it impossible.

'ARMY-TAJ!'

Later on this same friend had killed a man of another tribe. The army demanded justice. Armitage sorrowfully took his gun and fired it into the pleading face of his friend. The bullet merely nicked his friend's ear. 'I have spilled his blood. Now let us live in peace!' Armitage embraced his friend and the army embraced Armitage.

'ARMY-TAJ! ARMY-TAJ! ARMY-TAJ!'

He was in conference with a sad Arabian king:

'The Arabs were once a great people. I dream of the fountains of Cordoba, Armitage.'

'Time to be great again, your Majesty.'

'Do you think we can?' the King asked in a quavering voice.

'With my help, yes.'

'ARMY-TAJ! ARMY-TAJ! ARMY-TAJ . . .'

Armitage woke up to hear Captain Pooley calling him from the next bed.

'What? What? Is that you, Captain Pooley?' he asked in a daze.

'Well it isn't Mother Theresa, Armitage, I can tell you that for free,' replied Captain Pooley.

Armitage was thinking it all a bit thick being dragged out of his dream, but he did not have much time to think about it because he was suddenly very aware of an extreme pain in the vicinity of what had once been Moira.

'Ow! It hurts!' he said. Then he remembered. 'Charles! Where's Charles?'

'He's not back yet.'

'I do hope he's all right. Gosh, I'm thirsty, Captain Pooley.'

'Nurse!' called Captain Pooley.

A nurse came in at a fast trudge. 'Yes? What you want?'

20

The following morning Abdul Wahhab Higgins drew his car into the covered car-park of the Naffa industrial port. He noted with no small satisfaction the paucity of Toyotas. The Godless were otherwise engaged. Today, and for several days to come, the port would contain only the faithful. It would be an excellent opportunity for him carefully to draft what he knew would be a prize-winning memo to the Ministry for the Suppression of Vice and the Encouragement of Virtue regarding the logo of Surreal Airlines.

The previous afternoon, having with a sigh of no small relief deposited Faridah, Niramon the maid, the Noritake dinner service, the Sony Trinitron, the Goblin Teasmade, two Kashan rugs, a rice cooker, a canteen of Taiwanese cutlery, half a dozen green Cannon bath-towels and a half-bottle of Badedas at his ex-wife's mother's house, Abdul Wahhab Higgins had been overcome with a feeling of great relief which had grown to near-ecstasy as he returned home to his empty villa. True, he had failed to administer due justice to Faridah, but he had succeeded in escaping from the manacles of matrimony.

He had gone from room to room spraying Pif-Paf insect killer over everything. A foolish lizard, aroused from its slumbers behind a framed picture of King Fadl, received a five-second direct hit. The lizard had found the blast cooling and chick-chacked chirpily, before the poisons began to make it feel woozy. It gathered its family together and evacuated Abdul Wahhab Higgins's residence for good.

The evening had flown by. Abdul Wahhab Higgins put the finishing touches to a new pamphlet, 'One Hundred and Thirty Four Reasons To Reject Monogamy'.

Abdul Wahhab Higgins walked with a spring in his sandals to his office. Two items of mail awaited him, one from his mother and one from the Ministry for the Suppression of Vice and the Encouragement of Virtue. He wondered which to open first and selected the one from the Ministry. He did not discard his mother's letter, however. He felt more than a match for her today, but it could wait awhile.

Opening the letter from the Ministry for the Suppression of Vice and the Encouragement of Virtue, he read:

To: All Religious Policemen
From: The Ministry for the Suppression of Vice and the Encouragement of Virtue (Naffa Branch)
Date: 6 SAFAR, 1411.
Subject: Surreal Airlines Logo

This is to inform all righteous religious policemen that a loyal religious policeman of Fadlabad, Mr Mohamed Ali Ibn Abdullah, has drawn the attention of this Ministry to a heinous Zionist plot against the logo of Surreal Airlines. The fictitious cross of the Nazarene has insinuated itself into the symbol of our great and efficient airline. The Ministry awards Mr Mohamed Ali Ibn Abdullah with a sum of one hundred thousand jumpas in recognition of his holy watchfulness.

Be it known that from 5.00 p.m. on the 12 SAFAR, 1411, all planes in the fleet of Surreal Airlines will be grounded so that the work of painting out the present, Satan-inspired, logo can proceed.

It is incumbent on all righteous religious policemen to keep themselves on the alert to find and destroy all manifestations of the insidious logo that they may see.

May God give you the strength!

Before he knew what he was doing, Abdul Wahhab Higgins was tearing his garment. How could this be? He had been pipped to the post by some wretched colleague. It was unfair. It ought not to have been allowed. He had seen it first, hadn't he?

Abdul Wahhab Higgins paced his office from wall to wall, chewing his knuckles.

It took half an hour for him, by much repetition of pious phrases, to return to some semblance of normality. But it was a semblance only. Inside he wept. Inside he seethed. Inside he boiled and bubbled. Inside white hot pokers sizzled and burnt him up.

At last he tore open his mother's letter and read:

28 AUGUST (My birthday!)

Dear Patrick

I've been reading about all the dreadful things being done to the poor foreigners in Ras Al Surra. Father McNally came round to see me and asked me to beg you to do what you can to stop this wickedness. You, he said, must know that St Paul said that Christian men did not need to have it done. Isn't the world a bloody enough place already without you adding to it, son? Father McNally has organized a week of prayer for all the poor fellows you're carving up over there. I sit in the back pew and feel really giddy with shame when he starts the prayers, but he's a lovely man, Patrick, Father McNally! He sat with me and comforted your poor weak old mother. He said that perhaps your becoming a Mohammedan was all part of God's plan. Well, at first I thought he had had one too many of my Jameson's. (Don't you miss the Jameson's son? You always used to have a real taste for it!) Anyway, he said that perhaps the Lord was behind your conversion. According to his way of thinking he thought that with all this circumcising that's going on, it could be that the Lord knew in advance exactly what was going to happen – as He does, of course – and placed you there to stop the wickedness. Father

McNally has been reading up on Ras Al Surra. He told me that they didn't allow priests and nuns in and that there are no Catholic churches at all! Imagine that! The Lord works in mysterious ways, he said, and perhaps you were one of them. Anyway, a nod's as good as a wink to a blind heathen. Think about it, son, and when you come crawling back like the prodigal son you are, bring us a duty free bottle of Jameson's. Talking about duty free, Mrs McNabb said the most uncharitable thing to me last night. Remember I told you how threadbare her place is these days? Well I didn't mention her tea trolley on castors. Instead of cups of tea it's loaded down with duty free hootch! I remarked on how much she had, 'like the Blarney Bar sitting in your parlour, Mrs McNabb' I said. She said that she had twice as much before Father McNally began to visit. She says he's never away and not only that but he's got her roped in to clean the brass at Our Lady of Perpetual Succour's. Of course I knew exactly what she was driving at. It's dreadful to hear a woman with all those pilgrimages behind her, a missal swollen to double the size with holy pictures and signed photographs of the last four popes on her wall saying uncharitable things about men of the cloth! I told her what I thought. She ignored me at the Catholic women's meeting last Thursday. I feel terrible about it all. I wish I could believe what Father McNally says but it is hard. You're my own flesh and blood, Patrick, and yet you are doing these dreadful things. It's your mother, Patrick! Your mother! I appeal to you now to see your errors and return to the fold. You can't be happy there bleating out in the desert! Tell me, Patrick, as you read this, are you happy? Are you? Every time I walk along Castlebar streets, people look at me with sad, concerned expressions on their faces. Everyone feels sorry for me. And, you know, Patrick, I'm feeling pretty sorry for myself. The face of Our Lady is black from all the candles I've

burnt in front of her for your conversion.
Are you happy, son? Are you?

Love, Mother

A large tear pushed itself out of Abdul Wahhab Higgins's right eye, rolled over the cliff of his cheekbone and dropped with a plop on to his mother's letter. It blotted the word 'happy' and tendrils of tears and ink crossed out the words 'Love, Mother' like tiny rivers that flow for a while in the desert after rains, but then lose themselves in the barren sand.

'Hail Mary! Full of . . .' began Abdul Wahhab Higgins. But then he stopped, appalled at what he had said. He stood up, upsetting his swivel chair so that it fell back with a thud against the floor and tore at his garments again until they hung around him in tatters.

Then Abdul Wahhab Higgins fled along the deserted corridors of the port's administration building. Downstairs and along further corridors he walked, then he began to run. And as he ran and climbed stairs again and ran some more and descended stairs, lines came into his head from a poem he had often, when a priest, recommended to members of his flock tormented by doubts, and for all his movement away and away would not be dislodged:

I fled Him, down the nights and down the days;
  I fled Him, down the arches of the years;
I fled Him, down the labyrinthine ways
  Of my own mind; and in the midst of tears
I hid from Him . . .

21

'Well have you done anything yet?' Queen Noof demanded of King Fadl.

'To what do you refer, my dear?' asked King Fadl, swiftly closing a file as his wife approached.

Noof noticed. 'I refer to the accursed Zibda,' she said, eyeing the folder. 'And what are you attempting to conceal, Fadl?'

'I am not attempting to conceal anything, my dear,' replied King Fadl.

'You are not, are you not? Well, in that case you will not mind if I peruse that file; after all there should be no secrets between a king and his queen.'

King Fadl held the file close to him. Noof grasped it and tugged, but King Fadl hung on tight. 'Cease, Noof. Cease at once! I am looking at confidential photographs and they are for my eyes only.'

Noof stepped back and held out her hand. 'Show me that file, Fadl. At once!'

'The folder contains photographs of an extremely distasteful nature, Noof . . .'

But if King Fadl thought that informing his queen about how unsavoury the photographs were would discourage her from wanting to see them, he was very much mistaken.

Noof seized the file and opened it. She emitted a little cry when she saw the first photograph, then sat down at a desk nearby, opening the file on to it.

'I told you it was disgraceful,' said King Fadl.

Noof said nothing.

'Something will have to be done about it,' he added.
Still Noof said nothing.

'It brings shame and scandal to the Arab Nation in general and Ras Al Surra in particular,' he concluded.

Noof was silent for a further long moment. Then, having studied each and every photograph in the file, she exclaimed, 'Why, this is wonderful, Fadl. Wonderful!'

'What do you mean, my dear? I can see nothing at all wonderful about it.'

'Oh, yes! You old hypocrite, Fadl. This is glorious! The best thing that could have happened.' She held up the photographs and then spread them on the floor at her feet. 'Oh, yes, Fadl, this *will* do nicely.'

Fadl stood up from his desk and walked over to where Noof was gazing down at the photographs. They showed Sheikh Al Gaz in a variety of profligate poses in various locations in Bangkok. The old sheikh looked a decade younger than he ever had during his time as the Head of the Ministry for the Suppression of Vice and the Encouragement of Virtue. For a start, in most of the photographs he had a smile on his face. That was a transfiguration in itself. No longer was Sheikh Al Gaz the stern pillar of rectitude, the avenging ancient, the terror of erring humanity. The photographs showed him gentle – almost sweet – as he pinched and promised and patted his way through Bangkok, the City of Angels.

'From whom did you obtain these photographs, Fadl?' asked Queen Noof.

'From the Bangkok embassy. They came with the usual weekly reports.'

'You do realize what this means, don't you?'

'It means,' said the King, remembering his similar unfortunate lapse in London, 'that I shall be able to render Sheikh Al Gaz toothless upon his return. We shall, from this day forward, be able to keep religion firmly in its place, Noof.'

'No!' shouted Noof. 'You must do more than that. I want to see that dog Al Gaz publicly discredited and abjectly humiliated. I will be satisfied with nothing less than that. As usual, Fadl, you seem intent on doing things by halves. Why let him get away with it if we can totally destroy him? You must find yourself another chief of the Ministry for the Suppression of Vice and the Encouragement of Virtue.'

'Noof,' said King Fadl, mustering all the patience in his depleted arsenal, 'I know that you hate Al Gaz – and for good reason. You have never forgiven him for pushing his niece on to me as my second wife. Well, you have had your revenge. The poor girl is wasting her life unloved in the Al Wajja palace. But, don't you see, Noof? With this evidence against Al Gaz, I have a tame Head of the Ministry for the Suppression of Vice and the Encouragement of Virtue.'

'No!' shouted Noof again. 'It is not in your best interest to have a tame and permissive head of the Ministry. With regards to religion, Fadl, it must be given its head completely and allowed to pierce every door, nook and cranny in Ras Al Surra. It must be like an aerosol insect killer. No part of the room can be allowed to escape.'

King Fadl raised his hand to protest, but Noof was not to be gainsaid and pushed his objections aside with a wave of her hand. 'Oh, I know what you want to say; our pact with the Ministry is what keeps us on the throne. I could not agree more. But make that alliance *work* for you, Fadl! It will not work if you control the religious police and make them moderate and sensible – God, how I hate those words . . . so bourgeois. It is precisely their lack of moderation that makes them useful. They are mad dogs. The populace does not know who they will bite next. They make the people *anxious* and anxious people don't make trouble. You see, Fadl, the will of God – no doubt in a rather garbled version as promulgated by the Ministry for the Suppression of Vice and the Encouragement of Virtue – is hard to argue with. Give it its head! Make religion control the people. I see signs of decadence all around us, Fadl. The tape stores, the videos everywhere, the bored young men on every street corner, the airport coffee lounge. Softness and decadence is moving in. Do you remember that dreadful night in Park Lane when those disgusting punk people stood on the bonnet of the Rolls and spat and pulled tongues at us inside? Well, believe me, if we do not tighten up, the same thing will be happening to us in our own capital city. No, we need somebody more energetic, wilder, more God-drunk than the dog Al Gaz – someone who will be pliant, yes, but someone who will put the fear of God into the people.'

'But—'

'But me no buts! I will not be distracted.'

King Fadl sighed, then he smiled wheedlingly, 'Not by a penthouse in the Trump Tower?'

Queen Noof turned up her nose.

'An unpolluted water-source in the High Andes?'

Noof was unimpressed.

'The Star of Shiraz diamond?'

'I want you to think seriously about what I say. Proceed to your disgusting rumpus room right away and give the matter your complete attention. I have little time for baubles when the fate of my beloved country hangs in the balance,' said Noof. 'Still, if you would like to throw in the rest, I will not oppose it. My official birthday approaches.'

Zarina quietly closed the door of Daud's bedroom and walked on tiptoe down the corridor towards Nabil's study. She held a candle to light her way, shielding it against the breeze blowing through the open windows. It had taken her an hour to get Daud back to sleep after the Ras Al Surran F15 jets had flown low over Al Rahman that night. The other children seemed to have got used to the daily roar of the intimidating jets, but Daud continued to be terrified.

She opened the door of Nabil's study and went in. Nabil stood looking out of the window, his back to her. Without turning he said, 'Zarina, there are vast deposits of uranium under Al Bustan.'

She said nothing. For a moment she could feel only a great weariness at the prospect of having to provide yet more balm. Who ever comforts me these days? she thought. But then, before the protest could come, she had understood the implications of Nabil's flat statement.

'The Swedish geologists say that anybody could have discovered it,' he continued, turning towards her, holding a thick wad of papers. 'The Barefoot Geologists, it seems, took advantage of our trust and then deceived us.'

'Maybe they did it for our own good,' said Zarina.

'How can you say that? They came here with their Peace and Love and Joan Baez records and had us eating out of their hands.'

'But look, Nabil, could it not be that the Barefoot Geologists knew what a spot deposits of uranium would place us in? And they were right, weren't they? What are we going to do with huge reserves of uranium? Uranium represents everything that we believe is bad.'

'I could, perhaps, believe you. But the Barefoot Geologists did not just leave us ignorant. They went straight back to London and informed their paymasters of the find. That is certain otherwise how would Fadl know?'

'Well you were right not to sell to Fadl.'

'I am not so sure,' said Nabil. 'If I had sold the land then the damned decision would have been out of my hands.'

'Fadl would have at once exploited the uranium, sold it around the world, built processing plants on our doorstep and God knows what else. You can't want that!'

'No, but we should have had money and access to Ras Al Surra. Now we have nothing. We must ask for handouts, with a fortune laying in wait under our feet. What are we to do?'

'We do what we have always done, and that means that we leave the uranium where it is, where it will do no harm,' said Zarina quietly.

'A true daughter of the Barefoot Geologists!' shouted

Nabil, throwing the pile of papers in the air. 'You are aware, aren't you, that Fadl has tripled the price pilgrims must pay to go to the shrine of the Footprints of Aisha. Our people who come back with Ras Al Surran goods have them confiscated at the border. Fadl, hardly lifting a finger, has been able to completely emasculate us. The Swedes are bailing us out but they won't bankroll us into the indefinite future. It is a one-off thing. I tell you, Zarina, the more I think about it, the less harmful uranium seems.'

Zarina paced over to her husband and stood close to him, waving her finger in front of his face. 'Go and have a lie down, Nabil! But before you drop off think about what you have just said. Think how it casts doubts on the integrity of our lives, on the time spent trying to run a decent country.'

'But what about the Democratic Council? I have a meeting.'

'Let them manage without you for once. Let them agonize about things too. Do they know about the uranium yet?'

'They know.'

'Then see what the people think,' said Zarina. 'But, let me tell you this, Nabil. If the people decide to allow exploitation of the uranium, then I for one am going to do what we always dreamed of doing.'

'What's that?'

'I'm going to sail away. And I'm taking the children with me.'

'But what about me?' asked Nabil, in a childish whine that set Zarina's teeth on edge.

'You can stay here and become a middle-aged yuppie with your morality culled from the latest edition of Gentleman's Quarterly and the Surreal Airlines In-Flight magazines. You can sell the whole country to Fadl for all I care! But if you do that you do it alone.'

'And if I don't?'

'You become captain of a family of boat people, Nabil.'

'And then what?'

'Then we find out how it feels and where it leads. We won't be the first.'

Nabil opened his lips to speak, but then closed them again. Zarina, standing on tiptoe, gave those lips the quickest of kisses. Then, as a smile started to form there, she slapped his cheek and left the room.

22

Abdul Wahhab Higgins had been cleaning and polishing an Anderton Lash'em on his hands and knees at the headquarters of the Ministry for the Suppression of Vice and the Encouragement of Virtue when a servant tried to hand him a letter.

'Don't give it to me like that. Can't you see my hands are covered in oil? Put it on the table over there, by God!'

The servant did as instructed and left the room.

Abdul Wahhab Higgins continued his work. He did not feel he could face any further correspondence at the moment. Too much misery had found him through the mail. His work on the Lash'em was succeeding in putting thought to sleep, and he continued oiling and polishing with all available energy.

Such dark temptations had besieged Abdul Wahhab since the day before. He had been pipped at the post over the Surreal Airlines logo; he had been unable to prosecute his erring wife. In his eyes, these minor reversals cancelled out his recent successes.

Abdul Wahhab's Great Temptation – to return to Ireland and write a letter of apology to the Jesuits – had come back to besiege him with force. Childhood prayers had issued from his lips before he was aware he was saying them. He had dreamed of Christmas and climbing Croagh Patrick in bare feet. Satan was having a field day at his expense.

Abdul Wahhab turned his attention to the Sandhurst Stone'em and lavished all his attention on making the machine shine, the mechanism click satisfying through its action. As he worked he allowed himself to think of the machine in use. He saw himself in the centre of the King Fadl stadium, standing to attention next to the Stone'em. A capacity crowd filled the stadium and he heard 50,000 voices raised in the cry: 'God is the Greatest!' Then the crowd went silent as a procession of adulterers, usurers, murderers, apostates, perverts and blasphemers were led to the centre of the arena. He licked his lips, knowing that with the aid of the Stone'em and the Lash'em he could put on a show that would make the amphitheatre scenes in *Quo Vadis?* look like a cat food advertisement.

By the time he had finished with the punishment machines, Abdul Wahhab Higgins felt much better.

He Swarfega-ed his hands and at last felt ready to open the letter on the table. He pushed his index finger under the flap of the elegant envelope and tore it open resolutely. Seeing the royal coat-of-arms of Ras Al Surra at the head of the notepaper, his heart beat faster. He read:

> Dear Mr Higgins
> Your presence is requested for a private audience with King Fadl Ibn Abdullah Al Surra at the Fadlabad palace at 3.00 p.m. on Thursday the 20 SAFAR, 1411.
> Yours sincerely,
> Murad Al Meroodi (Royal Secretary)

'This is wonderful! Wonderful!' exclaimed Abdul Wahhab Higgins. 'When the Lord closes a door, somewhere He opens a window.'

He gave one last look of great affection to the shining array of instruments of punishment. 'Your day will come as mine has,' he told them. Elated, he left the Ministry building. So overcome with excitement was he that he did not stop to chide the servant whom he had seen ready to doze off in the marbled entrance hall.

King Fadl motioned Abdul Wahhab Higgins to be seated, then returned to a perusal of a pile of papers.

'All these islamic republics everywhere, Mr Higgins.

Well, I suppose we are an Islamic republic too except we are a kingdom.'

'Quite correct, your Majesty,' said Abdul Wahhab Higgins respectfully. 'If I may be permitted to add that it is a blasphemy against our religion to assert that kings are not permitted. Why the full flowering of our great religion occurred during the benign rule of the Caliphate.'

'Quite right, Mr Higgins,' said the King, pleased with the way Abdul Wahhab Higgins appeared to be so tractable. Then he shuffled a pile of papers into a neat pile, laid them aside next to a model of a solid gold Chieftain tank, and addressed Abdul Wahhab Higgins. 'The matter for which I have summoned you is one of some import. There has recently come into my hands materials of a most shameful nature. It reveals that the flower of the Ministry for the Suppression of Vice and the Encouragement of Virtue is, in fact, a poisonous and most monstrous carbuncle.'

'You do not refer to Sheikh Al Gaz, surely?' asked Abdul Wahhab, in a tone of deepest concern, mentally rubbing his hands, legs, and eyebrows together in glee.

'I do. I would have been the last to suspect Al Gaz of such conduct. As you know I am always the first to think the best of people. However, I regret to say that the evidence is indisputable.'

'Of what does the evidence consist, your Majesty?'

King Fadl reached into a drawer and produced the folder. 'Certain photographs. Please peruse.'

Abdul Wahhab Higgins perused, flying through the photographs at speed.

When he had finished, he stood up and tore his garment. He did not make a great tear, merely a couple of inches at the breast. Then he sat down again, feeling that he had made just the right pious gesture.

'Quite so,' said King Fadl.

'There can, I assume, be no doubt as to the photographs' authenticity?' Abdul Wahhab enquired.

'None at all, I fear. Anyway, that is why I have

summoned you to my presence. It is clear that Al Gaz cannot continue to occupy the great position of trust which he has so abused. I was wondering if perhaps you would like to take over as Head of the Ministry.'

Abdul Wahhab Higgins knew he had to work fast. 'I do not think I am worthy of such an honour—' he began.

'Then perhaps you would give me the name of someone who is.'

'I was going to say, your Majesty, that, though I am unworthy, I would consider it a great honour and would do all I could to make myself worthy. My every waking moment shall be given over to the spread of full religious observance in the Holy Land of Ras Al Surra,' added Abdul Wahhab Higgins at speed.

'So you want the job, do you?'

'Well . . . yes.'

'Why?' asked the King.

'I . . . I would like to see our holy religion deeply imbuing every aspect of life in Ras Al Surra.'

'And you do not believe it is already deeply rooted enough? You do not think that we are a beacon which every other country looks to as an exemplar in matters religious, technological and social?'

'Well, yes I do, your Majesty. But I think these pictures do go to show that one must be watchful. The Evil One is ever on the prowl seeking souls whom he may devour. Eternal vigilance is incumbent upon us.'

'The job's yours,' said King Fadl. Then, quite suddenly ignoring Abdul Wahhab Higgins's profuse thanks, he added, 'What do you think of our neighbour, Zibda, and its rulers, Nabil and Zarina?'

Abdul Wahhab replied boldly. 'I think that Zibdans are good people but that they are led by a misguided apostate whose inspiration comes more from decadent humanism than from our Holy Book and traditions.'

'You have answered well. And what do you think Ras Al Surra should do about the indecency on its doorstep?'

Abdul Wahhab Higgins thought for a moment. He knew what he would like to say. He would like to say that he thought the whole might of the Ras Al Surran armed forces should be turned on Zibda. But would the King like to hear that? Perhaps Fadl was testing him. He stroked his beard for a moment before saying, 'Holy remonstrances from Ras Al Surra might go some way to converting the wretched Nabil from his monstrous error. I would advocate that as a first step. Turn all the pressure at your disposal on to Zibda.'

'And if that has no effect?' asked the King.

Abdul Wahhab Higgins, after only a moment's hesitation, said with certainty, 'Jihad!'

'My thoughts entirely,' replied King Fadl. 'Now I want you with all energy to seek out the Evil One in all his manifestations in Ras Al Surra. Leave not one stone unturned in your search for wickedness. Should the wretched dog Al Gaz have the temerity to return, see that he is dealt with using all the rigours of the law. I want Ras Al Surra to be second to none in the practice of daily virtue. You may start with the airports and public places. Veils all round. I am giving you your head, Abdul Wahhab. Only if we are seen as a bright beacon of strictness can we be deemed worthy to bring light into the darkness of the wretched Nabil of Zibda.' The King gestured to Abdul Wahhab Higgins that his audience was at an end.

The new Head of the Ministry for the Suppression of Vice and the Encouragement of Virtue bowed deeply to King Fadl and walked from the chamber. Only when the great doors of the palace had closed behind him and he found himself outside in the God-calling dusk, surveying in front of him the skyline of Fadlabad with the freeway climbing the sky behind it and, twinkling in the distance, the lights of the Naffa industrial port, did Abdul Wahhab Higgins realize the import of what the King had just said to him. And when the realization had sunk in, he lifted his eyes to the sky above Ras Al Surra, shouting, 'O thou of evil intent within this city and its environs! O thou wicked licentiates and distillers in your nooks and crannies! O thou uncircumcised in spirit! O thou ill-clad wives! O thou unnatural ones wallowing in a cesspool of your own creation! O thou importers of Pornography and CTS pamphlets! O all thou throughout this Holy Land who sully its bridebed with the devilish spots of anti-religious plots! I, Abdul Wahhab Higgins, am coming to seek you out!'

Then he walked down the steps towards the palace car-park, fumbling in the deep pockets of his gown for his car-keys.

Part Three

Hard Tops

23

Two weeks passed. The circumcision edict and its effects on expatriates continued to be the main topic of conversation in the tea-shops, cafés and suks of Ras Al Surra. The people wondered what it all meant, then shook their heads and pulled their beards and looked heavenward and repeated proverbs about the strangeness of rulers.

Things became clearer to the average Ras Al Surran when it was announced that Sheikh Al Gaz had been replaced as chief religious policeman and they saw on their television screens the pale countenance of Abdul Wahhab Higgins. He took to speaking to the people every night, sitting in a room lined with books.

Abdul Wahhab Higgins spoke to the people in an avuncular tone which belied the content of his speeches. Each night he castigated sections of the community and informed the populace of new restrictions. Standing in a street outside one of the Fadlabad housing projects, it was possible to hear the yaaahs of disbelief coming from each of the twenty storey buildings as Abdul Wahhab Higgins held up the thin black veil in his left hand – proscribing it – and then lifted up the new thick, righteous version – prescribing it; and as he waggled his finger at the populace and announced that travel restrictions were to be placed on all people under thirty. What was wrong with Ras Al Surra as a holiday destination, he asked? Could one not have a good – and righteous – time at the shrine of the Footprints of Aisha? And if it were beaches you wanted, were not the beaches in the highrise holiday resorts of Jaheel and Saffina – an easy day's drive away – not good enough? 'Yaaah!'

He turned his attention to male dress. Decadence had even been allowed to infiltrate that most hallowed and democratic garment. In summer men had taken to wearing a dish-dash of light cotton. But Abdul Wahhab asserted that the material was translucent and gave a sight of leg, buttock and the organs of reproduction. Sale of such garments was to cease immediately. 'Yaaah!' Airports, he stated, were for travellers. One did not notice non-passengers sipping Pepsis and eating crème caramels at bus-stops, did one? Airports were, from now on, to be reserved for travellers with tickets. 'Yaaah!' Attendance at Friday prayers was compulsory as from next Friday. Dated stamps would be issued to all worshippers at the door and were to be stuck on to a card that would also be issued. Any person seeking medical or social benefits of any sort, or an exit visa to travel abroad, would have to show a full set of stamped cards to the appropriate authorities. Without a full set, neither benefits nor visas would be issued. 'Yaaaaaahhhh!'

Blissfully unaware of the veil upon veil of restriction that was stifling the daily lives of Ras Al Surrans, the expatriate employees at the Naffa industrial port hobbled back to work. It was easy to spot people who had had the operation because they took very short steps and kept their legs wide apart as they walked. Also, trousers bulged in front, due to the plastic codpiece an enterprising British company had sold to the Ras Al Surran Health Ministry when they heard of the circumcision edict. This gadget cupped the genitalia gently as in a padded jewel box. As the salesmen had said, it would allow those operated on to return to their work at least a week sooner than they otherwise would. It would pay for itself in no time and aid healing.

The insult which had been paid to the crippled expatriates did not heal, however, and while all forms of industrial action were forbidden in Ras Al Surra, several did their best to make their protests felt. Little jobs were left undone in the knowledge that they would cause large problems later on. Captain Pooley no longer remonstrated with employees he caught smoking, but rather hoped that their cigarettes might blow up a tank farm or two; while Trevor Armitage, though happy in his domestic life with Charlie Hammond, had his students spend much of their time copying page after page of 'Has Man a Future?' into their copy-books and was deaf to their appeals of, 'Very tired, teacher!'

However, in lighter moments, Trevor let them make their appeals to him (in English which he corrected with all possible pedantry) that he should convert. The students felt that, since their teacher had gone through the hard part, then the soft sentences required for converting should be no problem at all. After all, they said, if he converted, he would get 50,000 jumpas from the public purse and a King Fadl wrist-watch and his picture in the paper. To these ingenuous arguments, Trevor merely shook his head with a smile. Islam had been fine in theory. Before he came to Ras Al Surra he had thought that it might be nice to turn over a new page, find a satisfyingly simple set of dogmas and be accepted into a family that spanned the world. But, once in the country, that notion had quickly flown out of the window. Now he blamed the religion for the walls it erected between the sexes and between groups of people who should be getting on well together. He blamed it for all the petty restrictions with which his life had become surrounded. A part of him felt strongly that multinational creeds and their over-advertised products commanded too much clout in the world. His own little product did not stand a chance, of course. The list of ingredients started with 'Try your best to be nice'. There was quite a lot of 'Not sure' and 'Haven't the foggiest' in it as well. But, now the new improved version also liyted 'Charles Hammond'. Trevor felt Brand X would do for the time being.

Then, almost without warning, the new, improved

Charlie Hammond was standing in the wings of the Fadlabad National Theatre, his body covered in concealed nylon threads and his old friends, the worms. He kept his harmonica under his armpit to keep it warmed and he took sips from a glass of Perrier to keep the saliva flowing.

He had the programme worked out to the last second. First he had planned a rendition of a medley of patriotic English songs, followed by a mini-drama involving the worms. The violet one was in love with the blue one but the couple had to find one another across the desert of Charlie Hammond's front – encountering the wicked red, black, green and white worms as they made their journey towards union. The drama had a happy ending with all the wicked worms falling over the precipice of Hammond's belly, broken asunder on the rocks of the stage-floor. To round off the evening Hammond was going to do a rendition of 'Elegy in a Country Churchyard'.

He peeped through the curtains. There was not much of a house out front, but then he had expected that. Trevor had come, of course, accompanied by his class of Fire and Safety Officers; the Plunketts were there with a couple of Ras Al Surran friends. Captain Pooley, Pontin and McGregor, sat near the back. Otherwise, the hall was empty; its five hundred empty plush seats staring up at him like open red mouth's pulling tongues.

Charlie Hammond stepped on to the stage to loud applause led by Trevor Armitage. He hobbled to the centre.

'Good Evening, Ladies and Gentlemen. I would like to begin by playing you a selection of songs of the United Kingdom.'

Charlie took a sip from his Perrier and launched into 'Ye Gentlemen of England'; went on to 'The Vicar of Bray', 'The Bluebells of Scotland' and rounded it off with 'Land of Hope and Glory'. He made barely a mistake and bowed as low as his codpiece would permit to receive his applause. Quite comfortable now, he thought an encore was in order and gave his audience a rendition of 'Down by the Salley Gardens'.

He had been about to start on his worm play when a voice was heard from the back.

'Stop this immediately! Shame! Shame!' And Abdul Wahhab Higgins, accompanied by several religious policemen, strode down the central aisle. He mounted the stage and addressed the audience.

'This performance is at an end. All of you in the audience will leave here immediately. Music is a forbidden activity.' He looked towards Charlotte Plunkett. 'Also, the consorting of the sexes in a public place is an abomination. All present will give their names to the righteous religious policemen before leaving.'

And Abdul Wahhab Higgins descended from the stage and strode to the back of the auditorium where he stood watching stonily from behind his dark glasses as the meagre audience muttered and gave their names and addresses to the clipboard-cradling religious policemen.

Trevor was appalled and, not caring about what people would say, left his students, strode on to the stage and put his arm round a stunned Charlie Hammond, whispering comforting words into his ear.

'Don't worry, Charles! We might have guessed something like this would happen. They did exactly the same last week when the RASONGRO Drama Club tried to put on *Waiting for Godot* in their compound. I didn't tell you that before. The Arts are being stifled throughout Ras Al Surra. You must not think that you have been singled out.'

'But I had everything prepared! The worm play would have been such a treat for everyone!'

Trevor Armitage hugged Charlie tighter and then led him off the stage. They gave their names and address to a religious policeman and sadly left the hall, passing Abdul Wahhab Higgins as they went.

Abdul Wahhab Higgins had been a witness to the public intimacy of Trevor and Charlie and holy alarm bells were ringing in his head. When everyone had been checked and had left, muttering, he strode down to the policeman who had taken Trevor and Charlie's names seized and the clipboard from him.

He looked at the names, noting that they shared the same address. And he filed the information in the cold crypt of his brain.

24

'Well, if you want my opinion, I think our submitting to the knife was a big waste of time,' said Captain Pooley as he drank his own wine and endeavoured to chew his way through a steak au poivre prepared by Trevor.

'Why's that?' asked Charlie, a piece of steak, a morsel of potato and some squashed peas poised on his fork.

'Well – you've got a pea on your chin, old chap – I reckon the whole thing's going to blow up. You mark my words, before too long we'll be stuck in the middle of a war.'

Trevor laughed nervously.

'Don't laugh Trevor. It won't be funny let me tell you. With that madman Nabil hurling insults at Fadl it can only be a matter of time.'

'But Fadl could gobble up Zibda between breakfast and lunch,' observed Charlie.

'Maybe,' conceded Captain Pooley, 'but I doubt it would be as simple as that. Look what's going on within Ras Al Surra. The religious police are going berserk. There's not an expatriate woman who dares go out on the streets any more. Not a day goes by without a raid being made on makers of booze. The airport has become a no-go zone unless you've got a ticket and I hear that all those pretty stewardesses are going around in veils and bumping into baggage trolleys. They grounded the whole fleet of Surreal Airlines because the logo appeared to have a cross in it. Circumcision was just the start of the madness.'

'Surely, Captain Pooley, the story about the Airline

logo was just a rumour, wasn't it? You know how stories spread round here.'

'It was no rumour. I went for a paddle - swimming's out for obvious reasons - at Celibates' Beach just last Friday and the Manager of Surreal Airlines told me. That's what I call fact, Trevor.'

Trevor nodded politely and made off to the kitchen to put the finishing touches to his trifle. He made, he felt, the best trifle in the Eastern hemisphere. The home-made sponge cake was soaked in wine contributed by Captain Pooley, with brown sugar and some nutmeg added to mimic sherry. Then half a gallon of custard was poured on top, this followed by lashings of whipped cream. He poured hundreds and thousands over the top, along with pieces of cut glazed cherries and slithers of almonds. Then he took the heavy bowl into the dining room, where he heard Charlie ask Captain Pooley where to find Zibda's new radio station.

'Thirty-one metre band, short wave. It's almost bang on top of the World Service.'

'What's it like?' asked Charlie, making a mental note to listen in, suddenly recalling, as he still occasionally did, the reason for his being in Ras Al Surra in the first place.

'It's not my cup of tea but it might suit you two. Some woman with an accent you could cut with a knife was going on about some clause in the Education Act back home that forbade teachers talking about you lot.'

'Clause 28.'

'That's the one. She accused Britain of stifling free speech.'

'Which it does,' said Trevor. 'God, I wish I'd had a teacher who had explained things to me when I was growing up. What else did she say?'

'Don't know. I finally found "The Pleasure's Yours" on the BBC. They failed to play Doris's request again. She sends one in every week but they haven't played it. Not once. Still, one day. Now can I have an eyeful of what looks like excellent trifle, please, Trevor?'

'With pleasure, Captain Pooley,' said Trevor, pushing a big spoon into the trifle and feeling a wave of satisfaction as the trifle farted. If the trifle farted he knew it was going to be good.

Captain Pooley left at eleven. Trevor set about washing up, and Charlie started trying to tune in Trevor's battered Roberts radio to Zibda. After much static and the occasional sound of Jimmy Savile playing the top records of March 1958, Trevor heard, 'This new radio station is called Radio Desert Rose and we will bring you all the news that you cannot hear elsewhere. You, dear listeners, will hear much misery on our station. You will hear tales of greed and avarice and treachery. However, we also hope to be able to bring you stories of goodness triumphant, of biters bit, of decency enthroned, of peace declared and triumphant.

'We begin with a story that is very close to home. Although our radio station is called Radio Desert Rose we must tell you that the Desert Rose Fields after which we are named are the cause of conflict between Zibda and Ras Al Surra.' And Nabil went on to tell his listeners the history of the conflict and the aggression by which Zibda felt threatened.

Trevor, drying plates, walked into the bedroom to listen. Charlie sat on the bed engrossed, then groaned inwardly as Nabil turned his attention to exposing the Barefoot Geologists.

'It seems like an interesting station,' said Trevor. 'All the news we cannot hear elsewhere. That sounds promising, doesn't it, Charles?'

Charlie Hammond nodded without enthusiasm.

By twelve the two were asleep in one another's arms, codpiece against codpiece. They did not hear the landcruiser of the Ministry for the Suppression of Vice and the Encouragement of Virtue pull up in the car-park outside; nor the swishing robes of Abdul Wahhab Higgins and four other religious policemen ascending the stairs and stopping outside the door of their flat.

Abdul Wahhab Higgins inserted his skeleton key into

the lock and swung the door open noiselessly. Then, placing his finger in front of his mouth, he silently led his companions into the hallway.

It was not difficult for the group to locate the room where Charlie and Trevor were curled in sleep. Charlie Hammond's snores guided them as a foghorn guides sailors. The group tiptoed into the room in the dark and stood around the bed with its invisible occupants. Then Abdul Wahhab Higgins switched on the lights.

Charlie and Trevor woke simultaneously to cries of 'Shame!' and the sound of tearing cloth. They looked about them and saw Abdul Wahhab Higgins and his witnesses standing, torn but triumphant, looking down.

'There you are, my brothers. What did I tell you. Witness the iniquity. Let your seared eyes note and remember the base crime before us. Log it in all its gross detail!'

And Abdul Wahhab Higgins pulled the covering from Charles and Trevor, revealing their nakedness.

'What! What!' exclaimed Charlie Hammond. 'Now look here!'

'Now look here!' sneered Abdul Wahhab Higgins, mimicking Charlie's accent. 'No, you look, my fine fellow. I and my colleagues have witnessed your wicked and unnatural conduct. You do not have to say anything but anything that you do say will be written down and used in evidence against you. Now get dressed. You are coming with us to the Naffa House of Religious Correction. You will appear before a devout judge of the Ministry in the morning.'

Charles and Trevor stumbled into their clothes while the five religious policemen looked on.

Trevor, shaking, missing the hole in his trousers into which he was trying to fit his left leg, had on the tip of his tongue to say, to plead, 'It wasn't what you think! We weren't doing anything. I'm as straight as a die, honestly. The air-conditioning was a bit chilly so we thought we would share the same bed for a bit of animal warmth. Anyway, how could we do anything in our present state?' But he jumped around untidily on the spot and saw Charlie looking at him in a hang-dog way.

Quite out of the blue the bulldog face smiled and Charlie winked and Trevor stifled the utterance. It was true, they had not been doing anything except cuddling before dropping off. But the shame of being discovered and looked upon by these dour dogmatists he now knew would be as nothing compared with the shame of denying the only thing that promised to untwist him, to make him human. No, he would not deny. Neither would he confess. To confess would be to accept Abdul Wahhab's version of events, the version of a world he rejected – and this he was suddenly not prepared to do. That world was guilty of great sins which masqueraded as virtue. His only guilt lay in going along with that perverse world's view and ignoring his own nature. Charlie's smile and his decision quietened down his distress and he found that he was able to put on his clothes without too much trouble.

He was still shaking, knew that the men could see him shaking, but he would say nothing, deny nothing, affirm nothing. Silence, and his friendship with Charlie, would have to serve as anchor for his fragile bark. Bullies could puff and pant and tear their garments. He would no longer put up a pretence of subscribing to their codes. All those years of pretending had unmanned him, reduced him to a clown. Dishonesty and fear had brought down those dead years at Mrs Polletto's boarding house upon his head. A term in the Naffa House of Religious Correction was his punishment for his dishonest life. It might not be so bad.

They packed a few things into a bag. Trevor pushed his Roberts radio into one corner.

The religious policemen led Trevor and Charlie out of the flat and down to the car-park. There the two were bundled into the back of a landcruiser with barred windows and driven off through the streets of Naffa, deserted except for roaming packs of dogs and the Philippino and Sri Lankan road sweepers brushing away the rubbish from the gutters in their luminous uniforms, and thinking how each stroke was contributing in some tiny way towards the realization of their bejewelled dreams.

25

'I have a problem, Mr Higgins,' said King Fadl the following morning. 'While you have been chasing iniquity up and down the length of Ras Al Surra, I have been attempting to mobilize the might of the Ras Al Surran armed forces to start a punitive air-strike against unholy Zibda. I have encountered a major stumbling block, however. For reasons best known to themselves, the expatriate pilots are unwilling to bomb Al Rahman. I had thought that my mercenaries would prove loyal when tested, but this is not, apparently, the case.'

'Perhaps further pressure is required. Surely some persuasion could move the expatriates?'

'I doubt it. They have already resigned in droves. Asking them to fight my war for me, coming on top of making them undergo circumcision, would seem to have been the last straw. No, Abdul Wahhab, I do not think they will be open to any persuasion.'

'I see. However, I do not think it is an insurmountable problem. A punitive expedition by land would be sufficient and would give you, your Majesty, the opportunity to lead your troops into battle in the old way. Imagine yourself at the head of a great army. It would be just like the good old days of Islamic expansion. A real Jihad!'

King Fadl frowned. 'I am not sure I fancy the idea of leading an army, Abdul Wahhab.'

'But think what a sight you would be upon a white charger with your gold and silver scimitar unsheathed. The merest glimpse of you at the head of an army of Ras

Al Surrans on camels and horses would inspire abject terror in the enemy.'

'But what if the Zibdans fight back?'

'They will not fight back, your Majesty. When they see your might, they will also see the uselessness of opposing you. How can they fight? The pacifist Nabil has never allowed weapons into Zibda. There is no danger there. All that is needed is a grand gesture. You have it at your command to make that grand gesture.'

'Perhaps you are right, Abdul Wahhab. One thing is certain, I cannot stand by and let Nabil continue to broadcast his lies around the world. Something has to be done about Radio Desert Rose. I've already had to cut off relations with Sweden for letting Nabil use their satellite. If I allow him to get away with this daily besmirchment there is no telling what will happen to me at home.'

'You are right, your Majesty. However, I believe that the wise measures taken by the Ministry for the Suppression of Vice and the Encouragement of Virtue have been able to inspire circumspection and no small dose of holy terror among the people. Do not worry on that score. The few among your subjects who might be swayed by Nabil's lies are also in a state of fear for their own futures. I have been knocking on many doors, your Majesty. I and my loyal religious policemen have set about sucking up the vice-addicted of Ras Al Surra with the vacuum cleaners of our virtuous ardour.'

'Continue your . . . holy housekeeping, Abdul Wahhab,' said King Fadl. 'Meanwhile, I shall think of what you have said.'

'The matter is urgent,' counselled Abdul Wahhab Higgins. 'One must catch the tide at its fullest or miss the boat.'

'True, true,' replied King Fadl, quite taken with the notion of himself in full regalia, at one stroke putting to death all the wickedness on his doorstep and silencing the calumnies of those who thought him soft and decadent. 'I shall set about arranging everything this very day.'

Abdul Wahhab Higgins retired from the royal presence and went straight to the court-house next to the Naffa House of Religious Correction. If his monarch was to be active in setting the country on a war footing it was only right that he should do his best to see that all the sinners he had dragged in during the past week be dealt with at once.

When Abdul Wahhab arrived at the court-house, he treated the blind judge peremptorily and did not assist him to his seat in the large court room.

'We have much wickedness to chastise today,' he told the judge.

The judge nodded, stumbling to his seat.

Abdul Wahhab signalled to a guard, who opened a door and ushered in Trevor and Charlie, along with the witnesses.

Abdul Wahhab Higgins read out the charges against the prisoners in Arabic. The witnesses were called and answered questions put to them by the judge. As neither prisoner could understand the proceedings they tried to imagine themselves elsewhere. Indeed neither could really believe that what was happening was really happening. Trevor felt that at some point Abdul Wahhab would turn, smile, and say that it was all a mistake.

Charlie aimed glances at Plunkett who had turned up to visit the pair in gaol, little realizing the proceedings would be instigated at such a fast pace. Plunkett felt that his own worst imaginings about the visits of travelling thespians had come to pass. He had barely had time to inform the hapless pair that they had brought it all on themselves and that they knew the laws of Ras Al Surra and that they could not expect to be bailed out by HM's Government, before the call had come that the court was in session.

The witnesses finished their testimony and Abdul Wahhab Higgins asked the accused if they had any statement to present to the judge. Trevor looked at Charlie and stood up.

'All I have to say is that we have been spied upon and

brought to this court because we dared to express affection for one another. We do not deny the charge brought against us. What we do deny, however, is your right to judge us. Which of you is so pure that his conduct could be laid open to public scrutiny and judgement for every second of every day? Are all your thoughts so chaste, all your actions lacking in greed and malice and selfishness? Jesus is one of your prophets. He said that only the man who is without sin should throw the first stone. That is all I have to say.'

Trevor sat down and Charlie patted him on the back.

'Now hold on there just a minute,' said Abdul Wahhab Higgins. 'Your woeful ignorance of the tenets of religion cannot go uncorrected. While we accept that Eisa was a prophet, we do not accept that any of the Christian books are in any way genuine. So your use of a story from your false books can cut no ice with this court.'

He turned his back on Charlie and Trevor and spoke to the judge for a minute or so. Then, turning back to the accused, he said, 'The judgement of this court is that you are guilty of the grossest sexual crimes. You will be taken from this court and at a time and place to be named by the Ministry for the Suppression of Vice and the Encouragement of Virtue you shall be stoned to death.'

Plunkett stood up to protest. 'But that has never been the punishment for this crime!'

'It never used to be. Now it is,' replied Abdul Wahhab Higgins. 'Take them away!'

26

Across the border that King Fadl, at the head of a phalanx of Ras Al Surran troops, was about to cross in style, Sultan Nabil was having an excellent time.

For most of each day he sat before the controls of Radio Desert Rose playing tapes, reading Amnesty International reports, commenting on the day's news and giving his collection of sixties' broadsides a world-wide airing.

It had been a lonely job at first. But after a week letters started to arrive at Radio Desert Rose; letters of support mainly but also ones containing ideas for further broadcasts. Civil servants in a number of countries sent him information of secret abuses and encouraged Nabil to broadcast them. Bank employees in Switzerland sent him lists of the contents of numbered bank accounts and put names to numbers. Armies of the oppressed, the downtrodden and the merely put-upon wrote to Radio Desert Rose as their only hope. Every night Nabil and Zarina pored over piles of mail and sorted out the priorities for broadcast.

These times were the worst. The volume of mail in itself was distressing and despair was only avoided by the knowledge that Nabil and Zarina were certain that, if their radio station were able to survive, it might give tyrants pause.

Sometimes, however, the mail provided them with some mirth, as when an employee of American Express sent them photocopies of Queen Noof's itemized bills for her gold card. The bills were, they felt, eloquent. They itemized a pattern of conspicuous consumption: fifty pounds of caviar from Harrods; twenty solid-gold statuettes from Garrards; one hundred assorted wrist-watches from a shop in Zurich – the list went on and on. Zarina took a five minute slot for seven of the following days just to read out Queen Noof's purchases over the air to the accompaniment of 'Hey Big Spender!'.

It took Radio Desert Rose just a fortnight to build up a world following. Many hated the needling radio station, broadcasting the contents of supposedly secret Swiss bank accounts, fingering national hypocrisies, turning the dagger in the bowels of corrupt and cruel regimes, blowing the whistle on the secrets of the world's diplomatic bags. But another part of the world, a quiet part, made up of individuals everywhere, took Radio Desert Rose to its heart, sent it information and offers of support. They believed in little Zibda's integrity, sensed that Nabil was speaking to them and for them.

Zarina's record request show became especially popular. She played Joan Baez and Bob Dylan and Woody Guthrie and Pete Seeger and Cypriot wedding songs and she had her children give recorder recitals. Radio Desert Rose was far from slick. Mistakes were made all the time, but mistakes further endeared it to those listeners who felt that in Radio Desert Rose they had found their place on the dial.

Not only had Zibda espoused libertarian causes the world over, it had resisted a great temptation on its own doorstep: by refusing to allow the uranium to be mined that could have enriched Zibda beyond the dreams of avarice. So, when Nabil had broadcast an appeal for funds, cheques large and small arrived. Nabil began to feel that Radio Desert Rose could well become a means by which little Zibda would be able to keep itself without reliance on outside aid. He quickly employed his children in soaking off the stamps from incoming letters, and packaging them for sale.

So busy was Sultan Nabil that he gave hardly a thought to the trouble brewing back in Ras Al Surra.

*

Charlie and Trevor in their gaol cell – waiting for the day when they would stand in front of the Sandhurst Stone'em – also heard the broadcasts of Radio Desert Rose on Trevor's ancient Roberts. They would, had they been able, have written to Sultan Nabil themselves. Captain Pooley had been able to write to the station, however. He sent his letter to Doris in England who sent it on. Charlie and Trevor were surprised, therefore, on the day before they were due to be executed to hear Zarina read out the letter about their case, apologize that she did not have a copy of the Serenade from *The Fair Maid of Perth*, but played them 'Ramblin' Boy' instead.

That night, their last night, Charlie and Trevor sat together listening to their favourite radio station once again.

'It looks like I chose the wrong country to work in, Charles,' said Trevor. 'We should be helping them out across the border.'

'Looks like it. But, Trevor, we never had our talk. Remember the night before we went into hospital I tried to tell you something?'

Trevor sighed, 'All right Charles. Tell me now.'

'Well, I'm not really an entertainer. I work for an arm of British Intelligence.'

Trevor started laughing. '*You!*'

'Well, yes, I know it sounds absurd. It was absurd. Anyway, I was sent out here to look into the situation between Zibda and Ras Al Surra. But that's not really what I wanted to tell you. Part of my job for the last twenty years has been finding gay men throughout the intelligence service and then informing the authorities.'

'And did you inform on many?'

'Quite a number, yes.'

Trevor was silent.

'Are you sorry you ever met me?' Charlie asked him.

'So that is why you did nothing all those years, never tried to find a friend?'

'Yes, I suppose so. Believe me, Trevor, if I could undo what I've done, then I would.'

Trevor nodded. It was no easy thing to take in. He felt a self-righteous side of him rising up to attack Charlie. He said nothing for some time, just looked at the floor of the cell.

'It's funny, isn't it?' he said at last. 'If I were a good heterosexual I would probably approve of what you have done, think it was for my country's good. Well, I'm not and I don't. I'm saddened to hear what you've just told me, but I really can't get angry about it. I've done my share of betraying. I've denied what I am and tied myself in knots to conceal what I am. That is as much of a betrayal of other gay people as the one you describe. Being gay is a journey without maps. You and I, we both asked directions from strangers and then believed what they told us. But look at them, Charles! They don't know the way any more than we do.'

'So you're not sorry you met me?'

'Well, I'm sorry about what has happened. Who wouldn't be. But, no, I'm not sorry I met you. I wasn't happy before. Before we met, you and I were just a pair of wankers. We're not wankers any more. Also, I'm hopeful that the embassy will be able to do something. Don't give up hope, Charles.'

Just then Abdul Wahhab Higgins came into the cell.

'Your execution has been unavoidably postponed,' he said.

'How long do we have?' asked Trevor.

'We in Ras Al Surra are in a state of war with the evil Zibda. Our great and good King Fadl is at this moment marching into Zibda at the head of a huge army. When he returns, your execution will form part of our celebrations in the National Stadium.'

'You people have a funny way of celebrating,' said Trevor.

'There is, perhaps, one way in which you can avoid this fate,' said Abdul Wahhab Higgins.

'How?'

'You can embrace the True Religion.'

Charlie looked at Trevor, who looked back at Charlie.

'Think about it,' said Abdul Wahhab Higgins.

Trevor spoke up. 'We don't need to think about, Abdul Wahhab Higgins. We would rather die than embrace your religion.'

'Oh you would, would you?'

'Yes.'

'Then I'll see you at the stadium.'

And Abdul Wahhab Higgins left the hapless pair.

'Now we must pray that Zibda can defeat Ras Al Surra.'

'It's a pretty vain hope, Charles,' said Trevor.

'I know,' said Charlie Hammond.

27

The freeway along which King Fadl was leading his troops went due west before snaking south, aiming for the Eastern Region of Ras Al Surra. King Fadl's white stallion Euripides, flown in specially for the jihad from a stud farm in Kentucky, made a satisfying clip-clop against the black tarmac. Occasionally it bucked and snorted as the television trucks of the world's media panned the phalanx of his army.

'This is the life,' thought King Fadl. 'All the time I've been wondering what I wanted and all the time it was a war. Wars clear the head wonderfully. Foolish of me to breathe all that stale air in the rumpus room. This is what I was made for.'

King Fadl was wearing a white silk gown tailored to flatter his form. Such a perfect white was it that it seemed to glitter in the hot sun. He wore his matching head-dress, its ends drawn around his mouth, and topped it all with a gold-looped rope. At his waist, hanging from a silver-tooled belt, glittered the Al Surra scimitar, the very weapon used by his grandfather to slaughter the complete Al Kwasani family during the desert wars and normally kept in a display case in the Fadlabad Museum of Significant Artefacts.

Overhead whirred several helicopters. Following up the army came a battalion of supply trucks and a four-wheel-drive charabanc for King Fadl to eat and sleep in during the campaign.

Making sure that the eyes of the cameras were trained upon him, King Fadl took his telephone from the inside pocket of his gown and dialled Queen Noof's number.

'Is that you, Noof? It's me, Fadl, scourge of the infidels,' said the King.

'Are you eating the liver of Nabil in Al Rahman, Fadl?' asked Noof severely.

'Not quite yet, dear. I'm still on the Fadl Freeway. However, in a couple more kilometres we shall be turning off the road and sweeping down through the desert to Al Rahman. Then the fun begins.'

'Well, I want the Zarina woman's head on a plate. Is that clear?'

'Yes, dear. Is there anything else you'd like?'

'No, that will do. There is little in the way of souvenirs in Zibda, I'm told. So primitive.'

'Well that will all change once we've taken over, Noof. By the way, I'm wearing your handkerchief on my sleeve.'

'I'm touched,' replied Queen Noof, 'but just make sure you bring back Zarina's head. I wish it displayed at the victory celebrations.'

'You can rely on me dear.'

'I hope so, Fadl. Just don't mess up, that's all.'

'I won't, my queen. This is going to be my finest hour. I feel it in my bones. Goodbye, Noof.'

King Fadl put down the telephone, wondering whether he would be able to pluck up enough courage to sever a head. And doubting it.

The sun was setting behind the Ras Al Surran army as they turned off the freeway into the desert. The supply vehicles had sped on ahead to prepare the night's camp atop the desert rose fields that hugged the border between Ras Al Surra and Zibda. At dawn the following morning the invasion of Zibda would begin.

King Fadl spent the evening in his charabanc with his military advisers. There was not really very much to say. The generals were confident that Zibda would fall without resistance, due to the lack of an army or even an armed police force in Al Rahman.

'The main thing is to blow up that infernal radio station. We must stop their lying mouths once and for all. Is that clear? The wretched Nabil has not only offended Ras Al Surra with his broadcasts but also most of the leaders of the world. We are striking a blow for world stability,' King Fadl told his generals.

They nodded and told the King there would be no problem.

But, as King Fadl settled down to watch a double bill of war films on the video in his charabanc, three Land-Rovers passed along the freeway which the army had just recently left.

In the first Land-Rover sat Captain Ibrahim, the head of the Desert Regiment for the Eastern Region of Ras Al Surra. Beside him was Peter Drury, Captain Ibrahim's friend and adviser. Behind them sat three soldiers of the Desert Regiment.

Captain Ibrahim was seizing the moment. He had heard the news of the invasion on his radio that morning. Then, turning to Radio Desert Rose, he heard the calls for aid coming from Sultan Nabil. Now was clearly the time, thought Ibrahim. While Ras Al Surra's army was away, while the King was elsewhere, while the power that he felt was stifling the soul of Ras Al Surra was at its weakest, was the time for action.

Captain Ibrahim looked doggedly ahead of him along the black ribbon of road. His dream was going to come true. He and his friend, Peter, were either going to bring justice to Ras Al Surra or die in the attempt.

'Are you afraid?' Peter asked Captain Ibrahim.

'Yes, I am terrified. But I am ready for what will come. My life has been leading towards this moment, Peter.'

The three Land-Rovers parked by the side of the freeway when they saw the lights of Fadlabad glinting in the distance. Ten men got out of the other two Land-Rovers and came over to where Captain Ibrahim and Peter Drury stood.

'Now, you are all clear about what you must do?'

Ibrahim asked them. 'Once the television station is ours, the people will rally to our support. They are tired of the decadent tyrant, Fadl. Now Fadl, masquerading as a great military leader, is about to attempt to subdue Nabil, the only leader in the area who points the way forward for us. Steel your hearts, my brothers! Be courageous! If our plan goes well, no blood will be spilled, either in Ras Al Surra or in Zibda. When tomorrow comes it will dawn on a bright new day for our country and for the whole Arab Nation.'

The guards were dozing in their sentry boxes at the television station. When the three Land-Rovers drew up outside and a group of uniformed men leapt out, the guards stood up and aimed their weapons, but, seeing the Desert Regiment uniforms, were not sure what to do.

'There are rebels loose in the television station!' shouted Captain Ibrahim. The guards looked at one another and made to run towards the building, thinking that the soldiers had come to assist. But as the guards turned, two soldiers tackled them round the legs and brought them down on to the tarmac. Then another two sent the guards into unconsciousness with blows to the head.

'Tie them up and put them in the guard-house!' commanded Captain Ibrahim.

The soldiers grabbed the guards' weapons and walked into the television station.

Queen Noof had been watching filmed reports of King Fadl's day at the head of his army when the television screen went blank and the handsome face of Captain Ibrahim appeared. She fiddled with her remote momentarily, thinking she had inadvertently changed channels, but then she heard what Captain Ibrahim was saying.

'People of Ras Al Surra. A revolution has taken place against the corrupt regime of Fadl Al Surra. For too long has the house of Al Surra fed off our land. We have seized the time of his unjust invasion of our neighbour, Zibda, to unseat him from his golden throne and institute the rule of the people. We appeal to all of you who desire honest government in this Holy Land to go up on to your roofs, to lean from the windows of your flats, to go out into the street and bang your pots and pans, beat your drums, make all the noise you can. If we hear the city of Fadlabad erupt in sound then we will know we have your blessing on our endeavour. If there is silence, then we shall retire from your capital and await our punishment. The choice is yours, people of Ras Al Surra. Now, this moment, is the time for your first ballot. If you choose us, it will not be the last. We promise to make of Ras Al Surra a generous and tolerant land. Do you want this or do you want the continuation of the hypocritical religiosity of the Al Surras? We await your reply.'

Queen Noof scurried out on to the balcony of the palace and listened. For a moment all she could hear was the chirping of the cicadas and the drone of a thousand air-conditioners. Then, somewhere just outside the palace gate, she heard someone banging a pan with a spoon.

'Shut up!' cried Queen Noof, but as she spoke a car horn blurred. Then a tape recorder was turned on at full volume and the voice of Um Kalsoom competed successfully with the other two sounds. 'Stop it!' she commanded, but her voice was lost as, from the skyscraper apartment blocks down Fadl Drive, she heard a cacophony of bells and pots and cutlery and gold bangles. Then the people started shouting, 'God is most Great!' and 'Death to Fadl!' and the sound was of thunder, but, unlike thunder, it would not fade, but grew and grew until it was past bearing.

Noof fled back into her palace and slammed shut the double glazed patio doors. She lifted her telephone and banged out King Fadl's number.

'Yes?' asked King Fadl, drowsily.

'Fadl, it's Noof! Come back at once! There has been a coup.'

'There's been a what, dear? I can't hear you, there's such a din in the background. Are you washing up?'

'A coup. A revolution. Fadl! A man appeared on the television declaring that you are deposed. Now all the people of Fadlabad are beating pots and pans and making a most unholy row.'

'Whatever for?'

'To show their support for the rebels. Do something, Fadl!'

'Listen, Noof, and do not interrupt. I am sure there is nothing to worry about. It will all turn out to be a storm in a tea-cup. However, I think – just to be on the safe side – that you should evacuate the palace. Have the servants take all the valuables through the escape tunnel and out to the royal terminal. Telephone the duty emergency pilot. Then, when everything is loaded and ready, fly to Al Rahman airport. We will immediately advance on Al Rahman. By the time you arrive we shall have attained our military objectives in Zibda. Then we shall have the army return and do what has to be done. Did you understand all that?'

'Yes, Fadl.'

'Very well. Do it now. Do not delay.'

Noof called her servants to her and reminded them of the evacuation drill they had practised monthly. Then she went into her suite and collected a few of her personal belongings and piled them into a Gucci bag. The sounds outside in the city had increased, but Noof was becoming almost used to it. She took the lift to the basement and, pushing her way past servants carrying caskets and luggage and paintings and metal cash boxes and files and carpets and furniture and jewel boxes and trays of video tapes and compact discs, made her way through the underground escape tunnel – excavated at the same time as the palace was being built – and out to the royal terminal, where a 747 stood waiting.

She was welcomed aboard by the pilot. 'Fly to Al Rahman at once!' Noof commanded.

But the plane had been unable to land at Al Rahman,

even though, by the time it overflew the airstrip, King Fadl was waiting there with his army.

After receiving news of the coup, Fadl had at once ordered his army to march on Al Rahman. They had encountered no resistance and were able to walk into the radio station, where three Ras Al Surran soldiers heard Sultan Nabil, a headset on, announcing to the world that Radio Desert Rose had been invaded.

The soldiers led Sultan Nabil out into the night and set fire to the portacabins with small explosive charges. Nabil watched as his dream returned to the realms of imagination.

He had, on hearing of Fadl's army, sent Zarina and the children, together with much of the population of Al Rahman back to the coastal villages to the north. Resistance, he knew, was useless, but he had determined to stay and broadcast until the very last moment. When he had finished speaking he had set a tape playing on the console and, until the fire took hold and melted the cables, the world listened to 'Black is the Colour of My True Love's Hair'.

'We meet again, my brother!' said King Fadl.

Nabil said nothing.

'It was not nice of you to plough up your airstrip. Not neighbourly. Now my plane will be unable to land. And where will your children play football, may I ask?'

'Leave Zibda, Fadl! Leave now!' said Sultan Nabil.

King Fadl looked about him and curled his lip. 'I think I shall take your advice, Nabil. There is really nothing to stay for. No palaces to plunder. Not even an Intercontinental Hotel to billet my troops in. Of course I could plough under your bike tracks before I go but that would be churlish. We have achieved our objective. But tell me, Nabil, why did you start broadcasting all those stories about me?'

'Somebody had to. It needed doing, Fadl. The world cannot afford your sort any more.'

'I see. Well, Nabil, it looks as if I am having a spot of bother back home. There would seem to be a few people in the Holy Land of Ras Al Surra who have drunk in the lies of Radio Desert Rose.' And Fadl looked over to the red flames of the radio station, 'A splendid conflagration, is it not? I had not thought radio equipment burnt so well. It is worth remembering. Still, Nabil, I am prepared to withdraw and leave Zibda to its problems. I wonder if you could direct me to the next friendly country to the north.'

'Gladly,' replied Sultan Nabil. 'I am sure Saudi Arabia will give you refuge. It is just up that track, about a day's drive.'

'Right. That's where I'll go. As to the army, they will be sent back to Ras Al Surra to sort out my temporary difficulty.'

Then King Fadl gazed with distaste at the ill-lit capital of Zibda, twinkling before him. Above him the night sky was, he felt, vulgarly solid with stars. 'And what will you do?' he asked Nabil, though as he asked he wondered if the question were also addressed to himself.

Nabil shrugged. 'We shall manage, Fadl. We have always managed.'

'Ah, yes. I remember. You said.'

And taking three bodyguards, King Fadl got into his charabanc and made off along the bicycle track towards Saudi Arabia, leaving his army to march to Ras Al Surra to win his kingdom back for him.

28

Abdul Wahhab Higgins had seen Captain Ibrahim's broadcast, too, and had gone up to the roof of his house in Naffa to hear if anybody would dare to defile the holy silence of the night with rebellious outpourings.

Like Queen Noof, he had been reassured at first. The silence was almost palpable. But then, from the next roof but one, he saw some shadowy figures and then heard a tentative *think . . . think . . . think* – the sound of a pen on a bread tin. And, from the house opposite, a rather more animated banging of metal on metal. Abdul Wahhab made a mental note. These treacherous neighbours would pay dearly for their frolics.

Soon an element of competition entered into the noise from his neighbours. The women in the house next-door-but-one to his began to ululate and the pen seemed to be replaced by a wooden spoon, beaten with African abandon. Not to be outdone, the family opposite began singing in chorus, accompanying themselves with kettles and pots and cookie-shape-cutters and the sound of pop music on a cassette, its volume being raised to maximum then lowered to minimum by a dizzy, whirling finger. But now that was not the only sound that Abdul Wahhab heard. And it must have impinged on his two erring neighbours at the same time that something else was happening. For they ceased together and silence did not return. From all around came the noise of beaten metal, ululations and blaring stereos. The neighbours, taking in the fact that they were no longer alone, recommenced.

Packs of dogs joined in and a twittering of awoken birds, together with their darting flying shapes in the sky above, added to the activity. Layer upon layer of sound saturated the air, and though Abdul Wahhab Higgins tried to blot it out by covering his ears, it did no good at all. And, looking over the rooftops of Naffa, he saw the lights of Fadlabad in the distance and detected a shimmering, a beat, coming from the capital too. The sound rolled in like a breaking wave radiating from a distant storm centre; beating the flotsam of sound in Naffa against his very threshold. The ragged desert between Fadlabad and Naffa seemed to act as a sounding board and the house below his feet shook.

Abdul Wahhab Higgins stood on his roof appalled. Then, slowly, needing to concentrate all his attention on putting one foot in front of the other, he left the roof and returned to his living-room, where the television was still broadcasting the face of the rebellious Captain Ibrahim. Sound had penetrated even into the studio where Captain Ibrahim sat and smiled. As Abdul Wahhab Higgins watched, he got up and was shouting into the microphone, 'People of Ras Al Surra, I can hear your answer! Ras Al Surra is now a republic. Continue to make your views clear until they can be heard by the ex-King, Fadl, in humble Zibda!'

Abdul Wahhab Higgins turned off the television in time to hear a shout of acclaim coming from all around. Then, his ears aching, his heart breaking, he walked slowly, deliberately, into the bedroom.

He removed his clothing and reached into a drawer and took out his robe of martyrdom. He wound this robe around his body and left his house. King Fadl's troops, he knew, would be coming back to restore order. He would drive out along the freeway to meet them and encourage them in their Holy Purpose.

As he drove, Abdul Wahhab Higgins passed other drivers honking their horns happily. In Fadlabad groups of people had come out of their houses and were dancing in the street. At the corner of one street a fire had been lit and Abdul Wahhab could see a picture of King Fadl curling in the flames.

He left Fadlabad behind at last and the din lessened, though, even in the desert and out of sight of the city lights, he could hear the distant, ominous thunder behind him.

As he drove he took comfort from the thought that he was getting closer to the army. The army was huge and would surely have no trouble in restoring order. Then, with order restored, he, Abdul Wahhab Higgins, would have to work as he had never before worked. His knuckles would bleed from knocking on the doors of the rebellious. The Lash'em and the Stone'em would glow white hot from overuse. Truly, then Ras Al Surra would be his foot-stool! He would become as famous as Ayatollah Khalkali across the water.

At last he parked his car where the Fadl Freeway turned south. He got out and looked into the empty desert towards Zibda, straining, hoping to see a trace of King Fadl and his army.

Abdul Wahhab Higgins sat down on a rock and continued staring into the black desert in front of him. A warm breeze blew and faded, blew and faded. In the stillness between the breeze, he could hear the silence of the desert and his own heartbeat. But, when the breeze blew, it carried with it traces of sound – as insistent as memory – from the ferment of Fadlabad. When he caught the sounds, his trepidation deepened and fear took hold of him and shook him. Then, when the breeze ceased, the fear slowly, reluctantly, let him go. His heartbeat quickened and slowed. If only the breeze would stop, he thought, I could concentrate. So whenever the sounds reached him, Abdul Wahhab opened his mouth and covered his ears and howled like a wolf or a muezzin to block out the sound of life. Then he would stop, listen, look around, and perceiving that silence had returned, seek to wrest solace from the temporary stillness. But as time passed the respite of silence became less of a respite, and, instead of a slowing of the heart, a retreat into the hard core of the silence, the memory of his howl intruded and he wondered if he were losing his wits.

A strong gust of wind blew and the sounds it carried were louder than before. This time he did not make a sound, but listened, fascinated by the sounds of revolt that would undo his sweet routine. And, in the midst of the sounds, he heard a howling as from an animal caught in a trap. As silence returned, the howling did not abate, but climbed up the steps of the silence to a vantage point just below the stars.

Abdul Wahhab looked up and opened his eyes wide and gasped at the sound in the stars. The animal had escaped the trap and seemed to be bearing down on him, salivating damnation and salvation; unbearable anger and ineffable gentleness.

He could not stand the feelings the sound set off in him and he started to run out into the desert. His car-keys, clasped tightly in his hands, he let fall, and their loss did not for one moment impinge on his consciousness, which could only take in the howl. But the faster he ran, the faster the animal pursued and the howl . . . was it a howl for blood or for love? . . . grew louder and did not lessen, even though his breathing rasped and grated through him, his blood biffed its way – like balls against a squash-court wall – through his veins.

Dawn was inching up when Abdul Wahhab Higgins in his martyr's robe caught sight of the Ras Al Surran army approaching, raising a cloud of dust in its wake. He gesticulated and ran towards the still-indefinite shape. Stones cut his ankles; spindly, daggerlike plants tripped him up; the wreckage of the exploited desert rose fields of Ras Al Surra seemed to conspire to stop his progress, their broken slabs of silica petals shifting, robbing his feet of their foothold: ALL THINGS BETRAY THEE, WHO BETRAYEST ME! He blocked out the words of the poem as he had tried to block them out throughout the long night, but they kept coming back and he slid and fell and the sharp rose petals cut his face, arms and legs, tore his garment, like the teeth of a huge dog.

The phalanx of the Ras Al Surran army was passing him now. Soldiers looked down from their vehicles and saw a pale, bleeding foreigner standing mouthing words at them and then turning to look round – as if he were being pursued. Then, with a supreme effort of will, the tattered figure shouted, 'Thou warriors of God! Ras Al Surra is in the throes of accursed, godless revolution! Hasten, thou roses of the Great Ras Al Surran renaissance and put an end to this iniquity!'

The troops looked at Abdul Wahhab strangely and he realized that in his panic he had lapsed into English.

One of the generals came forward from the rank of troops. The sun was rising over the desert behind the general and Abdul Wahhab Higgins had to shade his eyes to see the man at all.

'I know you!' said the general. 'You are Abdul Wahhab Higgins!'

'Yes, I am! And I have come to tell you that Ras Al Surra has fallen to rebels!'

The general nodded and motioned to two of the soldiers standing nearby. They took Abdul Wahhab Higgins and bundled him into a truck.

'What are you doing? I am the chief of police for the Ministry for the Suppression of Vice and the Encouragement of Virtue! You can't arrest me!'

'You are a foreigner,' said the general. And he had not said the half of what he thought.

The army continued on towards Fadlabad as the sun started to sweep across the sky.

Trevor lay on the floor of his cell dreaming that the port was being bombarded by enemy forces. He was teaching his class of Fire and Safety Officers, and was glad that the invasion had come, though he felt guilty for being so pleased. He refused to let his students leave, or even to get up and look out of the window. There was a video lesson to be watched and Trevor felt that they were already far behind because of the interruptions caused by his operation.

As he taught, he thought of Charles. Was Charles all right? Yes, Charles was all right. Charles would be at home making the tea.

At last the noise of explosions, alarms and shouting humanity became too great to be borne and Trevor reluctantly turned off the video, covered it up with its plastic cover, removed the socket from the wall theatrically – turning to make sure that his Fire and Safety Officers had noticed his careful classkeeping – and said, 'Right! Stand! In single file we are going outside to see what is happening.' And he led his Fire and Safety Officers out of the classroom to view the battle in the bay between them and the town of Naffa. The guns chafed and boomed and hurt their ears.

'What are the guns doing?' shouted Trevor over the din.

'They are firing,' replied Salem.

'What are they firing?' asked Trevor, nodding towards a terrified Zayd.

'They are firing shells.'

As if to prove the truth of this, a shell whizzed over their heads and scored a direct hit on the petroleum jelly storage tanks half a mile along the port.

'What has the shell just done?'

'It has just blew up the petroleum jelly storage tanks,' replied Mahmoud.

'Not "blew up", it is "blown up". Repeat blown up!'

'Blown up.'

'No, the whole sentence, Mahmoud! I want the whole sentence!'

But as Mahmoud was gamely trying to repeat the whole sentence, a shell whizzed through the air and the sulphur prilling tower fell with a crash.

'There! Something *else* has just happened! What else has just happened? Salem?'

'The sulphur brilling tower has just blown down.'

'Well, yes and no,' opined Trevor. 'First of all it is the

sulphur P-P-P-prilling tower . . . or rather was. Second, you used "blown down". Now usually we talk about trees and notices and things like that "blowing down". The sulphur prilling tower has "blown up"! Or, perhaps, if one wanted to be more accurate, the sulphur prilling tower has just *been* blown up. Now I know it is a difficult example of usage, but you'll just have to . . .'

Then another shell interrupted Trevor's explanation and blew up the methanol storage tanks. The Fire and Safety Officers looked around them unhappily.

'There, you see!' breezed Trevor, 'blown up! Gosh it was a good idea to come out and see all these examples. Much better than blackboard drawings, though I must admit, my drawings of things blowing up are really second to none. Especially when I add my own sound effects.'

'Teacher, we scared!'

'You're what?' asked Trevor, scarce heard amidst the sounds of explosions.

'We scared!'

'Why fear you?' asked Trevor, smiling indulgently as he looked back down the causeway towards the mainland, his gaze taking in the fires and smoke as Lawrence's had once taken in the Devil's Anvil and found the crossing possible. 'I will lead you to safety! Do not fear!'

And Trevor Armitage strode away bravely towards the flames, knowing that his students would follow him.

'I'm coming, Charles! I'm coming!' he shouted.

Trevor woke himself and Charlie up with his shout.

'What? What?' asked Charlie.

'Oh, I'm here! I had a most peculiar dream, Charles. I dreamed that the port was being bombarded. I was teaching. Anyway, it doesn't matter. I've always found it to be one of the problems of teaching. I teach all day and then I go to bed and teach all night. I can't tell you how often that's happened. It can be really wearing.'

'I can never remember my dreams,' said Charlie.

' "Life is but a dream",' said Trevor. 'Can you play that one?'

Charlie reached for his mouth organ. 'How does it go?'

'No, don't bother, Charles. See if you can pick up Radio Desert Rose.'

Charlie fiddled with the radio but he could only pick up crackles where Radio Desert Rose had been.

The door opened and two soldiers came into their cell and told them to leave with them.

'Where are you taking us?' asked Charlie.

'Does this mean we're free?' asked Trevor.

But the soldiers did not understand.

King Fadl's army, upon their return to Ras Al Surra, had not taken to the streets to fight for their monarch, but accepted the fact of the revolution. They returned to families, families with stiff arms from banging their pots and pans.

The new government of Ras Al Surra decided that, if a new start were to be made, all foreigners would have to be sent away. Planes arrived to evacuate the expatriates from Ras Al Surra. Captain Pooley found himself next to a dishevelled Charlie and Trevor, both still in brown prison dish-dash and flip-flops. They had been taken straight from the prison to the airport. On the wall of the departure lounge only a dusty outline showed where the portrait of King Fadl had, until just hours before, held pride of place.

'This is not the way I would have chosen to leave,' Captain Pooley said. 'I had always imagined meeting up with Doris and going on around the world at the end of my contract. I don't like this at all.'

A child-guard poked Captain Pooley in the back.

'Excuse me, officer! I didn't realize I had stepped out of line!' said Captain Pooley from between tight lips.

Captain Pooley turned and nodded briskly at Trevor and Charlie. 'Still, I'm glad to see you two got off.'

'Thank you, Captain Pooley,' said Trevor.

The group of foreigners were ushered through passport control. Then two guards held them back so that a group of soldiers leading a dishevelled man in a stained white sheet could go ahead of them through passport control.

'That's Higgins, isn't it?' said Captain Pooley.

'You know, I do believe it is,' answered Trevor. 'He's in a shocking state, though, isn't he? You don't think they're deporting him too, do you?'

'Looks like it. Just goes to show.'

'Yes,' replied Trevor, feeling sorry for the bruised, bleeding figure of Abdul Wahhab Higgins, now standing on the far side of passport control with soldiers smirking at him. It was the first time he had ever seen Abdul Wahhab Higgins without his dark glasses and he was startled to see the man's cornflower-blue eyes, wide open, darting fearfully, madly from sight to sight, hunted, hounded, unable to concentrate on any one view of the chaos for too long.

But Trevor had little time after that to worry about Abdul Wahhab Higgins. Crowds of expatriates joined them in the departure lounge, until there was hardly room to turn around. Then the whole group was ordered over a tannoy to strip naked in order to be checked for arms and contraband.

A sigh went up from the group of men but all started resignedly removing their clothing.

Someone shouted, 'You'll be begging us to come back in a month or two! You'll never manage without us! Everything will fall apart!' and a cheer like a football crowd's arose from those who had heard the shout.

Trevor lost sight of Captain Pooley and stayed close to Charlie. They stood naked while the police searched for valuables among the piles of discarded clothing, and then gazed around the naked battery farm of humanity. In the midst of all this, as Trevor tried to keep Moira in repose while at the same time restraining his eyes from wandering, he thought he heard Captain Pooley's voice, 'Good God! Look at Higgins!' But quickly forgot amidst the other concerns of the moment. Five hours later, while stopping over at Larnaca airport, waiting for a plane to take them on to London, Trevor ran into Captain Pooley again.

'What happens now?' Trevor asked.

Captain Pooley took a swig from his duty free bottle of Scotch before replying. 'Well, for me it's home and no more to roam. I've learnt my lesson I can tell you. What about you?'

'Charles says he might be able to get me a job in something hush-hush,' replied Trevor.

Captain Pooley bit the inside of his lower lip diplomatically.

Then Trevor remembered, 'What did you mean at Fadlabad airport?'

'When?'

'What you said.'

'What did I say?'

'About Higgins.'

Captain Pooley beamed broadly, 'Ah *Higgins*!' he exclaimed. 'Abdul Wahhab Higgins has a foreskin you could wrap a fish in.'

Trevor looked back at Captain Pooley and felt tears coming to his eyes. Then they started to course down his cheeks. He was as much surprised by them as Captain Pooley.

Captain Pooley did not say anything. He frowned, worked his lips for a moment, then turned on his heel and walked away.

Trevor Armitage watched him go and then went off to find Charles whom he had last seen making for the duty free shop.

'Do you think Cyprus sherry passes muster?' Charlie asked.

Trevor shrugged. He wandered around the shop, trailing Charlie like a child his mother, his thoughts centred on Abdul Wahhab Higgins and what Captain Pooley had told him.

Charlie continued browsing, seemingly unaware of

Trevor's presence. Trevor left him there and wandered up and down the crowded departure lounge.

An hour later their flight was called. Trevor, who had said barely a word in the interim, looked at the board, saw that there was a Skyvan leaving for Al Rahman at midnight.

'Charles,' he said, 'do you want to go back to England?'

'Where else is there?'

'We could try Zibda, Charles. They seem to need help and it's a country that would accept us for what we are. Why don't we just change our tickets and go there? I think we could be happy, don't you?'

Charlie was not so sure. If Nabil and Zarina saw him and recognized him, then what? How much would it cost? Could he afford it? But he could pluck up neither the energy not the courage to prick Trevor's enthusiasm and allowed himself to be led away from the London queue, from Miss Glover, from his empty life in the full flat in Herne Hill – towards great uncertainty.

They had no problem in changing their tickets, but some hours remained before the flight left for Al Rahman. They filled the time by waving off the London flight. Then they sat close together on a wooden seat in the deserted departure lounge.

'So you didn't buy anything at the duty free shop?' Trevor asked Charlie.

'No, I decided I didn't want anything.'

'You surprise me.'

Charlie Hammond grunted.

'Play me something, Charles.'

And Charlie Hammond took his mouth organ out of the pocket of his grimy dish-dash, untangled the family of worms on nylon threads that had wrapped the instrument in a tight embrace, polished its surface and put his mouth to it.

Soon the Larnaca airport departure lounge was filled by the strains of 'Down by the Salley Gardens', to which Trevor added his light tenor:

'In a field by the river my love and I did stand,
And on my leaning shoulder he laid his snow-white
hand.
He bid me take life easy, as the grass grows on the
weirs;
But I was young and foolish, and now am full of tears.'

Sultan Nabil, a sadder man, returned to his duties and tried to think of ways in which he could improve the lot of Zibdans and get his message out to the wide world. The uranium lay – and would always lie – dead under Al Bustan, surrounded by its wreath of roses.

One day, consoled by overtures of sweet reason from the new regime in Ras Al Surra, he was repairing some mosquito netting in a classroom of one of Zibda's schools. Nearby, Trevor Armitage was teaching a class and Charlie Hammond, who had been immediately recognized and almost immediately forgiven, played the harmonica to entertain some of the volunteers who had come to help Zibda. Sultan Nabil found a spirit duplicator and some skins in a cupboard. There and then he sat down at one of the desks and with his Bic wrote on the top of one of the skins: THE DESERT ROSE MONTHLY. He chewed the end of his pen, listening to Charlie playing 'There but for Fortune', smiled at the mistakes he made and started writing in the hot little room.

King Fadl and Queen Noof, reunited and safely ensconced in their fairy-tale castle on a Norwegian fjord, found themselves missing Ras Al Surra. Noof would sometimes go out on to one of the balconies of her home and look east. Tears, those enemies of mascara, came to her eyes and she tried to think of a song to sing. Imelda had so many songs to serenade her homeland across the miles of ocean; but Noof found that she could not think of one.

Noof did not see much of Fadl. He spent long hours

alone in his tower with the door locked and a chastened Jeeves guarding the corridor that led to it.

There he spent his time removing the gold, silver, lapis lazuli, pearls, rubies and diamonds from the map of Ras Al Surra which the children had given him. It was no easy task to chip away the precious covering from the shells. In a day he might only manage to uncover a square centimetre of seashell. The ridges and furrows of the seashells caught the gold and silver fast. But, painstakingly, millimetre by millimetre, Fadl worked to restore the map to its original form. He could, of course, have sent the map back to Aspreys to have their work reversed. Aspreys have, perhaps, received stranger requests. But Fadl chose not to send it away. He felt that only when he had removed every last trace of the rich covering would his mind clear, would some relief to his pain come. For Fadl was in pain, though, as ever, he could not pin down its cause. But he longed for an end to it and restoring the children's gift was, perhaps, to be his start.

And in an ancient church in the west of Ireland, a black-scarved old lady lights a candle and kneels in front of a statue of the Virgin. She clasps her hands, around which are knotted rosary beads, in front of her face and prays doggedly as the candle burns down and its flame burns heavenward, as straight as a stick – or a missile – in the still, cold, air.

THE END

Sucking Sherbet Lemons
by Michael Carson

'A splendidly articulate and witty first novel'
SIMON BRETT, PUNCH

Benson is fat, fourteen and inspired with Catholic fervour. He dreams of heaven as a place where Mars Bars grow on trees . . .

Benson is also a founder member of the Rude Club, at whose meetings 'irregular motions of the flesh' set off attacks of guilt that send him scurrying to confession. After one such attack he finds himself pledging his unclean soul to the service of God.

But at St. Finbar's seminary the temptations put before the novices are as great as those of the outside world: especially from Brother Michael, who entices boys to the rubbish dump on cross country runs. Expelled from St. Finbar's, and back at school, Benson befriends the sixth form's star pupil. Together they attend Benson's first orgy. It is both the culmination of his sexual insecurity and the beginning of self-acceptance . . .

'Funny about two notoriously difficult subjects, catholicism and homosexuality. He is the real thing, a writer to make any reader, of whatever sexual or religious orientation, laugh'
JOSEPH O'NEILL, LITERARY REVIEW

'Graphic but not pornographic, humorous but never sniggering, this is a marvellous first novel'
FANNY BLAKE, OPTIONS

'A funny, gay, Roman Catholic bildungsroman'
PHILIP HOWARD, THE TIMES

0 552 99348 4

BLACK SWAN

A SELECTION OF FINE TITLES AVAILABLE FROM BLACK SWAN

THE PRICES SHOWN BELOW WERE CORRECT AT THE TIME OF GOING TO PRESS. HOWEVER TRANSWORLD PUBLISHERS RESERVE THE RIGHT TO SHOW NEW RETAIL PRICES ON COVERS WHICH MAY DIFFER FROM THOSE PREVIOUSLY ADVERTISED IN THE TEXT OR ELSEWHERE.

☐	99075 2	**QUEEN LUCIA**	E.F. Benson	£4.99
☐	99076 0	**LUCIA IN LONDON**	E.F. Benson	£4.99
☐	99083 3	**MISS MAPP**	E.F. Benson	£3.99
☐	99084 1	**MAPP AND LUCIA**	E.F. Benson	£4.99
☐	99087 6	**LUCIA'S PROGRESS**	E.F. Benson	£4.99
☐	99088 4	**TROUBLE FOR LUCIA**	E.F. Benson	£3.99
☐	99380 8	**FRIENDS AND INFIDELS**	Michael Carson	£3.99
☐	99348 4	**SUCKING SHERBERT LEMONS**	Michael Carson	£4.99
☐	99351 4	**BLUE HEAVEN**	Joe Keenan	£4.99
☐	99375 1	**WHEN SISTERHOOD WAS IN FLOWER**	Florence King	£3.99
☐	99243 7	**CONFESSIONS OF A FAILED SOUTHERN LADY**	Florence King	£3.99
☐	99376 X	**REFLECTIONS IN A JAUNDICED EYE**	Florence King	£3.99
☐	99337 9	**SOUTHERN LADIES AND GENTLEMEN**	Florence King	£3.99
☐	99377 8	**WASP WHERE IS THY STING?**	Florence King	£4.99
☐	99239 9	**BABYCAKES**	Armistead Maupin	£4.99
☐	99384 0	**TALES OF THE CITY**	Armistead Maupin	£4.99
☐	99086 8	**MORE TALES OF THE CITY**	Armistead Maupin	£4.99
☐	99106 6	**FURTHER TALES OF THE CITY**	Armistead Maupin	£4.99
☐	99383 2	**SIGNIFICANT OTHERS**	Armistead Maupin	£4.99
☐	99302 6	**THE LOVE OF GOOD WOMEN**	Isabel Miller	£3.95

All Black Swan Books are available at your bookshop or newsagent, or can be ordered from the following address:

Corgi/Bantam Books,
Cash Sales Department,
P.O. Box 11, Falmouth, Cornwall TR10 9EN

Please send a cheque or postal order (no currency) and allow 80p for postage and packing for the first book plus 20p for each additional book ordered up to a maximum charge of £2.00 in UK.

B.F.P.O. customers please allow 80p for the first book and 20p for each additional book.

Overseas customers, including Eire, please allow £1.50 for postage and packing for the first book, £1.00 for the second book, and 30p for each subsequent title ordered.

NAME (Block Letters) ....

ADDRESS ....

....